THE CORPSE FLOWER COLONY

KATHERINE DEMPSTER

1st Edition: 2023

ISBN: 978-1-7782049-7-5

Cover images by: SushiHue, Jazella, Monika1607 via Pixabay, and Katherine Dempster

Cover designed by: Katherine Dempster

Corpse Flower Illustration by Matilda Smith, public domain via Smithsonian Open Access

Dedicated to anyone who has found themselves lonely in a crowded room.

CHAPTERS

"Neither the hummingbird
nor the flower wonders how
beautiful it is."

-Unknown

Chapter One

Change will always come. Invited or not, change will arrive at your doorstep, and for better or worse, nothing will remain the same. Everything around us is changing before our eyes, from new life to new death; the cycle of change is a powerful force that pushes us along and reminds us that we're never truly still. It is the inevitability of existence.

In the middle of choppy dark waters, which was ice cold more than found to be comfortable, was a small, forested island that held a community who decided to fight the change they saw coming as if the very idea of that arrogance would not enflame the Universe around them. Five generations had dug out a life on the rocks that held them before Amelia came to be a part of the village as the oldest of three children in the Taylor family.

The history of the village's creation was myth steeped in superstition at best by the time it had been passed on to her and the others who had come to the age of attending classes in the steepled structure of mud and straw that made up their church—the center of their village and an essential space in an overly crowded environment.

At a young age, Amelia Taylor had been told of the founders turning their backs on the quickly advancing world around them. That they were sure it had nowhere else to go but deep into war, sin, and suffering. The greed and quick pace of the country they knew would swallow them whole or push them out. When they could take no more, they chose to leave while they still had the chance to do so in the manner they wanted. Start a life on their terms. They would find a place to change their world into what they wanted, not what was forced on them by their weak-minded neighbors.

Amelia had wondered how lousy life could have been if the hard work of service and grueling labor that was their everything had been a better choice. She had just turned eighteen, and the whimsy of childhood had started to fade, revealing what life entailed for the adults who dedicated their lives to honoring the founding families.

The worn fabric of their hand-me-down clothing matched the dusty clearing in the thick evergreen trees that held their entire existence. Leaving the island was rarely done. There was no return once that choice was made. The outside world was not welcome within, and once one stepped foot outside of their sacred space, they would forever be sullied by the disgraceful existence they had chosen over righteousness.

Amelia was aware of only one exception to that infrangible law. The younger brothers of a spinster named Molly, who had been cast to the outer realm of the village, tucked in among the trees, to live a life of solitude as repentance for her family's actions. Malcolm had left and never sent word of his new life. On the other hand, John felt responsible for the life his sister had fallen upon by their choices. Amelia had only cast eyes on him but once when he was passing through the dense forest after a visit. Molly was uncomfortable discussing either of them, even with her only secret confidant, Amelia. She wasn't sure if the old woman spared her words out of anger or her fear of what could still happen to them.

When they had left decades before, it had been decided that Molly, the last remaining member of the Clark family, would be allowed to remain, yet only as an outcast outside of their crowded village.

Amelia knew it was taboo to visit with her in the crumbling cottage that she rarely stepped foot outside of. That did not stop her from going whenever she could sneak away. The punishment could be time in the box, a tight wooden cell in the center of the square that would cook you in the summer and freeze you in the winter, or worse, banishment. It was worth the risk to spend time with the only person she had ever known who could pass a thought entirely outside of the church's word.

Her parents were kind, which was not something she could say for all the village elders, and she was grateful to be under their roof. However, her mother's position on the Privy Assembly held her close to the cloak of those who spoke on behalf of the power of the church. Jane Taylor was a realist as best as she could be, having spent her life under the veil of the village, even as she toed the line. Amelia had learned from her mother's actions that there needed to be space to press against rigid rules if you were to know the difference between right and wrong.

Jane had spent her youth wishing for the strength to discover what lived beyond the white-capped waves that pushed against the shore of the island, a shimmering guard that held them within the Privy's teachings. Amelia had admired her mother's will even as she held the responsibility of being the keeper of the Taylor seat on the Assembly. Thanks to her similar mindset, Molly had become Amelia's closest confidant outside her mother.

Unfortunately, due to the politics of an archaic community, Molly was punished for her views simply because she dared to voice them. Either way, living in her run-down cottage never seemed to bother her. If anything, she found peace being on her own without the buzz of superstitious rules.

Amelia pulled at her thick braid that was swung over her shoulder, hating how it pulled at her scalp. "Have you heard from him?"

"Not since the last time I spoke of it," Molly sighed, straightening the tattered apron she wore to cover a new rip in her dress, "and it would be best if you did not ask after him, Amelia. Even here."

Tossing her hair back, she sat softly on the edge of Molly's bed, the only place to perch in the tiny home other than the chair the plump, white-haired woman currently occupied. "I don't see why the others can't know of his kindnesses, is all. Doesn't seem like something that should be kept to yourself."

Molly let out a heavier sigh even as she smiled at the young woman. "You know better than to go against the Privy, girl. You best be getting your head right with that before you have your own seat at that table to worry about."

Amelia frowned at the dirt floor that she shuffled her feet over. She did not like it when her imminent spot on the assembly was brought up. The eldest child of the previous member would inherit the seats, which could be traced back to each original family. Being the oldest was obviously not her choice, nor was the rule. The position was one that she did not aspire to. The fact that it would be her future upon her mother's death made her life feel even more bleak. Her mother had the family name of Allen when she married Gavin Taylor, yet she had been set to take the Taylor seat from birth, being the direct descendent and next in line for the place Joseph Taylor had claimed upon the creation of their new land.

Molly never had anything good to say of the Privy. After all, they had been the ones to force her to the edge of humanity because of the choices made by her family. On top of that cruelty, they had the gull to invalidate her family's seat, disrespecting all members of the Clark clan that had worked alongside them from the day they crashed into their new lives. The Privy Assembly would be a completely different entity if Molly's rational mind was still being voiced among the women who currently bowed down faithfully to the Shephard's armored rules.

Amelia learned not to bring that point up to her. Even though she would brush the fact away as if it was of no importance, the sadness that comes from betrayal would darken her eyes. It broke Amelia's heart to see such a kind, intelligent woman treated so poorly by her own people.

Molly pushed herself from the chair and sat the blackened kettle on the fire grate. Picking up a glass jug of water to fill it, she put a finger to her lips with a mischievous grin.

"You have heard from John! He has come to see you, hasn't he?" Amelia declared, bouncing in place and looking about the room for the treasure.

"My brother is smart enough not to come to see me unless it is of importance," Molly reminded her, "but he is good enough to leave me gifts." Molly pulled out a small paper box with delicate pictures of flowers decorating the edges. She handed it to Amelia, who inhaled the sweet scent of the contraband tea.

"I don't understand how he can bring whatever the Privy demands, and wonderful treats like these must be hidden." Even though she felt guilty when Molly shared the rich flavored teas that would explode against her tongue, she had gladly accepted a taste every time it had been offered over the years. "Sometimes, I think I should stand in the middle of the square and let everyone know about John as loud as I can. They shouldn't think the Shephard is managing to bring us such riches when you and John bring us the blessings. It's not right. It's certainly not fair for her to keep it a secret."

"When you're on the Assembly, you will be quite surprised by the unfairness of it all; I will tell you that much for free." Molly shook her head, frustration crumpling her kind face. She stumbled a step, lifting the clay mugs from the crooked, wooden shelf that held her worldly goods.

Amelia caught them before they hit the floor. "Molly, you need to be careful." She helped her back to her seat. "I hate the idea of you living out here on your own." Looking around the tight space, she noticed the cracked hole in her roof had been mended. "Now, I know John has been here!" Amelia set the cups on the overturned wooden bucket that served as Molly's table and poured the hot water over the tea bags the tired woman had placed inside. "He takes such good care of you. I know you don't want to hear it again, but why don't you go with him to the mainland if you won't fight for a spot in the village? It cannot be as bad as they say if John has made a go of it for so many years."

"I am perfectly fine here, thank you. I am far too old to find out what devil lives across those waves when I am already settled in with the devil that makes his home here," Molly chuckled and sipped her tea with a toothless grin. "John looks after me. I have what I need. I have you as well, my sweet girl. Until they marry you off, I suppose."

Amelia glared over the hot steam in the mug that she softly blew into. "Let's not ruin a pleasant visit with those awful thoughts."

"That's fair," Molly nodded, agreeing to change the subject, "Did you read the book I gave you? He left a few more for us to take a gander at."

"It's still under my pillow. I haven't had a moment to myself in days," Amelia moaned. Her mother was aware of the books that Molly would share with her, even though they were strictly forbidden. They had never spoken of their existence except for the moment Jane had caught her reading about the aching heart of a young woman in a Jane Austen novel, her absolute favorite author. Her mother had made it sternly clear that she would never be seen with a tome that the church or Privy did not provide. Her small, proud smile told Amelia that she was not to be caught, not that she should stop reading.

Knowing how much it meant to her, John had been kind enough to include books in his secret deliveries to his sister. Amelia felt indebted to him for the worlds he was able to bring to her fingertips. People and places that her mind struggled to picture with the plain and tiresome existence that she woke up to every day. Living within the days that played on a loop in her mind was far more pleasant than anything that made up her reality.

"I would welcome you to read them here if it wasn't for how lost you get in them," Molly teased and swallowed the last of her drink, "It is dangerous enough for you to be out here sharing a chat with the evil 'ol witch in the dark, spooky forest."

Amelia did not share the laugh that Molly barked. She knew very well that Molly Clark was nothing close to a witch. Accusations of witchcraft were not uncommon, with the origins of their community starting with just that, and she did not believe a word of it. The wart-covered witches in the stories that lay on the soft pages of the loaned books were laughable with their dramatic spellcasting and moonlit nonsense.

It was the mention of the dark forest that had her eyes dart to the smudged, cracked window that sat halfway up the wall beside the cottage's front door.

The idea of witches among them may have been challenging for her to accept, but evil was something that she truly believed in. Something that she had witnessed with her own eyes. The dark beings that would drift on the edge of the woods were well-known to everyone. Quietly observing them, they never breached the edge of the forest. Their dark masses would flit about, murmuring amongst themselves. At times, a giggle would drift towards her, putting the hairs on her neck on end. The seasons turning from icy stillness to fresh, warm breezes was the first sign that the frightening visitors would increase in sightings.

The sun lowering on the skyline let her know it was time to head back.

Leaving Molly alone in the forest and at risk made her feel horrible every time. The thought of luring the darkness back into the village and putting everyone at risk felt worse.

Amelia had tried to talk to Molly about that threat many times, only to have her wave the idea away with a flick of her wrist. She would always repeat that if the Devil himself were too frightened to come for her, she wouldn't waste a thought on the shadows of the trees.

It always made her squirm to hear her talk so lightly of the Devil. It seemed as if she was calling danger upon herself for no reason other than tempting him to challenge her. Being in her nineties, it was not wise to so lightly play games with her soul. Even so, Molly had a toughness about her that made it hard to decide if it was for the best or worst. It was hard to imagine anything that could go up against her and win.

Molly noticed her attention on the window. "Well, dear, it would be best if you got on back. I think I will spend some time giving a look at the new books before the light leaves for the day."

Amelia rose to kiss her on both cheeks and give her a tight squeeze before making promises to return as soon as she could with the book she had tucked under her pillow fully read. As usual, Molly handed her a jar filled with water, which was sweetened with a splash of the sugar that John secreted to her. Not for Amelia but for the crystal bowl that sat just outside her door. For as long as Amelia could remember, that dish had sat out on a weathered wooden stool to serve the generations of delightful hummingbirds who would hover over the treat. Opening the door, she found one awaiting the top-up of the dish, its gorgeous green feathers glistening in the last of the day's sun. Tipping the jar over the bowl, she emptied its contents before setting it just inside Molly's door. She watched the swift bird buzz about its reward for a moment, lingering in the happiness that the cottage brought to her.

Setting out, her eyes scanned the woods as her feet carried her as quickly as possible while keeping each step silent. Getting caught coming out of the forest was not something that she wanted to add to the list of wrong-doings she had been scorned for as of late. Every crack of a twig or rustle of leaves in the late spring breeze caught her breath in her throat, her heart pounding as quickly as each of her footsteps.

When she came to the clearing that led to the bustling village, she squared her shoulders and strolled out from behind the outbuilding that held the sparse gardening tools. Picking up a rake which was haphazardly held to the handle with rope, she acted as if it was the most interesting thing she had ever laid eyes on as footfalls approached.

"Amelia! Where have you been?" A sweet voice called out with concern. She was in luck. The only one to see her arrive was her dear friend Elsbeth, whom she affectionately called Ellie.

Tossing the rake against the wall, she stepped away to greet her. She ignored the disappointed look on her delicately pale face. "I was looking for...," she trailed off, looking for an answer. Ellie narrowed her eyes at her friend's obvious lie. "Oh, shush now. I finished my chores for the day before I went to check on her. I shouldn't have to sneak off to see her, anyways."

Ellie was also fond of Molly, although she was fonder of following the rules. She had a chronic need to please that seemed to keep her nerves vibrating throughout her short, waif body. They could not have been more different in mind and body, yet they had been as close as sisters for as long as they knew. More so than Amelia was with her own blood-born sister. Where Amelia had a mass of deep auburn hair that refused to be contained by the braid all girls in the village were to wear, Ellie had a tiny wheat-colored plait as thin as her fingers. Amelia's crisp teal eyes, inherited from her father, were in contrast with Ellie's wide hazel eyes that currently looked back at her with concern. The near extra foot of height Amelia had on her caused her to bend in order to pull her friend into her arms, consoling her worriment away.

"You are going to find yourself in the box, Amelia. Today is not the day to anger the elders."

They started for the fenced garden, making themselves look occupied. "What has angered them today?" Amelia queried, knowing it would only take the most minor discomfort to throw them into a fit of unnecessary frenzy.

"Shephard Ward has been having the scent again," Ellie whispered.

"Where?" Amelia asked, uneasy with what was to come, no matter the answer.

"The woods behind the barn," she responded, opening the small, latched gate to the gardens and following Amelia in, "but it's worse than last time. She's seeing the big flowers again and says that something big is on its way. They're cloistered in the church now."

Shephard Ellen Ward held the Stewart seat on the assembly and took her role as head of the Privy as seriously as a heartbeat. The community members knew they had no choice but to take her as seriously as well. Amelia's mother had made hushed comments in the safety of their home that there were times that she questioned the visions and decisions made by the austere, middle-aged woman. Words that she would never speak outside of their walls or from her own seat in the Privy.

To go against the Shephard was to go against us all.

To move against the grain of the Privy's word was not done. It helped that the universe, through death or disappearance, had created an Assembly made up solely of docile women who bowed to the orders of Ellen Ward. If Jane Taylor, in all of her rebellious nature, did not have the gumption to speak out, the others certainly would not either. To question her was not to even be thought of. When Shephard Ward made her ability to smell the decrepit smell of the cursed flower known, those who found her mad were wise enough to cast their eyes down and swallow their opinions.

The scent was something no one had experienced before, even though Shephard Ward insisted that all women in her family had since Eleanor Stewart had set foot on the island. Since taking up the leader's seat, Ellen Ward had insisted on many things. To Amelia, most of it all seemed more deeply rooted in fantasy than what she read in the books that the Shephard was so violently opposed to.

"I'm sorry, Ellie, but the curse is just a story," Amelia said in a hushed voice after a group of men, tools over their shoulders, passed by the fence. "There is no way that Flora Edgar was a *witch*." She said the word as quietly as she could. Speaking of Flora Edgar was a direct trip to the box.

"I don't see how you could say that. It's not something they would lie to us about. You have seen the painting she had of that cursed flower. There's a reason it was the only thing from her family that survived the shipwreck. A flower that is said to smell like death can not have anything but evil in its roots. Death, Amelia," Ellie hissed and turned her to face her, "If that isn't a flower of a witch, what is?"

"It's a painting of a ridiculous flower, Ellie. There is no such thing as a flower bigger than a grown man! The whole idea is silly, and even if it could be real, it's Shephard Ward who can smell it, is it not? It's our leader who has visions of them growing up around us. What does that make her?" Amelia countered and regretted it as soon as Ellie pulled away, tripping into a patch that had been tilled for planting.

She shook out her thin leather shoe with a groan before scolding her friend, "Talk like that is dangerous, and you know it. Why must you always push against the elders? We've known about Flora's curse on us since we were smaller than the chickens, Amelia. What will you say next? That the Watchers aren't real? For goodness sake. We have seen them together!" Ellie placed her slight fingers over her lips when she raised her voice, her cheeks reddening. She looked about to make sure her words had not reached anyone's ears before she continued, "No matter what you want to believe, now is not the time to press them."

Amelia opened her mouth to argue with her friend when her name rang out. Peter, her eleven-year-old brother, was skipping up the pathway towards them. His arm was outstretched over the short fence to graze his hand along the tall weeds that had yet to be pulled in preparation for the next round of planting.

"Papa wants you home to help with dinner. Mama is still doing business with the Privy," he announced when he reached them.

"All right, Peter. I'll be there in a moment," she said quickly, wanting to finish her conversation. He stood rooted in place, shredding a long blade of grass with his dirt-crusted fingers. "I heard you, Peter. Run along now."

He twirled the ripped grass around his arm. "I don't want meatloaf."

"Fine, Peter. Head home and tell Father I'm on my way," Amelia ordered with thinly veiled impatience.

"I want corn chowder," he stated, still not taking his leave.

"Fine. I will need to check the jars, but I think we still have some. Why don't you head home and check the cellar? I'll be right along behind you."

Amelia shook her head with humor when he smiled broadly and turned to run home with the grace of a boy still growing into his legs.

The need to prove her point faded as quickly as he disappeared into the village. "Ellie, I'm sorry. You're right. I should not be making trouble where trouble doesn't need to be," she apologized truthfully.

Ellie's shoulders loosened, the weight of her friend's misdeeds lessening on her conscience. "I know you're just full of spirit," she conceded, "It's one of the things I love about you, Amelia. We just need to keep good while the Shephard is in the state she is. It's best for everyone in the end."

"You are right as you always are, Elsbeth," she declared, making her friend's nose crinkle at the mention of her given name, "I will walk in your shadow to the path of righteousness as always."

They shared a laugh and a hug before parting ways for the evening. Her stomach rumbled at the thought of dinner, and she realized she had not eaten since her breakfast of two eggs and a glass of milk. Her lunch broth would have most certainly been gobbled up by Peter when she had not arrived to claim it. She thought it was better for him to have the extra meal since he was growing more quickly than the weeds they walked through. He was going to be a tall member of the Taylor family, just like their father Gavin and herself, although he shared his fair hair and dark eyes with their mother. Sarah, Amelia's seven-year-old sister, did as well and was growing slowly into their mother's petite height, looking more like Jane Taylor's twin by the day.

Walking through the unassuming cottages toward her own, the silence sent a buzz of tension over her skin. The

Privy Assembly still had the doors to the church firmly closed, and the white candle set on the porch symbolically said they were in council with important business.

The Privy was responsible for every decision made within the village. The church's Cleric, Fredrick Gordon, was even at the mercy of their power. From crops to punishing misconduct to deciding who would marry and when it was left to the nine seats of power.

Being that the entire population was descended from only ten families, it was a bit of science to match up couples in order to keep bloodlines from crossing too severely. Amelia was sure that a more significant issue with controlling the pairings was to hold the power of the families unbalanced and in favor of the Shephard. Ellen Ward did not even try to shield her biases in favor of her own. She had warped rules and ordinances that fit her narrative so deeply that fact and fiction had blended together to create a society that hardly resembled the memories of the elders nor the early writings of the settlement.

Amelia could not help but see Ellen Ward as something dark that should be feared, not followed. When that thought had once crossed her lips to Ellie, the response was swift and severe.

The Shephard is to be respected above all others within the realms outside of Heaven. The Shephard leads the good within the Good Land. To turn your cheek shall bring the darkness that burns all in its sight upon us. Keep good and follow the path to light.

The words were a part of every villager's mind as profoundly as the need to breathe. When the original eleven families set out to find a new world that would be their Good Land, they did so with hope, faith, and love. The shipwreck that found them on the land they now existed on, which caused the death of the Edgars, including their precious children, spoke of a darkness in their hearts that changed the path—one without light and goodness. Amelia believed blaming the Edgars, especially Flora, for whatever befell them was unfair. Dishonest, even. They had suffered such tragedy, never even reaching what they had all hoped to be the Good Land. It was cruel to damn them as nothing more than evil and the source of their suffering.

The door to the church creaked open as she passed, and she paused to watch Ellen Ward pick up the white candle to snuff the flame. When the smoke rose from the wick, the other eight members of the Privy filed out, with her mother leading the line. She looked to Amelia with tired eyes as she stepped from the porch and fell in step with her back to their cottage. Soon, the others split off to go home to their own families before the sun slipped away for the night.

Evil walked among them; she knew that much. Watchers, witches, or one of their own, she could never tell.

CHAPTER TWO

HER MOTHER MOVED SILENTLY about the tight kitchen, putting together the nightly meal for the family. Amelia followed along at her side, helping where she could to ease her workload. After slicing the day-old bread, she set out the places at their heavy round table, which was the pride of the household.

A similar table had been lovingly built for each of the first ten cottages as soon as they were constructed. As the community expanded with each new generation, more homes were built, extending the village further toward the dense forest that circled and concealed their world. Although tables were made for each and every one, they did not have the craftsmanship of the original ten, which included Amelia's. Louis Gordon, one of the first settlers, had been behind the delicate carvings that swirled along the edges and down the legs, creating a working piece of art. Unfortunately, for Gordon and the generations that followed, he had been one of the first to perish under the conditions they were forced to live under when the Good Land was being developed. The flowers, spirals of vines, and delicate leaves that were still crisply visible on the table that sat in Amelia's home were a way for him to live on in a place he had had such high hopes for.

"Sarah, go wash up, please," Amelia called out to her sister. She was pleased when she set her doll aside and walked dutifully to the wash basin.

The tension that pinched at her mother's petite shoulders radiated to every surface in the house. When she came from a Privy meeting and remained silent, it was known that she was not to be pestered. Amelia was desperate to know what they had been discussing, and she chewed her lip to contain her questions. Her mother would share what she could when she was ready. If she could share anything at all.

Amelia was now eighteen; she and her friends were all around the age that the decisions of marriage pairings would be announced. In the books that she had devoured, marriage was romantic and could never come soon enough. Couples would fall passionately in love, and there would be a celebration of the union's welcomed joy. She had never experienced such feelings for anyone, let alone someone she would want to spend her life with. If the choice were hers, she would be happy to stay with her family as her life was forever. Even living as an outcast as Molly did seemed better than being forced to marry someone chosen for her, without any say on what her future would hold. Being separated from her family would be a hard choice if it came down to it, so at least with marriage, she could remain close to them. She always tried to find the positive when life seemed impossible to understand.

Unlike Amelia, Ellie was very much like the girls in the novels. She would be madly in love with one village boy or another every other day. She spoke of her inevitable marriage with whimsy and excitement, even though she had no idea who would be selected. Whoever it was would be lucky to have such a pure spirit as their partner.

Amelia's parents seemed to be in love. As in love as she could comprehend. They were friendly and playful with each other, working well together with every crisis that would arise. So many others were not as fortunate, with many cold couplings under unhappy roofs.

She dragged her spoon around the corn chowder, pushing the thoughts away. There was no way to know if the meeting was even about engagements; it could have been a million different topics if the Shephard was having visions again. There was no reason to fall into a pit of worry before it presented itself, and Amelia tried to think of anything else.

Her father cleared his throat, startling the group, "Have you been practicing your hymns today?" he asked Peter. "I was speaking with Cleric Fredrick, and he told me how well you've been improving. Enough to join the front of the choir if you keep at it."

Peter smiled widely as he swallowed a mouthful of chowder. "I have, Papa. I really like the new ones he's written. I get to sing them really loud," he giggled and filled his mouth again.

"That's good to hear," he nodded. Looking to his wife, who stared into her bowl, lost in thought as she ate, he cleared his throat again and returned to the silence.

Whatever had been discussed was not something that had pleased Jane Taylor.

When they finished their meal, Amelia helped her mother clear and clean the dishes and got Sarah and Peter settled for bedtime before slipping away to her room. With the mood her mother was in, she would soon be retiring to her bed with mumbles of another headache.

That would mean Amelia would be left alone for the evening.

One of the only benefits of coming of age was having a bedroom all to herself. It would be Sarah's once Amelia was married off and settled in the home of her husband's family. For now, it was a place to secretly consume her books under candlelight. The lard used to make their candles was not plentiful, as the meats that created it were used sparingly. She would give herself a chapter or two before snuffing it out to save it for another night. On evenings when the moon was full, she would take advantage of its soft glow through her window and read until it moved onto a place in the sky out of view, forgoing a good night's sleep for the escape of her stories. When the sky was moonless, as she currently found it, she would make quick use of a stone flint in hopes of not being heard.

Jane Austin kept her company for the time being, telling her all about a young woman named Elizabeth, whom Amelia wished she could be friends with. She seemed perfectly happy to live her life on her own, being independent and finding joy in her days rather than chores. Her mind soon drifted away to the rolling meadows of Elizabeth's life, seeing a world outside her confinement on the island.

A knock on her door made her jump. She slid the book under her pillow and passed a quick breath over the candle. "Sorry, Father, I was finishing a few chores. I have the candle out now." She glanced about her and snatched up an apron she had been mending as an excuse to be awake.

The door opened, and her mother's head peered into the dark room. "It's me, Poppet," she whispered, using the pet name she had called Amelia since she was a baby.

Amelia sat up in bed, surprised to see her. "Is everything okay, Mama?" She could see that the sadness on her face had lessened when she sat beside her. The sweet smell of dandelion wine was on her breath.

"Everything is right as rain. I just wanted to have a chat with you. I missed you today," she answered, putting an arm around her eldest daughter.

Amelia wanted to ask her all about the meeting and what had caused her to be so sullen. She still kept her lips tight, knowing her mother would tell her what she could in her own time. Questioning her would cause her to close up and return to her silent brooding. That sat quietly in the dark until she spoke again.

"Are you happy, Poppet?" She pulled her arm back from her daughter and fussed with the hem of her nightshirt. "What I mean is, are you happy with your life? As it is?"

Amelia was not sure how to answer such a loaded question. She twisted her fingers together on her lap, worrying what would cause her mother to need to ask such a question in the middle of the night. "I'm happy, Mama. I'm happy here with you – and with Papa, and Peter, and Sarah," she added quickly.

Jane sniffled and blew out a tiny breath. Her head bobbed in a tight nod. "I want you to have the life you want, Amelia. All I want is for you to be happy. For all of my children to be happy."

"We are Mama. Don't worry about us," Amelia offered, trying to ignore the quickened pace in her chest thanks to the ominous tone in her mother's voice. They sat side by side for a moment before Amelia worked up the courage to ask the question herself. "Are you happy, Mama?" Her voice was barely a whisper.

Jane turned to her daughter, a tight smile on her face. Even in the near darkness of the room, Amelia could see the damp glisten in her eyes. "I'm happy, Poppet. You make me very happy. I want you to know that."

Worry started to overtake her with the intensity of her mother's gaze, "Is everything okay, Mama? Are you okay?"

"It was just a very long day," she offered, looking away. "You know how spring is always so hectic."

She knew that to be true and hoped that was all that was burdening her. She watched her mother stare out the window in thought and took her hand in hers. "If there is anything I can do to help you, you know I will."

Jane shook herself from her thoughts and pressed a smile to her lips, "I know you would, Poppet. You always make me proud." She pulled her into a hug and seemed to shake away her heavy mood in her daughter's embrace. When she leaned back from her, the usual mask of contentment had returned. "Are you ready for planting tomorrow? We are blessed with an abundance of seeds this year. We should have a hearty harvest this year," she chimed, standing from the bed.

She was used to the mood changes of her mother. It would always make her siblings happy when the jovial spirit suddenly returned to her. Amelia felt otherwise as she grew older, learning that it was merely her mother pushing her upset further and further down into her soul. There was no way anyone could maintain that much weight for long, and she knew that one day, it would drown her right before their eyes.

"I am, Mama," was all she could muster.

"Good...good," she mumbled as she moved to the door. "Best get some sleep, then. I will see you in the morning."

"I love you, Mama," Amelia called out to her as she disappeared down the hall.

"I love you, too, Poppet," she echoed and shut the door behind her.

Amelia stood from her bed and moved the candle jar from the small table beside her to the low dresser, the only other furniture in the room. The thick, sour smell of it was turning her stomach. Returning to the side of her bed, she looked outside. The low light of the moon's sliver warped the view of the trees through the wavy glass of her window. Other than the nightly calls of birds, everything had stilled in the village. She preferred the abandoned state, finding peace with everyone tucked away from her.

She reached down for her book, hoping for enough light to read a few more pages. When her eyes strained to decipher the letters, she hid it away again and returned to gazing at the forest. The branches of the trees gracefully swayed in the night air.

Her heart sent a wish out into the cloudy sky that she could take her family and slip away into one of her books forever. She pictured her mother sipping tea with Elizabeth Bennett while Sarah romped through fields of wildflowers. Father and Peter would be laughing along the shoreline, fishing for a scrumptious supper they would all share. No worries of a Privy Assembly, no Shephard, no backbreaking chores, no rumbling stomachs when the food ran low. They would read books, discuss art, and live freely wherever they chose.

That was how she would picture her life if her parents had left the island before she had been born. Not the horrible pit of war and hatred that the outside world was preached to them to be. She refused to believe that the existence outside of the village was as terrible as they warned of. Her parents, as open-minded as they could be, disagreed with her. It was a conversation that was quickly shut down whenever Amelia brought it up. As rebellious as her mother could be, there was fear that was palpable at the very mention of leaving.

Amelia stretched her arms over her head, fatigue overtaking her. If only her mind would be as ready to rest as her body. Giving one last look at the peaceful scene outside her window, she started to crawl into bed. She froze in place when a rustling in the trees caught her eye. Squinting, she struggled to focus through the blurry glass. It was too far away to hear any snap of twigs that the motion created, but she could plainly see the tree's branches bending unnaturally. A dark shape started to make a shadow in the dim moonlight that was breaking through the clouds, and Amelia's body went cold.

The Watchers had returned.

She ducked down low enough to still be able to keep her sight on the tree line. Could this have been what had her mother so upset? Could they have known they were returning? As insane as she believed the Shephard to be, she did say that something big was about to happen. Amelia worried that she may be witnessing the start of that threat.

The veil of darkness the encroaching phantoms cast moved slowly along the edge of the village, never coming into the light. Her lip began to tremble when she noticed that it was not alone. Two, and then three, and then four other shadows joined it behind the trees, casting dark ribbons against the tall pines.

Her body became rigid, unable to run for help. The only sound in her room was her pulse thumping in her ears and her raspy, quick breath that tightened her lungs. The shadows would bend and stretch as they slipped about until they all moved together and stopped. The darkness they made swooped around like a giant winged bird stalking its prey. Amelia stared at the huge mass they created as it became smaller the further it away, back into the forest until they disappeared completely. Her eyes scanned the village for minutes that felt like hours, looking for a trace of them. The stillness of her world had returned.

Crawling under her quilt, the weight of it did nothing to quelch the shivers that had overtaken her body. Playing the scene over in her mind, she wondered if she should alert her parents to what she had seen. Her body refused to move. If she were to call out to her parents, it would only upset her brother and sister. They did not need such a deep fright when they were sleeping peacefully in the assumed safety of their beds. She pictured them terrified and crying when they saw the frightened state she found herself in.

When she could catch her breath, she slowly slid the blanket off and set her feet on the cold wood of the floor. Steadying herself against the tremble that remained in her legs, she stood. Looking from the window to the door, she tried to decide what to do. As her nerves calmed, her mind took on a different perspective. Her rational side told her that her tired eyes did not see what she thought she did. She had been reading too long, and the moon's new light had played tricks on her. She was upset by the encounter with her mother. She was still nervous from the walk home through the woods earlier.

She turned back to the window while thinking of even more excuses. The trees swayed only by the power of the breeze. There was no sign of intrusion among the forest floor, and the birds once again called out to each other into the night.

It was just a trick of her eyes.

There was no reason to alarm her parents and upset her mother further. It had been a long, strange day, and all that was needed was a good night's sleep. Even as she started to believe the rationalizations she was feeding herself, she could not pull her eyes from the window. She wished Elizabeth could jump from the pages and stand beside her, holding her hand until she found her bravery again.

She pushed away the thought of Molly alone in her cottage and told herself there was nothing to worry about because nothing had happened. When the work in the garden was done, she would sneak away to see her, and everything would be fine. Molly would greet her with another book to become lost in and a hot cup of tea.

Oh, how she wished she could have a steaming mug at that moment to calm her nerves.

Her exhaustion overcame her fear, and she settled under the covers, staring at the bare wooden boards of her ceiling.

Nothing but a trick of her eyes, she told herself again.

If she was of any use in the morning, she needed to get some rest. Her mother was counting on her to pull her weight with the long day that waited for them. Tossing and turning until she found a spot that soothed her, she pushed the images of the forest down until all she saw was the darkness of her eyelids.

Sleep took its time coming to her, and the morning came too soon.

The next day's heavy chores took its toll on her after such a restless sleep. She chose not to mention what she had witnessed among the trees, finding it easier to deny its reality the further away from the fright she got. That did not stop her eyes from tracing along the woods at the sound of any movement. As far as she knew, the Watchers had never appeared during the day, so the threat was done until evening. At the same time, she had also never seen as many at once. Not that she allowed herself to believe she had seen them. The lies became more empowering the more she repeated them.

By the time the seeds were in the soil, she had decided to keep the entire affair to herself. Her mother had been pulled away with more issues with the Privy that would undoubtedly cause undue stress, and Ellie was already on edge with the news of the Shephard having the scent again. Giving the nervous young woman more to worry about would be cruel.

"Amelia," a voice called out in a whisper. Amelia turned to see the young man peeking around one of the crumbling sheds that held the communal tools. His mop of brown curls that matched his eyes bobbed as he gestured for her to come to him. Although friendships between boys and girls were frowned upon, Amelia, Ellie, and Adam had been joined at the hips since they were toddlers.

"Why are you sneaking about over here, Adam? You look like a naughty raccoon," she laughed when she reached him. The smile slipped away when she saw the serious look on his face. Ellie stepped out beside him with a matching chagrin. "What has you two so solemn?"

"Haven't you heard yet?" Ellie asked, pulling Amelia behind the shed, shielding them from the prying eyes of the villagers who still milled about finishing their day's work.

"Arthur Allen has gone missing!" Adam exclaimed. He peeked around the corner to ensure he had not been too loud before he continued, "His wife was pacing about and ranting in front of the church before they pulled her inside to calm her down. I heard Annie Wilson talking to the others as they arrived, and she said Mary Allen was mad with worry, saying she couldn't find him anywhere. They had gone to bed, and he was not there when she woke. Now, he's nowhere to be found around the village."

"It's even worse than that, Amelia," Ellie rasped. Her body was trembling from head to toe. "They were back last night. A whole mess of them," her eyes welled with tears, "I saw them."

Amelia stared back at the two. Adam shook with excitement, and Ellie was almost paled to the point of transparency. There was no denying what she had seen. She had not been the only witness to the intruders, and now Arthur Allen had disappeared. Guilt for not coming forward with what she saw out of selfish fear slumped on her shoulders. She tried to move past her denial and admit what she had observed.

It had been a few years since someone had gone missing from the village. Alice Stewart, the only child of Edith and Charles Stewart and Ellie's cousin, was only seven years old when she disappeared in the middle of the day. A shoe and her stuffed doll were all that was found in the woods. It was decided that she had wandered off and become lost, the wild animals of the forest taking care of the rest. Edith and Charles had never stopped mourning her loss and had never borne another child.

The Watchers had not been considered as a possibility as to the cause of young Alice's unfortunate end. It had happened during the day and in the cold of winter when there had not been a sighting of them on record or in the spoken fables that were passed among them all.

This time, Arthur Allen, a hard-working man well-liked by all, had disappeared the same night as a spotting. Amelia's stomach turned at the thought of what could have come to him.

She did not have a chance to tell them she had also seen the frightening visitors in the dark of the woods. The three jumped when the clang of the small heavy bell struck by the Shephard rang out. Four quick smacks followed by one and repeated until all had gathered filled the air and made Amelia quicken a step toward the crowd. Word of Arthur had made its way to most of the villagers as they murmured their thoughts on the news among themselves until Shephard Ward hushed them and began to address the worried group.

Her face was not one of concern or upset. A smile glowed on her face as she raised her hands above her. "My friends, please. I need you to settle and listen. I have news."

"How can she look so pleased with herself?" Adam quipped with disbelief. They watched Mary Allen at her side, dabbing her red, swollen eyes with a hanky already doused in her tears. She stood with a numb stare that spoke to the grief that had overcome her entirely. "She has some nerve to smile when poor Mary is suffering."

"Adam, shush. You'll get us in trouble," Ellie chided. She wrung her hands with worry, turning her skin red.

The Allen's three children, Walter and Rose – both grown with Rose already married off to sweet Gilbert Morrison – and Neil, only sixteen years old, stood a few paces back from their mother. Rose and Neil mirrored their mother's mute sadness while Walter stood stiffly, staring up at the sky, avoiding the glares of the villagers.

"I know there has been gossip among you about our dear Arthur Allen. I will address the inappropriate chitter chatter at another time," Shephard Ward said with a poisonous grin and an uncomfortably forced eye contact with those already gathered before letting a serious mask slip over her expression, "The truth of the matter is that our dear Arthur has decided to leave us," she paused as a ripple of reaction rose up from the crowd, "Now, now. Your judgment is not needed at this time, and it is not our place to cast evil thoughts upon this family because of one man's choice."

"I don't believe it," Adam croaked, "Arthur would never leave his family," he glared at Ellie when she nudged her elbow into his side, "It can't be," he added, watching Neil attempt to hold himself together. He clung to his sister's hand as if it was all that could hold him up, "What will happen to them?"

Ellie's eyes begged him to stop speaking. If the Shephard was already in the mindset of punishment, catching her eye was not a good idea.

"Mary and her children have suffered a loss, and the weight of Arthur's shame will be carried on their backs for years to come. That being said, I can say that the cause of my visions was most likely based on the betrayal this man had planned and, sadly, has brought down upon us," Shepard Ward declared as Mary stifled a sob into her hankie. "I have seen things within my visions that cannot be shared with you. What I will say is that because of this, there will be mercy." Another wave of commentary whirled about the villagers. "Mary will not be cast aside and shall instead be mercifully declared a widow."

Mary's knees betrayed her at the word. Walter reached out to hold her on her feet, his eyes remaining locked defiantly at the sky above. His jaw was tight with the anger that held his body tightly.

"How could she know that he wanted to leave? If Mary didn't know...," Adam's query was cut short by Ellie's tight grip on his arm, her attention straight ahead to the Shephard.

"In repentance for his transgression, Mary and her children, along with their future children, shall pass unto us all but the bare essentials of belongings and rations until declared redeemed by the Privy Assembly. In addition, Walter Allen and Neil Allen shall not be considered for a marriage pairing until it has been decided that the stain of their father has faded to the point of no longer bringing their shame onto another family," the Shephard declared, confirming her decision with two swift knocks on the heavy bell in her hand. "I ask you to keep them in your prayers this evening when you gather with your families and praise be the grateful."

She turned and walked into the church with the Privy members, shutting the door heavily in the face of the Allens. A few villagers braved stepping forward and taking Mary by the hand, tugging her along to the safety of her cottage, which she was incredibly fortunate to have still.

"It doesn't make sense. Arthur had never made word of wanting to be a Mainlander. If anything, he spoke of them as nasty people that were beneath us," Amelia voiced as the trio parted from the crowd, moving quickly to the large stump at the edge of the woods that had become their meeting place.

"I can't say that I'm not jealous of Walter and Neil's situation," Adam mused and shrugged when he saw the judgemental glares from the girls, "What? Could you say that you are looking forward to being paired? I would rather be banned from a wife than pushed into marriage, is all."

Amelia could relate to that feeling with all of her being.

Ellie shook her head and perched on the edge of the old stump. "I don't understand it either. Mary did not look like she knew he was going to make such a big decision – and why would he leave her behind? They had always seemed to be settled well in their marriage."

"What if it was the Watchers?" Amelia posed, barely above a whisper, "What if the Shephard doesn't know they were here?"

"I can't bear to think of that," Ellie said, a shiver visible along her skin, "I can't stop thinking about seeing them creeping about in the dark."

"I saw them, as well," Amelia admitted, looking at them shyly.

"What?" Adam and Ellie squawked at once.

"Last night, I saw them in the forest." She watched their eyes widen at her revelation.

"Why didn't you say? We need to tell someone! What if they have harmed Arthur? They could be looking to harm us all!" Ellie shouted, stepping toward the village as if being pulled.

"You want to tell the Shephard that the Watchers have been seen again, just as she finished having her visions? Ellie, think for a moment," Adam demanded and pulled her back to them. "She has made the declaration and decisions already. To challenge her would lead to a punishment you do not want."

Amelia chewed her lip in thought, "I think he's right. There has to be a reason that Shephard Ward knew he had left. They have knowledge far out of our reach. They'll say we're making stories to favor the Allens if we tell them." She didn't know if her fear of the Privy or the fear of the Watchers was greater. Either way, it was easier to push it away and deal with whatever came next when it came.

"We would be punished along with them now, Ellie. It's too late," Adam conceded.

Ellie made a few more weak pleas to come clean to the elders before finally agreeing with the two. Mercy had already been shown to the Allens that day. Mercy that Shephard Ward used less than sparingly. When the sun dipped below the treeline, darkening the spot where they sat and bringing on the cool early evening air of spring, they made their way back to their cottages for the evening.

For now, the sighting would be kept between the three. They hoped it would be the last but knew their eyes would be on the treeline for nights to come.

Chapter Three

After the disappearance of Arthur Allen, it had been difficult to sneak away to spend time with Molly. The eyes of the villagers were rarely on their work anymore. Attention was drawn to each other with assumptions, suspicions, and distrust. Some were consumed with the worry that there could be others who would uproot their peace by turning traitorous like the likes of Arthur. Some with the unease that they were not told the truth about his fleeing the island for a life on the mainland. All were busy with an opinion on the remaining Allen family every time they would pass by.

Spending time away from the tension was worth the risk, and Amelia made a point to sit down with Molly at least every other day. When she visited the day after the announcement of the Allen family's situation, the usually happy woman grew pensive and cut their teatime short, requesting to be alone. During another visit, she waved away Amelia's concern about the Watchers she had witnessed in the woods as paranoia and nonsense. She knew the land around her better than anyone, even though she never stepped outside and insisted the only threat to her resided within the village circle.

"What is to be afraid of? They gave them a name that means they have eyes," she snickered, "The birds watch us, too. Should I be afraid of them?"

"You can laugh all you want, Molly, but I have laid my own eyes on them. There is something unnatural about them. Something frightening."

"Frightening? Oh, my girl, you have yet to see frightening in this world," she cautioned. She cleared away the empty tea cups and folded the cloth that had carried the sweet bread Amelia had snuck away with. "There was a time they said those shapes they see in the trees were my doing. I was doing some sort of witchy work to punish those weak-minded nillies," Molly chuckled. "Louisa Miller told me that when she was bringing me out my rations. I suppose she was Louisa Ward then. She stopped coming out here once she married. How is she fairing nowadays?"

"She's well enough. She has three grandchildren now. Two are already grown and married," Amelia replied, not liking her attempt at changing the subject. "Why would they think that you were the cause of them?"

"Who? The Watchers, as you call them?" Molly asked and clucked her tongue when Amelia nodded, "Why wouldn't they? They need to cast evil on others so they don't have to take a good look at themselves. They don't have the stones to see their own darkness. It's how they've always been. Just look at the mess they made of poor Flora Edgar's memory."

"The Elders are pretty clear that she was a witch. Ellie agrees, but I think she was a witch as much as you are," Amelia mused, earning a grin from Molly.

The hunched woman shuffled among some papers that had been tucked within a book until she found the one she was looking for, "You know I love you visiting, dear. I see so much of myself in you," her smile drifted away as she sat in thought as she considered the papers in her hand. "I try not to say too much to affect your life in the village, even though I know I already say too much. It's just my way. Always has been," she admitted as she sat on her rickety chair with a heavy sigh. "I think it's time to pass this on."

Amelia sat at her feet on the hard dirt floor, her eyes narrowed with curiosity, waiting to see what Molly held in her crooked fingers. She watched as she turned the papers over, flattening the creases against her knee. "What is it, Molly?"

She passed it to Amelia and remained silent while she read. It was a print of a flower she knew well. A long yellow point that was wrapped with a delicately rippled, deep red petal at its base. It was the flower that was said to be a symbol of Flora's curse.

'*Royal Botanic Gardens Kew 1889*' was written in a fancy script above and '*Amorphophallus titanum*' below.

Opening the folded paper, she found more drawings of the flower. "What is this?"

"That old piece of paper was the reason that Flora is called a witch," Molly said flatly, pointing angrily at it.

She flipped the paper over and then over again, trying to find what it was that Molly was talking about. "This is the flower that the Privy have painted on their books. What's magic about this one?"

Molly crossed her arms across her chest. "Absolutely nothing."

Amelia looked up, confused. It was just a print of a flower. The small words inside welcomed people to come and see the giant flower that would amaze your eyes with its size and your nose with its smell.

Come and take witness of the exotic Corpse Flower and its pungent smell of death!

Amelia reread the line and looked up at her with wide-eyed shock, "That's what Shephard Ward says her visions are! She says the big flowers smell like death!" She looked down at the page and back to her, "Shephard Ward is a witch? Is that why they draw this flower on their books?"

Molly's shoulders shook with her amusement, "No, she is not a witch, sweet girl. Not the kind that has magic, at least. She is just as full of sheep dung as every Shephard before her. Including the first who decided Flora was a witch. Ellen Ward has just put her nutty twist on it like she does everything," Molly stood with a pained groan, muttering, "How anyone believes a word out of that woman's sauce box, I'll never know."

Amelia had wondered how the Shephard was able to describe the flower in the picture right down to the disgusting smell if she was not a witch. She had been doing nothing more than describing what was written on the old card invitation to a flower show. That is, if she had ever been able to see what now sat lightly in her hands. By doing so, she had made herself out to be the all-powerful savior between the villagers and the lasting threat of that poor woman who had lost her family and her life in the cold waters off the coast. The water that flowed just a mile away from where she now sat. "What is this?" she held up the paper, "What exactly am I looking at? What does this have to do with Flora?"

"That is one of the few things belonging to Flora Edgar that survived the shipwreck. That's where the founders learned of Flora's so-called death flower," Molly huffed and shook her head. "You know the legends of her yelling out curses as she lost the battle against the current. Not that anyone in their right mind wouldn't have something to say to the folks that had put her in the spot she was in," she scoffed. "I don't know if you've been told how much the Edgars did not want to take the journey."

Amelia was surprised at the revelation. "The original eleven families decided together to begin our community," Amelia insisted. Myth and rumor ran rampant among them, but this had been a consistent fact. "We came as one, and we live as one." She knew the words as easily as the tunes to the hymns they were required to set to memory. The Good Land was created by a communal agreement on the right way to live.

"Do you really think they would like to remember that they pushed the Edgars to go so they could take advantage of the land they owned overseas? That they were more or less forced to go along with the mob and then ended up losing their lives because of their foolishness? Her children, gone without a trace into the waves because the self-righteous wanted a place to live as they pleased?" Molly twisted a washcloth in her hands, her anger clenched in her jaw. "Making Flora the reason for their unfortunate situation took away their guilt and gave them an excuse for every horrible thing that happened once they found themselves stranded. This cursed land is exactly what they deserved, not the healthy land of the Edgars. I hope it still lies free of nasty people. Wild, with animals claiming it all."

"What does the flower have to do with it? I don't understand," Amelia pushed, pulling her back from her tangent.

"Flora's love of flowers and nature was not just in her name. She was renowned for her gardens and the wonderful creations she could make from them. Her balms and medicines were very popular in their town," she said with reverence. "It was another reason why they wanted her on that ship. The Edgars were of more than one use for the fools who thought they knew better. It was easy to change that around to potions and curses once she was no longer of use." She shifted in her seat and took the page from Amelia's hands. "This was in one box of Flora's that made it to shore. It was from a trip she had taken to England, like in your favorite books," Molly added with a nod to the stack along her wall. "It was to see the spectacular gardens. A memento – nothing more – and they used it to turn the sweet woman into a monster."

"How do you know all of this? Why doesn't everyone else know this?" Amelia asked, anger rising from her gut. The lies were beyond unkind; they were dangerous.

"My Grandmother Alice was her friend. She survived the wreck, of course." Molly wiped at her nose and loudly cleared her throat, "She watched them die and could do nothing to help. The guilt ate away at her every day she lived on this land, and she never forgot how they twisted her memory. She often spoke of her to my mother, and then when the time was right, the truth was passed on to me." She shook her head gently with pursed lips when her eyes grew damp with the emotions of her memories. She returned the print to Amelia's hands, "My Grandfather, Francis Clark, was the first to hold the Clark seat in the Privy, as you know, even though he's probably forgotten by the sheep in the village," she scowled at her window as if she could see the people she spoke of. "This was locked away with the remaining few things left of Flora and the Edgars. He snuck this out for my Grandmother, hoping it would bring her comfort. At the very least, he had hoped they would stop using drawings of that flower to frighten everyone into settling into the palms of their hands. As you can see, that did not work. After my grandmother had kept it safe, it was then passed to my mother and then to me. It helps us remember not only her dear friend who was sacrificed but how this entire place is built on lies. Nothing here is to be trusted, Amelia."

She looked down at the picture in her hands. It was a strange-looking flower. Nothing that looked like it could bring death or curses, no matter the name or how the Shephard used it. Tracing the flower's stem with her fingers, she pushed away the thought of how terrified the Edgars must have been in the cold, stormy waters. "Those poor people."

"It's a terrible shame all around, and that is what they built this community on. That's what gets my goat," Molly lamented. Silent thought held her for a moment before a smile lit up her eyes. "Here's something that might make you smile," she started with a slap on her legs, "Flora's name is from a language called Latin, and it means flower! The universe seems to always know what it's doing, doesn't she?"

Amelia smiled at what she thought to be nothing more than a coincidence. "Good thing she wasn't named something more menacing than a flower then, I suppose. Who knows what the curse would be made of then."

"It gets better. See that name there? The name of it?" Molly motioned toward the print. Amelia looked at the words - *Amorphophallus titanum* – unable to pronounce them. Molly leaned down to her, a mischievous smile dancing on her lips. "That's Latin, as well. It means giant, misshapen penis!" she whispered and erupted in a belly shaky laughter.

Amelia could feel the heat rise up her neck and cover her face when Molly spoke the word. The conservative villagers did not speak about things like that. Being that her outcast friend was about as free of spirit as she could imagine, it did not surprise her that she would know that fact and have the tongue to share it. There was little that Amelia had in her education about the workings of the opposite sex, yet she had enough to lose herself in a giggle when she braved a peek down at the flower. "Molly! Oh my goodness, you're terrible!" she spat between snickers.

They both stood when what sounded like footsteps were heard outside the door, losing the moment's merriment. Standing as still as beams, only their startled breaths were heard. Amelia moved to the window and saw nothing out of place. She looked over the inert flower pictured in her hands. It seemed impossible that everything she had been taught of her ancestors and their very purpose had been cowardly based on something so innocent. She looked out of the window again, straining against the hazy glass. Molly had taken the fear out of a history that had kept Amelia on edge for eighteen years and replaced it with a more profound fear of the present.

"How does Shephard Ward know about this flower if you have the picture of it?" she asked, feeling the guilt that came with a twinge of distrust for her friend.

"That I could not tell you. With all of the writings that they have stored in that church, I'm sure there is something about it that she came upon when looking for a way to control you all. They are most likely copies that had been drawn before my grandfather squirreled it away," Molly ventured, putting a hand on Amelia's shoulder, "I am sorry if this is a lot for you to be burdened with. I have been fighting with myself if I should take it to the grave or pass it all on to you. There's no one else on this rock that I can trust but you."

"What am I supposed to do with this all? Should I tell the others?" The idea of going against the Privy Assembly and the Shephard herself was terrifyingly impossible.

"All I want is for you to see the truth. Your life is about to become thicker than mud in that village now that you're of pairing age. Mix that with your destined seat in the Assembly, and you are going to find yourself stuck in a permanent way. The truth will be with you now when you start making big decisions. I want you to have that before I'm gone down to the worms."

"Molly, don't talk like that. You're as healthy as a work mule, and you know it," Amelia asserted. She hated when Molly would talk about her time coming. She had been doing it more often than not as of late, which worried Amelia.

"All I want is the best for you. Maybe you make it better here, or maybe you make yourself better somewhere else – while you still have the chance," Molly returned to her chair, sitting back down with a heavy exhale of fatigue and emotion.

Amelia knew what she meant. She had been pushing for her to leave the island for some time. She had even hinted that she would have her brother John help. Amelia knew that was not an option. She could not imagine what would happen to her family if she turned against the village to live in a world she knew nothing about. Molly was right that dealing with the evil you knew was easier. "You know I can't," she lamented.

"Well, you take care of yourself however you see fit. You're a smart little whip. I know that much. You will land on your feet," she gestured for Amelia to bend down for a hug and gave her an extra long squeeze. "Now, you take that with you if you feel comfortable with it. I don't want to add to your worries. I just want to find a way for it to not get lost in time like Flora's good name."

Amelia gently folded it and tucked it in her dusty work apron pocket. "I'll keep it with me if that's what you want, Molly. It's not right what they are doing. I don't know how I can help, but I'll do my best to keep this safe."

"That's all an old woman can ask for," she cackled, waving her away for the day. "Best get back before they notice you. I don't want you scrunched up in the box just for visiting me."

Amelia gave her a tight smile and headed out the door and down the path to the village. If there was not a witch's curse, and Shephard Ward's visions were not real, maybe there wasn't anything dark to the disappearance of Arthur Allen. Maybe he did just up and leave. Perhaps he somehow learned that she was making it all up and wanted out. If that could be true, there was possibly a simple explanation for the Watchers as well. It was all just stories made up to keep them in line.

The relief of that thought drifted away when she pictured the menacing shapes in the trees. Beings that she had seen more than once with her own eyes. Maybe it was not so easily explained. Good and evil lived side by side just as light and dark. If they were real, could Shephard Ward be more than Molly believed? The more truth that was uncovered always led to uncertain questions of what was real. Could Arthur really give up his family just for a try at life on the mainland?

Her hand stayed on her pocket as the thoughts whirled about her mind so deeply that she was nearly knocked over by Ellie when she came running around a bend in the path. Her face was blotched red, with tears pouring down her cheeks.

"Ellie! What are you doing out here? What's wrong?" she asked as her friend crumpled into her arms.

She pulled her palm across her eyes and then under her nose, trying to catch her breath to speak. Her eyes scanned around her, seeming to look for a path even further away from what she was running from. Amelia held her tightly to her chest, trying to still the shaking girl who had little strength left in her legs.

"They've told me! They've told me, Amelia!" she burst into more harrowing sobs and went down to her knees.

"Who told you what? You need to calm down and tell me what's happened." She looked behind her to see if anyone was following her and then back toward the path to Molly's, wondering if it would be wise to bring the distraught young woman to the safety of her cottage.

"They announced my engagement! I've been looking all over for you! I couldn't find you!" she cried out to her. "I don't know what I've done to anger them so." Another sob erupted from her chest, "I don't know what I'll do, Amelia! You have to help me!"

Amelia was stunned into silence by her outburst. Ellie had been spouting excitement about her eventual pairing since they had been small enough to play dolls. This was not the reaction that she could have imagined.

"What could be so horrible, Ellie? Who is it?" Amelia could think of many options that would be the worst for herself. Almost every young man in the village, in fact. It was more the loss of freedom than an issue with the men, really. Conversely, Ellie could find something extraordinary in everyone she met. It was unimaginable that someone among them could cause such a reaction. "Ellie! Take a breath. Who is it?

"Walter!" she bleated and fell into another fit of tears.

"Walter? Walter Allen?" she questioned. Ellie could only nod. "How is that possible? Shephard Ward just decreed he would not be up for marriage consideration for some time."

"They're outcasts, Amelia! Why would they make me join into a family of outcasts? What could I have possibly done to anger them?" Ellie pulled at the shoulders of Amelia's dress, tugging her tightly to her as if she could crawl inside of her friend and hide from the world.

Amelia rubbed Ellie's back as she struggled to compose herself, gulping air as deep as her lungs would allow. Walter would have been a wonderful match for Ellie just a few days before. Tall, with his father's dark hair and eyes, he had a quiet, consistently kind manner. With the scandal of his father abandoning them, it made no sense to put him at the front of the line for marriage – and with Ellie, at that. Ellie Stewart was from a hardworking, well-respected family, not to mention she was one of the most lovely girls in the village. It was a perfect match in every way but one. How could she start a marriage with a member of an outcasted family? More importantly, what was she being punished for? Ellie had every right to be upset, and Amelia understood the reason for the uncontrolled tears.

"Come on. Let's get you put back together, and we will head home. I'm going to ask Mama what she knows about this," Amelia directed, pulling out a hankie from her pocket, making sure not to drop the print of the flower she had hidden away.

Ellie wiped her wet cheeks and blew her nose while calming herself down. When she had composed herself to only the hiccup of sniffles, they started back down the path. Amelia walked her to the cottage where her mother was pacing at the door for her distraught daughter. She could only give a tight nod to the woman who was nearly as rattled as the bride-to-be.

Walking past the murmurs of gossip that had overtaken them all, Amelia headed straight home, praying that her mother would be there and not behind the confines of the church's door. When she slammed the door open and burst inside, her mother's calm reaction told her she knew what she was about to say. She held a finger to her lips before Amelia could begin her assault of questions and pointed to her room. Amelia stomped inside and stared at her mother as she shut the door behind them.

"Please, Poppet. Do not start with me right now," she ordered. The frustration darkened her face, and her tone was stern yet exhausted. Amelia clamped her mouth shut, the rage she wanted to rain down on her mother disintegrating. "I know. Ellie is crushed. Before you say anything, know that it is not as you think. You need to trust me when I say it truly is for the best."

Amelia sat on the edge of her bed, watching her. She had a deep fondness for Ellie, almost as if she were one of her own, and would not want to see her unhappy. How it was for the best, she could not imagine. "What will happen to her, Mama?"

"She will be just fine. I promise you. She and Walter will flourish in their pairing."

"I don't understand how this happened with what the Shephard decreed. How is this happening?" She did not expect answers to be laid bare to her, but her lips could not hold her questions.

"There are always things happening outside of your eyes, Amelia." She rubbed at what looked like a burgeoning headache. She joined her daughter on the edge of the bed. "There are many cogs in the wheels that you do not see. Things that are much bigger than almost everything that you are aware of. Situations that are for adults to manage," she stated, raising her eyebrows with warning when Amelia started to contest. "I know how hard it is for you to give your blind trust, but I need to ask you to do just that. I need you to trust me. I wish I could tell you so many things, to explain so many, many things to you. Being on the Privy Assembly can sometimes be an unbearable burden, and the weight of secrecy is unimaginable." She reached her arm over Amelia's shoulders and pulled her against her side.

"You can trust me with your secrets, Mama. Maybe I could carry some of the weight for you," she volunteered. Her mother had been aging before her eyes in the past few months. Seeing the fatigue trace deep lines on her face broke her heart. The dark bruises of stress under her eyes had been deepening and stealing the sparkle that used to dance in her gaze.

"I know I can, Poppet. Unfortunately, these aren't my secrets to share," she sighed. Kissing her head, she gave her a squeeze before standing. "I need you to trust that I would never let anything happen to Ellie. Can you do that for me?"

Amelia nodded slowly, knowing she was telling the truth. As she started out the door, she called out to her, "Mama, can you promise me that Ellie won't be made an outcast? I mean, can you tell me honestly that she will be okay?"

"I can tell you that she will not be cast out, Poppet. I can promise you that. A happy marriage is waiting for her. Stop your fretting and try to help your friend do the same. That's the best thing you can do for everyone." She gave a weak smile and slipped back out to the common room of the cottage.

Amelia sat for some time, attempting to find the words she could say to Ellie to help her become excited about the surprising turn of events. Since her mother had not told her why it would be all right, her mother's good heart was all she could offer as proof.

Regardless, it would be so strange to see her best friend married. She would soon be living with a man, sitting with the wives at church services, and someday soon, having babies. It all seemed too quick, making her own pairing feel closer than ever.

Moving to her bedroom door, she looked to see if any-one was nearby. Her mother hummed a solemn tune she did not recognize as she moved around the kitchen. The rest of her family appeared to still be out and about in the village. Gathering gossip, no doubt.

She closed the door, leaning her back against it, and slipped the flower print from her pocket. Tracing her finger over the strange-looking bloom painted in soft colors, she read the description of the exotic flower and the Royal Fair it had been a part of over and over again. The paper in her hands had been all the way to England.

The land of Jane Austen and the strong women in her stories. The furthest she had been was four brave steps into the water along the shore on the other side of the forest. She thought of the feeling of standing there, the water lapping at her legs, tempting her to sink further in. To drift slowly away from the prison of her life and finally see something other than the horizon. Water that could take her anywhere in the world.

The water that had taken Flora Edgar and her family for its own.

Amelia gently folded the print and tucked it inside her pillowcase. She did not know what was expected of her now that she possessed such a dangerous piece of contraband. All she could understand was that if Molly wanted her to keep it safe, that is what she would do. Letting Molly down was not something she would ever let herself do. The rest of the village had taken it upon itself to do just that for years.

She laid back on the pillow with the paper folded as thin as a fingernail. That did not stop her from feeling like a rock was tucked in among the feathers.

Chapter Four

"Just think of how lovely you will look, my love," Ellie's mother, Florence, cooed with a little too much effort. She held up a dress covered by lace that had seen better days. Having Ellie hold it against her front, she pulled in the waist and rolled up the sleeves. With her tiny frame, they would not need much of the ragged dress to cover her.

The few days that had passed since her marriage was announced had seen her red-rimmed and swollen eyes slowly return to normal. After having a private council with the Privy Assembly, Florence, and her father Gilbert, Ellie seemed exceptionally more upbeat about the news. Their smiles were still tight, and their eyes shifted when they met with others, but they did not carry themselves with the world's weight as they had upon hearing the news. It gave Amelia further faith in her mother's words to see that the pairing did not look to end the Stewart family's reputation and standing thanks to the Allens' actions. If anything, the disdain cast across her betrothed's family seemed to lessen with the news. There had not been a chance she could find to pull her friend aside, hoping to inquire the reasons for the change of heart. Every second of every minute seemed to pull the bride-to-be this way and that. That made the chance to be with her while she sorted her wedding attire all the more special. There was nothing more she would wish for Ellie than all the best, so to see her and Walter sharing happy glances in church or when they would pass in the square gave Amelia peace of mind that better days lay ahead.

She had never assumed to understand the politics of the Privy. The hushed decisions were the powers that held everything together, yet they were rarely explained. Since Arthur Allen disappeared from the village, the strange turn of events was beyond confusing. All but Ellie, of course.

The Shephard had not made mention of the rotted smell of the flowers and had not thrown down any new punishments in days. If anything, she mostly remained cloistered in the church, no doubt plotting for her next inexplicable decision.

"Ah, our blushing bride is starting to prepare for her big day, is she?" a slithering voice called out into the Stewart cottage, along with a quick rap on the door that was already being opened. Fredrick Gordon, the village's

Cleric and the Shephard's go-to man, stepped his stubby body inside without invitation. He slipped a hand up to his greasy hair and pressed it down even more flat to his scalp. He had a way of darting his tongue to lick his lips before and after speaking, which turned Amelia's stomach.

"She is, Cleric, and she will be the most beautiful bride we have ever seen," Florence boasted.

"She will be a handsome bride indeed, yet never forget to heel your pridefulness, Mrs. Stewart. No need to draw an evil eye on the future of this young dear," the cleric scolded, helping himself to a seat at their table. His thin lips smiled when he saw the woman's face redden. "I have just been to see our Shephard. She is quite pleased with this pairing. I'm not sure who is more in luck, your scrumptious young daughter or the Allen family," he laughed as the ladies grimaced at the sound.

"We are sure they will live a fruitful and happy life together, Cleric," Florence answered quietly, folding the yellowed white dress over her arm. "Ellie, why don't you and Amelia go outside and get some air? A little sun on your cheeks will do you good."

They did not have to be told twice. Any chance to escape the company of Fredrick Gordon was to be taken.

The sun was high in the sky and unusually warm for it still being spring. They followed the worn pathway down to their familiar stump to find Adam already perched in his usual spot, enjoying the weather.

"There's the bride-to-be! How are you doing today? You look like you've been crying a little less, so it must be love," Adam teased, knowing he would be the only one to find it funny. Even still, his lips downturned when Ellie sent him a chilly glare. "Things could be worse, Ellie. I'm going to have to be matched up with one of those snooty birds swishing around the village like they're something worth turning your head for. At least Walter is interesting."

"He is a good man. I can't deny that," Ellie confessed. "Two weeks ago, I would have been over the moon for the news. But...," she sighed and sat in a patch of dried grass, "why do you think they were forgiven so quickly? They were on the sharp edge of being shunned, and then Shephard Ward acted as if nothing had happened. Their standing is just restored as if nothing had happened. I was sure I was being punished for something even though I'd done nothing, and then she changed everything with our engagement. I still worry that she will change her mind once we're married, and I'll be swept out like dirt with the rest of the Allens. It can not be this easy. None of it makes sense."

"If we ever try to understand the word passed down by those on high, we would go mad within a blink, I'm afraid," Amelia reasoned. She sat beside her friend and started to re-braid her hair in the back as she liked. It would be all hands on deck to keep Ellie from going mad just from the what-ifs that were currently drowning her.

"Maybe you and Adam will be paired," Ellie teased and yelped when Amelia gave her hair a playful tug. "What? There are much worse choices. At least you are friends already."

"What do you say, Amelia? Want to come over here and give me a big smooch, my bride?" Adam laughed and ducked the wad of grass that she tossed at him. "I guess that's a no," he snorted.

Amelia could think of much worse choices as a husband when she thought of her options. Adam was one of her best friends. The thought of him as her partner was strange because he had become as equal a brother as Peter was by blood. As next in line for a seat on the Privy Assembly, her pairing would undoubtedly be a well-thought-out political decision. Nothing like the heart-pounding love that ripped at the souls within the pages of Molly's books. No one had ever made her feel as deeply as those characters were blessed with. She pushed away the gloomy thought and frowned playfully at Adam, "You would be so lucky to marry me, giggle-mug."

He laughed with a shrug and a nod. "Either way, I still think Molly has the best lot in life. No spouse, no living under the thumb of the Privy. She could walk around the woods in the nude under the moonlight like a true witch, and no one would know."

"Molly is not a witch, Adam," Amelia shot sternly. She would not stand for the words to be spoken in jest or otherwise. Molly was the person who held the most goodness and wisdom in the world in her eyes.

"You know what I'm saying. She really takes the egg out there. Almost as good as if she had the nerves to get off this damn island altogether," Adam chuckled until he saw the looks on the girls' faces. Amelia was giving a warning with furrowed brows, and Ellie was on the verge of tears again, "Sorry. I know that it's not a good idea to...," he blew out a breath that seemed to come from his toes and ballooned his cheeks. "I can only taste my foot in my mouth today, huh?" He gave them an apologetic grin, "Well, I think I'm going to finish my chores before I say something else stupid. I'll see you both at Hymns later, okay?" He raised a finger dramatically, comically copying Shephard Ward, "Now ladies, be the harvest that feeds from the earth, not the tide that *bleeeeeds* from it."

He was up the trail and out of sight before another word could be spoken. Amelia wrapped a piece of loose string from her hem on the end of the braid and stood up from beside Ellie. She raised her face to the sun, letting the warmth wash away her worries for just a blink. She pictured herself standing in one of the rolling fields, taking in the scent of the imagined wildflowers dotted along the landscapes of the stories she loved.

"Have you put much thought into your pairing announcement?" Ellie asked quietly, bringing Amelia back to reality. "I've heard word it will be soon."

This was news to her. "Nothing that my mother has said."

"When the Cleric and Shephard came to speak with Mama and Daddy about Walter, I was listening from my room," she looked down, embarrassment at breaking the rules plain on her face. Amelia knew she would never be able to be as rulebound as her friend.

"What did they say?"

"They didn't say a name or anything. I just heard them talking about how it's been something the Shephard has been working on," Ellie stood and brushed the grass from her dress, "I'm sorry I didn't tell you sooner. I didn't know if you already knew...or if you would want to know."

Amelia took Ellie by the hand and started down the path. The Cleric would have to have slithered back to the church by now. "It's out of my hands. It will be what it will be. You know that more than anyone right now, don't you."

Ellie wrapped her arm around Amelia's as they walked, "Hopefully, you get someone as handsome as Walter," she wished, letting herself smile for the first time since the announcement. Ellie was an eternal optimist, and Amelia was happy to see that spirit return to her. She did not think she could survive in a world where Ellie felt hopeless.

They easily blended into the small crowds of people working their way through the day's duties when they returned to the main square. Amelia was still on garden duty and headed to the space that held their vegetables. Not much was to be done since the planting, so she walked the fence line, making sure there weren't any spaces open to allow critters in to cause damage. She always felt it was unfair that the animals were not allowed to partake in the leafy greens if they so pleased. The land was just as much theirs as hers. The smaller animals' ancestors would have to have been there before their mess of a group crashed onto the shores of that island, anyway. She made her eyes skip over a board that had cracked just above the ground.

Ellie had gotten out of garden duties thanks to her upcoming nuptials. The rest of her week would be spent preparing the flowers, food, and attire for her big day. Part of the time leading up to the wedding would be her lady's education, as it was called. She would be told the secrets of the marital bedroom and all of the things under the roof that a wife would need to know. Amelia wondered if Ellie would brave to tell her what had been revealed. It was against the rules, so she assumed not. She had already started her education, albeit much more bluntly, thanks to Molly. She giggled out loud when she remembered the flower's name on the print.

"What's so funny, bird-brain?" Finley Ward's voice tore her from her silly thought. The eldest son of Shephard Ward's three children, he was known for his cruelty as much as his ignorance. Already into his thirties, he had yet to be married off. It was common thought that she could not let go of her favorite child, as if anyone could ever favor such a man. Amelia liked to think that keeping him from becoming some poor girl's husband was the only kindness in her cold heart. He had his father's sweet baby face, yet you could never forget who he was by his inheritance of his mother's dark, predatory eyes. The juxtaposition of his poor, kind father and his powerfully frightening mother complicated his appearance.

"Nothing you would understand," Amelia barked at him. Turning her back to make work of a small weed, she hoped he would take the hint and leave. Luck was not something that shone on her.

He stepped into the garden, snapping an emerging plant that had started to bloom. "So, I guess you're little friend isn't going to be around for you anymore now that she's getting married."

"She's getting married, Finley, not getting locked in the box," Amelia retorted, snatching the leaf from his hand

and shooing him from the garden. He obliged but leaned on the fence, his eyes on her.

"A married woman has a lot more to do than go off giggling with her little friends," he sniffed. He kicked at the fence board when she did not acknowledge him. She looked up at his pleased face when he knocked the cracked piece free. She held her smile in, not wanting him to know his action had the opposite reaction that he wanted. "I could have had her, you know? Mother offered her to me, but I'm not about to marry down. She may be pretty, but her family isn't exactly impressive."

Amelia turned her head when her eyes rolled in response to his nonsense. "That's fascinating, but I have work to do."

"She seems more suited for the Allens. You know - how they are now," he pushed. She could tell it was his goal to get her goat.

"Walter Allen is a wonderful man," she said tightly, "and they will be very happy together."

"Oh! Am I detecting a wee bit of jealousy? Did you want to be the one to lift your skirts to him?" he rudely teased.

"Don't be so crass, Finley! You should be ashamed of yourself," Amelia shouted, throwing open the gate to the garden. If he would not leave, she would – before she said or did something that she would be punished for.

His laughter rang out behind her as she stomped toward her cottage. She roughly wiped at the tears that had betrayed her by trailing down her cheeks.

How could this be all that life could hold?

There had to be more to life than waiting to be married, waiting to have babies, and then waiting to die with back-breaking work weaved within it all. She had never wanted to leave the island more than at that moment. Molly preferred the devil she knew. Amelia was starting to think any other devil, regardless, would be better. Anything different from the bleak monotony of the generations of residents of the Good Land. She scoffed at that name. They were undoubtedly trying to fool themselves by calling that place *good* in any way.

Any bluster that was building the courage to cross the water blew away when she set her eyes on her young brother and sister chasing each other around the exterior of the cottage. Their sweet laughter was the antithesis of what had yipped from Finley Ward.

Leaving the island would mean leaving her siblings for a very uncertain yet most definitely unhappy future. The few times she had mentioned the idea of the family making a start of it on the mainland had been furiously shut down by her mother. Her father had not even acknowledged her words.

Her family did not notice her thoughtful silence during supper or the walk over to the church for the evening of hymns. Her mother sat in the front pew along with the others of the Privy, her father sat with the other married men, and Amelia sat with Sarah and Ellie in the back where the children and unmarried were sectioned.

Peter stepped forward from the rest of the church choir to sing his very first solo, his face glowing with pride, and she tried to lose herself in his sweet voice. The congregation remained silent, as always. The choir members were the only ones permitted to sing the holy words within the church, and the quiet allowed his voice to reverberate around her. Words of hope and promised lands filled her heart yet settled her melancholy deeper within her spirit. His angelic voice made it all seem possible. The smothering roof she sat under told her it was not.

Amelia looked down when she felt Ellie's hand take hers. Following her eyes, she saw they were locked on the section of the church where the wives sat. Where she would soon sit; it was hard to read the expression on her face. There was a slight smile that twitched on her lips. Her eyes, on the other hand, were filled with fear. Amelia squeezed her hand and turned back to Peter.

She would try to enjoy the last time they would sit together in that pew, listening to hymns. The last time Ellie would listen to the sweet melody as an innocent young girl.

As if reading her mind, Ellie gave her hand a squeeze back. No matter what the future brought, they would always be there for each other. That thought slightly lessened the knot that had been growing in her chest. If nothing else, she could lose herself within the ending of the book hidden away under her bed. If she had to live in her head, creating the worlds she read of, it would be better than dredging helplessly through the rest of her life. She pictured Ellie and Walter as characters. He would spin her around in a lush garden filled with exotic plants and perfumed flowers so beautiful her mind could not imagine them in detail. They would smile and kiss over sweet cups of hot tea in a large manor home far from the dusty cottages they now called home. She would wear dresses soft as a rabbit's fur, and Amelia would dress in the same finery when she came to visit and hear all of Ellie's romantic stories of married life.

A sigh and a smile escaped her at the thought, and it carried her through until she could escape to the happy solitude of her room for the evening.

CHAPTER FIVE

THE SUN BLAZED A smothering heat onto Ellie's wedding day. After dressing and starting the wait until the ceremony, she used a paper fan her mother had fashioned as if it was providing her with the only air in her lungs. Her mother had been right. She made a beautiful bride. The lace looked less shabby after the alterations and a good cleaning. The days leading up to the big event had been filled with gathering flowers, her secret matrimonial lessons, and the preparation of the food selections. Ellie had found a calm in that, which, in turn, calmed Amelia. She had a feeling that the large jugs of dandelion wine being passed around had a little something to do with her glow, as well.

"Can someone pass me my bouquet? It's wilting in the sun," Ellie requested, inhaling the sweet, pink blooms when her mother handed them to her. "Aren't they beautiful, Amelia?" She gave them another smell for good measure before holding them out to her to admire.

"They really are. Almost as pretty as you!" Amelia gushed, sending her friend into a fit of giggles.

"I've never seen flowers so pretty – and a wild pig roasted for our supper? When was the last time we've been lucky enough to have something so scrumptious?" Ellie pointed over the wooden reception tables set around the pit of coals that were preparing the pig.

Amelia knew when. It was the last time Molly's brother John had brought one across from the mainland. All the decadent touches they enjoyed that day were quietly brought over at Molly's request. The thought of all the folks who easily kept their backs turned on the sweet old woman enjoying the treats she had provided made Amelia angry. It was a perfect example of the kindness that lived within Molly's heart. It did not matter if those who turned against her were spoiled with her gifts; it only mattered that Ellie had the perfect day. The Privy knew very well who had provided it all yet kept their mouths tight. Amelia's father, himself, had helped bring the pig to the main square under the cover of night.

There was no reason to stew about the unfairness of it all when Ellie was twirling about in her dress. Walter's mother, Jane, had come over to admire her soon-to-be new daughter and wish her well. In barely more than a week, the Allens had lost their patriarch, had an engagement announced, and gone from near outcasts to hosting the most lavish wedding Amelia had ever set eyes on. There was no other answer Amelia could find other than a true miracle had taken place. With the breaking sorrow Ellie had started her engagement with, Amelia was overjoyed that her dearest friend was now finding it a blessing.

The wedding itself was as formally stuffy as all others that had happened before, except for the looks on Ellie and Walter's faces. There was a sweet wonder that lit up their eyes when they would brave a peek at each other. When it was time to take hands, they held on to each other as if they had always had their fingers interlocked. As they proceeded, the required hymns and prayers seemed to go without their notice, lost in whatever they were saying to each other through small smiles.

Even the Cleric's inappropriate leers at Ellie could not distract them from each other. The farther into the ceremony, the deeper they would look into each other's eyes, and when they returned from the Allen family cottage after sharing their first kiss, which was done privately to solidify the marriage, they looked as if they were walking on air. It was a scene that Jane Austen would be proud to witness, and Amelia was alight with happiness for her best friend's good fortune.

"Looks like that was quite the kiss, huh?" Adam asked Amelia, his eyes on the blushing couple sitting at the long table before them.

"It seems like it was," Amelia chuckled. "I am so glad it seems to have all worked out."

"Walter, as an outcast or even a Cleric, would still be a blessing of husband," he gulped from a stein of wine, "Ellie is a lucky gal."

"Where did you get that?" Amelia demanded. Alcohol was not allowed to be consumed by the unmarried, or at least not until they were well into their twenties. The latter rule was more for the male residents, as not many girls made it far into their twenties without being paired off. Adam, being seventeen, fit into neither of those categories.

"Have you seen the barrels they're filling the jugs with? I doubt they'll miss a mugful or two," he insisted and held the stein out to her. She declined with a flick of her wrist and a matronly glare. "Come on, Amelia. Bend an elbow with me. Don't be such a wet blanket. It's a happy day, isn't it?"

"It's not going to be so happy if someone catches you with that," Amelia chided with a hush. His father would give his ear a good battering if he caught wind. "Let's go wish the new couple well," she ordered, pulling him along with her. It seemed it would be her job to keep an eye on him for the rest of the night.

"Amelia!" Ellie squealed, "Wasn't it just the perfect ceremony? Wasn't it?" She wrapped her arms around her and pulled her tight. The excitement kept her in a tiny, constant bounce, even as she hugged her.

"It really was. I'm so happy for you," Amelia managed to say with her ribs being compressed. Ellie may be a waif of a thing, but happiness gave her the strength of a bear.

"I'm a fortunate man," Walter boasted with a shy grin. "I'm sorry to have stolen your friend away, though."

"You did nothing of the sort, Walter. She'll be a little busier..." She stopped to elbow Adam when he laughed at her phrasing, and he spit his mouth of wine back into his stein, "She may be spending most of her time with you, but we will always find time for just us girls."

"Gee, thanks, ladies. I guess I'll just get back to the barn," Adam jested and laughed a little too loud. "Ladies only, now, huh? Hopefully, Walter will make time for me," he snorted again into his stein.

"You know what I mean. She'll always have time for her friends, you included, of course," Amelia said, suddenly realizing that she hoped it would be true. Until she was paired and married, there would be a hole in their friendship in which she was not welcomed. She felt selfish for such thoughts, with her friend's joy glowing before her eyes. "You best getting along to receive everyone's well wishes," she announced, pushing a bright smile across her cheeks. "There are still so many to get to before we can sit down for your feast." Amelia gave them both a quick hug and took Adam by the hand again to find a seat along the edge of the gathered crowd.

"I think this wine has been sitting in the sun too long," he murmured with a burp when they sat on the edge of the old stone fence.

"I think it's been sitting in you for too long, you silly boy," Amelia chided with a laugh.

He joined her laugh as he poured the remaining wine to the ground behind them.

The villagers had the light energy that comes with a day of celebration and some much-needed time off from work. The men who had imbibed in much more wine than Adam had started to entertain the crowd with shanty songs that had been passed down for generations, much to the chagrin of the Cleric.

Looking around, she noticed that the Shephard was not seated at her usual place at the head of the table. Scanning the crowd, she did not find her even among the revelers. When she pointed it out to Adam, he gave only a shrug and mumbled about needing the outhouse.

It was unusual for Shephard Ward not to want to be the center of attention, regardless of the situation. Jumping to her feet from the wall when Adam wandered off, she made a full circle around the group and found no sign of her. Finding her mother, she made an inquiry, only to be told to mind her business with a worrisomely tense voice. Jane called her back to hug her, apologizing that she was not feeling well. Amelia was sent on her way again when her father approached the duo. They walked from the crowd, whispering between themselves. It all made her very nervous.

As she made her way to the table laid with treats and sweet juices, her eyes swept around, landing on the other members of the Privy scattered around. The same tight expression, void of the merriment held by the others, sat on their faces. She casually popped a berry in her mouth as she watched the Cleric slip away from the crowd. Without Ellie, her eternal conscience, at her side, there was no one to stop her from following him at a distance.

The church door was propped open when he climbed onto the porch, and he pulled it quietly closed behind him when he entered. Amelia was sure a creak of the porch boards would announce her arrival, so she chose to go around to the small window at the rear, hoping it would be open. She let out a quiet groan of frustration when she found it was not. Reaching up on her tip-toes, she tried to peer in. She came up a few inches short and could not even make out the mumbles of whoever was meeting inside.

Sitting on the dusty ground, she leaned back against the chapel wall. The sounds of the reception drifted through the air around her. Something was going on; she could feel it in her bones, and she prayed it would not be for the worse. The Shephard had been acting unusual since Arthur Allen up and left. Unusual even for a woman who predicted upcoming misfortune with visions of rotting flowers. The taut shoulders of her mother held the secrets of whatever had been happening, and her lips had, as always, been sealed.

For someone who had been adamant about not wanting her mother's seat within the Assembly, she was surprised at how intensely curious she had become. Molly had always said that knowledge was power, and she had never really understood what that meant. Seeing how quickly things can change while at the same time staying precisely the same had her head spinning with curiosity that was new to her.

Deciding it had to be for the worry she had been carrying for Ellie and the outcome of her marriage, she pulled her legs to her chest and tried to change her train of thought, enjoying the quiet away from the crowd.

If it was something terrible, there was no need to rush it any sooner than it needed. She told herself she needed to see Molly and request more books. It was better to keep her mind busy than to insert herself where she did not belong. Whatever was happening was out of her control. The thought made her smile as it sounded like something Ellie would have said to her. Not having her be a constant at her side may not be so bad if she had already made such an effect on her.

She quietly and quickly made her way from the church wall, not wanting to be discovered as a snoop. When she reached the edge of the tree line that she would follow back to the reception, she noticed a broad smudge of dirt on her dress's skirt. Being that a wedding called for church attire, her mother would be livid to see her best dress ruined. It was something to be expected of young Sarah, not her eldest.

Scurrying to the older well that stood beside the gardening shed, she pulled up some fresh water to swipe at the mess she had made. Luckily, it had not sunk into the fabric, and she would not put more undue stress on her mother. Fabric was not something that was freely available, even to the families of Privy members. Not that Shephard Ward ever seemed to struggle to find new clothing for herself and her miserable clan.

She was relieved with her dress back in order, except for a large wet circle where she had splashed the water. It would not take the sun long to dry it, and no one would be the wiser that she had taken it upon herself to try snooping around the church.

A large boulder near the trees was the perfect perch for her to wait. She wiped the surface with her hands to ensure no more dirt ruined the back side of her skirt and sat. After dinner, she would try to sneak some of the treats to Molly's cottage. It was unfair for her to miss out on the good fortune she provided the rest of them. She would, of course, tell Amelia that she did not need all the fancy foods; she was perfectly fine with what was provided in her rations. Amelia would insist she take it, and Molly would reluctantly stash it away for later. It was a dance they had done many times before.

Ellie's sing-song laughter rang out above the noise of the crowd, and Amelia found herself wanting to return to the party to take part. It was rude not to give her full attention to her best friend on her big day. Her skirt was dry enough not to be noticed. She gave a look around to make sure she was alone and then lifted her skirts to flutter and fluff them for good measure. Her breath caught in her chest when she heard more laughter. It was not Ellie, and it was much closer. Looking past the tree line, her ears picked up more smothered giggles.

"Who's out there? You're going to get in a lot of trouble for leaving the square!" she bluffed, hoping whoever was there did not see her under things. Another fit of giggles trickled out from behind the trees. "It's not polite to peek at girls!"

Her eyes tried to focus on the darkness of the woods. Her body lurched back, almost stumbling her to the ground when she saw the shadows move.

The Watchers!

She was sure it was them. They raced between the trees before gradually becoming smaller as they moved further away into the dark. Amelia had never seen them during the day. As far as she was aware, no one had ever seen them outside of the cover of night.

Her feet were moving back to the main square before her lungs recovered from the fright. Stars danced before her vision as she gulped in the air to keep her moving. Adam, just leaving the outhouse and giving his mouth a wipe, was the first person she saw. They both toppled to the ground when she reached him, unable to stop her momentum.

"What on earth is wrong with you?" he shouted, still looking green, "You could have killed me?"

"They're here," she panted, "In the woods. The Watchers!"

Adam struggled to his feet, pulling her up with him, "What are you talking about? It's the middle of the day."

"I just saw them! They were in the woods. They were laughing at me!" Amelia held onto his suspenders, steadying her feet.

"So it's okay for you to dip into the wine, but I'm the sinner for taking a sip?" Adam chortled and started back to the party, this time being the one to do the dragging.

Amelia shook her arm free of his hand. "I have not had any wine!"

The tone of her voice stopped her in his tracks. "You couldn't have seen Watchers, Amelia. Your eyes had to have been playing tricks on you. You're probably too warm from the sun. Let's get you some water."

Amelia started back toward the site where she had spotted them, the courage building with the company of another when Adam reluctantly started behind her, "My eyes and my ears, Adam?" She kept walking, relieved, when she heard his feet still shuffling with her. "I'll show you where I saw them. I think they may have left when I yelled out to them, though."

"YOU scared away Watchers? Amelia, if this is some joke, I'm not in the mood. I just spent twenty minutes with head in a very disgusting place doing something even more abominable."

"It's not a joke, I swear to you," she promised as they reached the edge of the trees. Steeling her nerves, she took a few steps into the forest, her ears trained on any little noise. When silence met them, she braved a few more steps with a nervous Adam at her side.

Reaching the spot where she saw them moving about, she stopped, turning in all directions for any sign of them.

"What's that?" Adam asked, pointing to the ground between their feet.

Squatting to get a closer look, Amelia found several sticks with the bark cleaned away. Each one had been ground to a sharp point and tossed onto a pile. She handed one to Adam, who turned it over in his hands.

"What do you think it is?" Amelia asked, scanning the woods around them.

"It's a stick, Amelia," Adam jested, yet his eyes shifted uncomfortably around them.

"Obviously, it's a stick. But why would someone leave a pile of sharpened sticks here?" Amelia asked, picking up a few more to inspect.

A crow called out loudly, and it echoed along the trees.

"I don't know. To be creepy? If so, it worked," Adam guessed, moving back towards the light of the clearing. "It was probably just the Morrison boys out causing trouble. You know how strange Wilfred and Nathaniel are."

Amelia stuffed one of the sticks into her pocket and followed Adam back to the reception. It would make sense for those boys to get up to no good. It was what they were known for. However, the idea of a knife in their hands in order to widdle the sticks gave her worry, being that they were only seven and five years old. They could do a lot of harm to themselves in the blink of an eye – or harm to a hapless passerby. Two little boys causing trouble was much easier to digest than the idea that the Watchers were now comfortable flitting about in the day.

They only allowed themselves a side glance at each other when they saw the Morrison boys were still running about the revelers, their faces covered in jam. Perhaps it was other children that had slipped away. She could not help but take a head count and decided they must have already returned when she found all present and accounted for.

Amelia brazenly slipped a stein from the table when no one was looking and took a healthy gulp of the dandelion wine. She knew well that it was against the rules, but her frazzled nerves required a little help to get her through the rest of the evening with a smile firmly on her face. It wasn't very pleasant against her tongue before a honey-sweetness took over the bitterness, and she went for a second mouthful. She set the stein down with a thump when she found Adam watching her with amusement.

Pushing her worries away, she gave herself every small excuse to explain away the mysteries of the day and joined her family's table to partake in the best meal she had ever had. The juices of the meat soaked into the large helpings of potatoes, and the berries they presented as dessert were sweeter than anything she had ever eaten.

Once the plates were emptied and cleared away, the flutes were pulled out, and the dancing began. She spun Sarah around and around to the music until her little tummy could take no more. Once she settled on her mother's lap, Amelia returned to the dancing, losing herself in the shared happiness of her neighbors. Ellie and Walter swayed to each song in each other's arms as if they heard music all their own.

When she finally spotted the Shephard among the crowd, even she was grinning at the scene before her. She took her seat at the head of the table to watch a few songs before rising and signally for the music to pause.

"What a beautiful day we have had with a beautiful new family blooming before us," she announced to rousing applause. "Congratulations to Walter and Ellie and to the entire Allen family. I give hope for peaceful happiness for years to come!"

The crowd whooped with agreement. Ellie raised her hands with excitement but did not notice when Walter avoided looking in the direction of the Shephard. Amelia watched him wash a thought from his eyes and smile down to his new bride.

"I would like to have the joy continue if I may. What is better than one happy union, I ask? I believe that would be two!" Shephard Ward shouted over the cheers. Everyone looked among each other, wondering who it could be.

Adam moved to Amelia's side, a look of disdain on his face. "Please, Lord, don't let it be me. I've been sick enough for one day," he groaned, earning a laugh.

"No need to draw this all out. I'm sure you all would like to return to celebrating." Sounds of clunking steins circled the crowd. "Cleric, if you could join me?"

Fredrick shuffled along behind the chairs of the head table, jostling each one as he passed and causing more than one person to spill their drink, "A blessed day, indeed, Shephard!" he called out to less cheers. He scowled at the faces that frowned back at him.

"Blessed in all things, Cleric, blessed indeed. If my sweet boy Finley could come to join us," she requested, eyeing the crowd until she set eyes on his smug face. He pushed his way through to his mother's side, a sly smile dancing on his lips.

"I want to be thankful, but some poor girl finally being cursed with that fool is nothing to celebrate," Adam murmured into Amelia's ear, and she gave a snort of amusement.

"I'm pleased to announce that it is finally time for my dear Finley to settle down," she said lovingly, stroking his cheek only to have him slap her hand away. She cleared her throat before she continued, "So if we could have Amelia Taylor join us, we can make this match official!"

The digesting wine pulled up into Amelia's throat at the Shephard's words. The world silently imploded around her. The only sound she could register was the *noooo* hissing from her own lips.

CHAPTER SIX

HER FEET BETRAYED HER by moving on command when the Shephard requested she join her side. Any faith that a mistake had been made disappeared when she saw the misery darkening her mother's face. Her father stared at his feet as they made their way to the front of the stunned crowd, not word from either of them.

"I would ask you all to raise your glasses and toast our next union. One that will come sooner than later if I have my way," Shephard Ward announced as if there was a way other than her own.

Amelia could only lock eyes with Ellie, who shared her wide-eyed stun. This new revelation muddied the joy that ultimately came to her friend's wedding. From a new beginning of love to a nightmare ending of dread. One more feather in the Shephard's cap of cruelty.

"A blessing over Finley and Amelia!" she shouted, pulling the two together in front of her. Glasses were raised in the air without the jovial excitement that had filled the rest of the evening.

The conversations that broke out around her blended into one deafening hum that quieted as she was moved away from the reception and back to her cottage. Once inside, behind the closed door with a few of their meager candles lit, they sat at the Taylor table to discuss the decision. Finley sat roughly beside Amelia, tossing his arm over the back of her chair with a grin. Except for a quick peek at her mother's devastated face, Amelia's eyes remained on the polished wood of the table.

"I do have to say how pleased I am that Finley has finally decided on a bride. My boy has a very discernable taste that has been hard to appease," Shephard Ward gushed.

Amelia could not for the life of her understand why he would have any interest in her at all. He had never been anything but cruel to her for as long as she could remember. It was strange enough to hear the Shephard make it seem as though Finley had a say in who his partner would be. No other pairing had been given that grace. Another perk of the Ward family, she conceded.

Her parents remained silent.

The tension that had been wrapped over her mother finally made sense. She had been aware of the news and had had to keep it to herself. Amelia wanted to be angry with her for not giving her warning. Try as she might, she couldn't. The ways of the Privy were not taken lightly, and Jane Taylor would have been severely punished if she had spoken the words of the Assembly without permission. Shephard Ward had been quite fond of a more brutal, physical style of punishment ever since the visions had become more frequent.

Amelia thought of the folded picture that sat under her pillow. Could there really be a curse attached to it, something that Flora Edgar manipulated from her cold ocean grave? She could not understand how she would be a target of her wrath other than she now possessed the paper the original families had decided was the source of it all. If anything, Amelia was in agreement with Flora. The creation of The Good Land was a terrible idea from the start to the present. If Flora really had otherworldly powers, why would she not use them to help Amelia instead of punishing her? Perhaps she was being used to save other girls from the fate she now faced. As much as the idea of Finley Ward as a husband repelled her, she would not wish it on anyone else. She gave her head a shake for letting herself fall into the supernatural beliefs she had spent her life trying to ignore. There was a reason for why this was happening, and a curse was not it. Shephard Ward rarely did anything that did not benefit herself.

"Shall we let them have a private chitchat?" the woman asked in a sickly sing-song voice, standing from the table and gesturing to the door.

Amelia's parents tugged her into a tight hug when they passed her. Their eyes did not meet, and a word was not spoken. Finley kicked his feet up onto the table when the door shut, leaving a smudge on the table from the mud on his boot.

"I hope you cook better than you garden, Amelia," he admonished while picking at his teeth, "I have a healthy appetite, and I'm used to a certain quality of meals." She stared back, her supper stirring in her stomach. Looking about the modest room, he continued, "I guess you're going to be happy to live in the nice house now, huh? I told Mother we will stay with her and Father until a suitable new cottage is built for us."

A new house had not been built in over a decade. Supplies of that nature were not readily available, and when they were, they were made to extend a home or to house multiple families. A new cottage for only two people was unheard of. When so many families lived shoulder to shoulder, the waste of it all was unimaginable. As was the idea of leaving her family to live all alone with Finley.

"I don't understand why this is happening," she managed when she could steady her voice, "Why would you want me as your wife? I've always assumed you hated me." She kept that the feeling was mutual to herself.

"Before you get a big head on you, it wasn't so much that I picked you. I'm doing Mother a favor. *Your* mother has been getting a little too loose with respect lately, and she felt it was in our best interest to start preparing the next in line in a manner more suitable to how she prefers the Privy Assembly to behave. In return, she's promised me the new cottage, extra rations, and her full cooperation to turn you into the wife you should be."

Amelia could not find the words to continue the conversation. Her mother had always had strong opinions, yet she always seemed to toe the line when it really mattered. What could she have done to make the Shephard react in such a way? The idea that she was being taken from her family to be molded into someone who would bow down to the privy when the time came was absurd. If she had the choice, she would not even accept the seat when her mother inevitably passed away. Unfortunately, choice was not something she ever found in her quiver.

"This is…," Amelia's mind spun.

"This is what it is. I have made quite the sacrifice here," he bragged. "You're not as special as you seem to think you are and don't think this makes you anymore so. You should thank me for taking you on. Although, you will have plenty of opportunities to do just that." He leaned over and tucked a finger under the hem of her skirts, attempting to lift them over her knee.

She slapped his hand away and jumped from the table, knocking the chair behind on its side. "Keep your hands to yourself, Finley Ward!"

"See? It's that attitude right there that we need to remove," he lamented with an arrogant laugh.

Amelia could find no other words than profanity to hurl at the despicable man who was sat at her family table. Words that would only get her into further trouble. Before she could even breathe, she was out the door and running to the darkness of the woods path, wanting nothing more than to be with Molly. If anyone had any sense left, it would be the only one who lived outside of the reach of the Privy Assembly. Her wise advice had never been needed more urgently.

When she arrived at her cottage, a dim candle flickered through the window, and she knocked furiously on the crooked door.

"What in all that is holy is wrong with you, girl?" she shouted when she found Amelia panting on her stoop. "What's happened? Come in. Get out of the dark."

If only she could, she wished. Within the dark was where her future now lay.

"They've paired me, Molly," she managed through deep breaths to steady herself, "With Finley Ward! They're going to make me marry Finley Ward!" She erupted in tears, and her knees betrayed her, taking her down to the dirt floor.

"Finley Ward? Ellen's blunderbuss of a son? I didn't think she would ever get him off of her teet," Molly quipped. She kneeled down beside Amelia with a grunt. "Don't let yourself fall apart. We'll figure this out. It's not the end of the world, now."

Amelia dragged the edge of her skirt over her wet eyes and stared back at her, "How is this not the end of the world? Molly, did you not hear what I said? I have to marry Finley Ward!"

"Oh, I heard you. My ears still work fine," she chided, pushing herself back up to her feet and shuffling to her chair beside the embers glowing in her small fireplace. She added a few twigs and set the kettle on the hook. "What I mean is that there are worse options. He may be a blathering fool, but he's a blathering fool with unlimited resources. Better to eat with the devil than to starve with the angels if you want to survive, Amelia. There's no helping anyone if you make a martyr of yourself."

"Is that even surviving? It's more like lifelong torture."

"It is not ideal, I agree, but it keeps you on their side. Ellen Ward keeps her family close and away from her own judgments. She is a spider that has cast her web over this entire island. We're trapped in that sticky net exactly where she wants us all. Some she will eat, some she will simply keep. I know which one I prefer to be," she nodded her head in agreement with herself, "This could also bode well for Peter and Sarah in the future. Sacrifice is never easy, Amelia. That's the point."

"What are you talking about?" she raged with betrayal, "How can you take this so lightly? It's easy for you to say! You get to live here! You don't have to live under their thumb and be married off to a monster!"

"I'll ask you to watch that tone when you're in my home, girl. I understand you're angry, but I am not your enemy in this."

Amelia was awash with guilt with Molly's words and the hurt that grew in her eyes. She knew she wanted to yell at Finley, and the Shephard, and at her mother, and mostly at the universe. Taking it out on her only truly faithful ally was foolhearty and wrong. "You're right. I'm sorry. I'm just still in shock."

They sat quietly with their thoughts while Molly prepared the tea. She was right when she said it could be beneficial for her siblings to be in well with the leader of their community's decisions. Lord only knew how many sacrifices her mother had silently made over the years, and now that she was of age, maybe it was just her time to do the same. Amelia had admitted that there was not one boy over the others that she would want to be engaged to. It was bound to happen with someone. Her chest spasmed lightly with the tears that were slowing. Just being with Molly in her tiny cottage was enough for her to find her center once more. The scent of the tea in the kettle warmed her heart further.

"Why can't I stay here with you, Molly? Who's to say that I can't?" she asked when handed a hot mug.

"Me, for one!" Molly cackled. "You don't think they'd miss a chance to rain fresh hell down on me if one of their own turned their backs on them for me?" She blew into her tea with another chuckle. "You would go mad living under this broken roof with a crotchety old woman, anyways."

"I would not! I could help you. I could make your meals and clean. I could be very helpful to you."

"And what would we do when they decided to punish your deeds by cutting off my rations? Rations that I would already be generously splitting with you in your little dream world, mind you."

"Your brother John could help us. I'm sure he would have no problem looking after what we need," Amelia insisted.

"I don't know how you picture the mainland, but it's not trees to be shaken with all that you require. John has himself to look after. He already lives thin with his misplaced kindness to those fools."

Amelia knew it was wrong to put her needs onto others. John already did so much for the people who only took from him with their backs turned. It was too much to ask him for even more.

"Well, how about I go to the mainland and help him? You and I could go and leave all of this behind. It has to be an easier life there. Wouldn't you like to live more comfortably?" she asked, stopping before mentioning her waning age.

"Not this again," she croaked. "If you want to up and leave your family, I will help you. You know this. You have always known this. I know, however, that you would not be able to leave them and let them suffer whatever punishment would be put on them. If you leave and return, things would be much worse for you than they are now; I can tell you that much – and as for me? I won't pick up and start a new life at the very end of the one I'm quite settled in. This cottage is my life. That village is yours. If you want a new life, you must accept that it will be permanent and have repercussions."

Amelia sipped at her tea, knowing she was right. They had had this conversation too many times to count, and Molly knew her too well. If she were to go ahead and marry Finley, she would at least still be able to see her friends and family. She would be able to sit with Ellie in the wives' pews at hymns, and they could start the next chapter in their lives together. One in which Finley would share her bed. The nausea returned.

"You'll find a way to make this all work," Molly assured, getting up to rustle through her books.

"I'll do my best," Amelia said through a sip of her tea. "Why do you think life is so unfair?"

"Why shouldn't it?" Molly asked without turning back to her. "Who are we to demand life be fair and as we want it? Why would we be owed that, silly girl?" she laughed and moved on to another stack of books. "What you should ask yourself is, what are you doing to make it better? Things will never be perfect because that's not for our time on earth but for after we go to reap what we sow."

Amelia set her mug down and digested her words. She wasn't as innocent as Sarah still was. She was now eighteen, and it was time for her to shoulder some of the burden carried by her parents. Life would be as good as she made it, whether it was with Finley Ward or not. Having time to sit and process the evening's events away from the smothering press of the village gave her a perspective that there was still hope.

"Elizabeth Gaskell! Here it is!" Molly whooped and presented a well-worn novel. She handed it to Amelia, who read the scrolled letters trailed across the cover – *North and South*. She knew not to ask whether it was good or not. Molly had never given her a story that she did not love. "This one may be just what you need right now. Margaret has a strong mind and a soft heart, just like you. She may be the one to offer advice."

Amelia turned a few pages, not wanting to let any of the words grab her as she would not be able to put it down once she started. "Thank you, Molly. I just finished the last one. If I had been in a better mind, I would have remembered to bring it back to you tonight."

"There's no rush for me, dear. I've read them all so many times I only need to sit in the quiet, and they're all there in my mind waiting for me," Molly mused. "When you get a little more settled with the idea of marriage, I'll introduce you to a little lady named *Lady Chatterley*. She knows enough even to make an old lady blush."

She couldn't imagine what was in that book. Either way, she was not in a rush to think about her upcoming nuptials yet. It was enough that Molly had found a way to get her to stop weeping like a frightened child and set her spine a little straighter. Between the time with her friend and whatever lay in the pages of the new book, Amelia was sure she would find the bravery to navigate anything.

The thought of marriage brought Ellie's shocked face to mind, and Amelia knew she needed to excuse herself to return to the gathering. It would not do Ellie any peace to be sitting worried about her when she should be focused on her own celebration.

Making sure Molly was settled in her chair with her favorite quilt, she tucked the book into her skirt pocket and headed back after filling the crystal dish outside for when the hummingbirds returned in the morning's light.

The peace that she had found during her visit would be short-lived; she was well aware. The escape of the rickety old cottage in the woods always was. The break from village life was something she treasured. As far as she knew, it was something that no other neighbor had the blessing of.

The night sky was clear between the trees, and Amelia enjoyed the twinkling stars that peeked through the branches. The full moon cast a bright glow on the trail before her, making everything appear soft and calm. The flowers were in full spring bloom, and their scent danced on the warm breeze that told her summer would arrive soon. The sweet aroma was nothing like the decrepit flowers described during the Shephard's visions. She wondered if they had been if she would be a gentler woman to her flock. It would be better if they never returned at all.

Amelia pushed the what-ifs from her mind and transported herself to the imaginary world she had created for herself and her loved ones. The wedding she would return to would be in a beautiful stone manor house, even grander than the ones she had read of, with flowers more enormous than any bloom on the island set in bunches across the garden. Ellie's dress would be fit for a princess, and Walter would stand proudly at her side in a suit covered with polished buttons and a sword at his hip to protect his new bride and her best friend. After finding himself lost in the dreary woods around the estate, Finley Ward would not even know how to find the glorious party and would return home to his wicked mother.

Music would fill the air, and they would dance into the night, their whole happy lives awaiting them the next day. She started to hum a made-up song and shuffled her feet along the path.

Her song stopped suddenly, and she was brought back to reality when she heard a rustling off to her side. More followed, along with the quick snap of a branch. It sounded too close for comfort and too loud for it to be nothing more than a small critter.

If it was a Watcher, there was nowhere to hide.

The moonlight was the only weapon against the darkness that surrounded her. The shadow of whatever was watching her slipped between the trees, moving along beside her, just out of view. Quickening her pace, she kept her eyes straight ahead, willing the village closer to her with each step.

When she made it to the edge of the clearing, she stopped with her ear turned in the direction of the intruder. The sound of footfalls disappeared into the distance until they were no longer heard at all.

She had never heard the Watchers make so much noise. She had also never been so close to one. Taking one last look at the forest, she was satisfied that whatever it was, it was gone.

Braving a minute to compose herself, she decided that she would find Ellie to quash her worry and then take leave of the party to put herself to bed. If the party lasted into the night, as they sometimes did, she could devour her new book under the moon's light before anyone arrived home. She owed herself a treat after the evening she had been thrown into. Evenings to herself would soon be a thing of the past.

Finding Ellie in the nervous state that she did, Amelia felt guilty for taking so long to return to her. Walter had been doing his best to console his sensitive new wife as best he could. They were both relieved when she stood before them in a better condition than when she had left. Only so much could be said with the noise of the gathering, but she felt she had calmed her friend enough to allow her to enjoy the rest of her party. Finding her parents in much the same concern, she put on her best smile, told them that she would be all right and that they could speak of it all in the morning. Thankfully, it was not too much to expect when she excused herself as exhausted and headed home to the quiet of her room.

Even though it was a risk, she pulled out the novel to take a peek before she was even in the door. Looking up from the pages as she approached, the candlelight that flickered surprised her. Her parents were not ones to be wasteful. Sarah and Peter had been kicking up their heels to the music when she left, so no one should be home. Entering, the mud still smudged on the tabletop caught her eye.

"Is that you, darling?" Finley's voice called out from her bedroom, "You left before I could say goodbye."

Her first instinct was to run. That would not do her well in the future as there was only so far she could run to. Stomping to her room and opening the door further than it was already, she found him lying on her bed, her beloved Jane Austen novel in his hands.

"What are you doing? Get out of here!" she bellowed, closing the space between them. "Give me that!" Seeing her prized treasure in his hands caused a wave of fury to crash within her. She tried to snatch the book from his fingers, but he was too quick. His eyes landed on the new novel she clenched in her other hand.

"Well, well, well. Someone is still breaking the rules, I see. This is going to be harder than I thought," he growled and snatched her book away. "What are you doing with these? Where would you even find such garbage?" He flipped open the pages as he stood, holding it above his head when she tried to take it back.

"It's none of your business, Finley. Hand them over!"

"Oh, I don't think so. Mother and the Cleric will need to see these. This is quite a bit worse than back talk, young lady. I will not have a bride that can hide such improper materials. Any book that is not held within the church should have been burnt years ago. Have you gotten your hands on some of those Mainlander's sins? Are you a traitor, just like John Clark?"

Amelia stopped struggling for the books when he spoke. What would he know of John and his possessions? The only thing ever spoken of the Mainlanders were their evil ways and their hatred of the purity of the people of the Good Land. The Privy was well aware of what John could bring to them, but as far as she knew, Molly and her parents were the only others who knew of John. She had assumed all of the others were completely unaware of his existence. It had been naïve to think that if her father were in the know, those under the Shephard's roof would—especially her favorite child. Hearing John's name mentioned along with the books was another worry altogether. Those were a secret she was sure was only shared by John, Molly, her mother, and herself. If word had spread of Molly's contraband being within the village, all four of them would be in danger.

"How do you even know what those are?"

"I'm not a mule-kicked fool, Amelia. I know what a book is," he snarked. "I also know that all acceptable books are kept in the church under lock and key. I'm guessing this nonsense has no use to the Privy or the Cleric. Where did you get it?" he demanded again. He stepped forward, causing Amelia to step back.

"I found them in the woods," she lied, trying again to grab them away. He kept walking until she had backed her way out of her room, moving all the way to the kitchen and against the family table.

"If you think I will stand for this, you have another thing coming," he raised his arm and swung. The back of his hand that held the books cracked against her cheek. She crumbled to the ground at his feet. "If you think that's bad, wait until I tell Mother."

Chapter Seven

She was still crumbled on the floor, hand to her cheek, when the front door burst open. The Shephard held the books in her fingertips as if they would burn her flesh. Her eyes locked on Amelia, who looked past her to her parents. They chased behind helplessly into their home. Sarah and Peter tried to wrap themselves around their mother's legs, looking even more frightened. They reluctantly went to their room when Jane insisted. Amelia felt no more secure seeing the anxiety taking hold of her mother.

"Well, Miss. Taylor. I don't know if this is a sign that my decision to bring you into my fold was correct or if you are too far gone to be saved," Shepard Ward hissed, standing above her. Her smile was poisonous; her lips pulled too tightly over her teeth.

Amelia struggled to her feet without the hand she offered. She could feel the heat that remained on her cheek from Finley's hand. He looked pleased when she ran her palm over the redness, seeing that his anger had caused her pain.

"I think we may have to have a few more talks if you expect me to take this one on, Mother. We've only been engaged for a couple of hours, and she is already being a handful," Finley sniffed.

"I would ask you to keep your mouth shut, young man," Shephard Ward snapped. His eyes flashed with embarrassment before he straightened his shoulders and stepped back against the wall, glaring daggers at Amelia, holding out the books. "Where did you get these?"

The room was feeling too full and too warm. Amelia straightened the chair that had remained on its side when she first left and sat, trying to find a way to make it all seem harmless. She would never forgive herself if Molly were to find trouble from her kindness. Her rations were too small as it was. "I found them. They were in the woods."

"In the woods in a certain cottage, I suppose?"

Her mouth ran dry, and her stomach sank. Molly's voice echoed in her head – she's a spider...some she will eat, some she will simply keep.

Amelia forced herself to look the Shephard in the eye and held her voice steady, attempting to sound light. "No, I found them when I was collecting berries for Ellie's wedding." Keeping up the lie was the only option her spinning mind could produce. "I know I should have turned them over to you or the Cleric, but with all of the excitement, I forgot." Her voice was trite and embarrassed, but inside, she was filled with hatred for even having to justify her private belongings. Was it that important to her to see all of her flock so desperately unhappy? She was willing to be unhappy if that meant Molly would be left out of her mistake.

Shephard Ward's eye narrowed. "Did you take it upon yourself to read this filth?"

"I won't lie to you, Shephard. I did read a few lines when I found them," she said, casting her eyes down with an attempt at embarrassment. It was easy to admit to. She had, in fact, read a few lines when Molly had given her the books. It was hard to wait to consume them. "When I saw what they were, I closed them up and vowed not to read another word. It was wrong of me not to bring them straight to you, and I am truly sorry for that." She peeked up at her with contrition.

Finley stepped away from the wall. His lips snarled into a bitter frown. "Why did you have them under your mattress like a dirty little secret then, hm?" he quizzed her. Another look from his mother had his lips sealed, and his body pressed back against the plaster.

"I was worried that Sarah and Peter would see them before I could bring them to the church. It would have been awful for them to be exposed to them. Hidden away, I guess I forgot they were there." Amelia was feeling more confident the deeper into the lie she dug.

"If that's true, then why was only one...," Finley piped in with a whine.

"Finley, I will not tell you again. Be on your way now. I'll speak with you at home," his mother ordered. He stomped his foot like a child, not a grown man in his thirties. The door slamming behind him rattled the windows.

"Shephard, I think she has explained things as best she can. It's all a misunderstanding, just as I said," Amelia's mother said softly, moving to her daughter's side. "Let's not let this ruin such a blessed day."

"Do you really think that I'm going to let this stand?" she bellowed as if enraged by the benevolence being shown by Jane. "She is set to become a Ward and will join me on the Privy Assembly!" Spittle gathered on her lip as she shouted. "She is expected to behave!"

Jane took a step toward the outraged woman. "Shephard, my Amelia is set to become a Ward by marriage, not blood. When she is one day on the Assembly, she will have the *Taylor* seat." She spoke slowly and tightly. "My daughter will not be an extension of your fist over the Privy, Ellen."

The informal use of her name set her blood boiling. All reason left her eyes as she closed the space between herself and Jane, her thin finger pointed in her face. When the anger swallowed all words from her tongue, she turned to Amelia's room, rushing onto her private sanctuary. She moved over every inch of the space, turning over her furniture and few possessions with wails of furious frustration.

"Shephard Ward! Please! What are you doing? Please stop!" Amelia's father pleaded. He reached for her arm and received a solid blow of her palms to his chest. He stumbled back a step more from shock than her strength. "Shephard! This is madness!"

They watched as she stripped away the blankets from the bed, her candle, and Sarah's charcoal drawings, the only decoration in her simple room. Amelia watched her pillow launch into the air, willing the flower picture to stay safely tucked away. Finding it in her current state would lead to punishments for everyone that Amelia could not even fathom. Landing on the wooden floor, the pillow was kicked under the bed when the Shephard spun around to them with Amelia's few belongings clung tightly to her chest.

She took a calming breath and exhaled quickly, tucking back a lock of hair that had slipped from her tightly twisted bun during her outburst. "Young lady, you are under castigation until further notice." She folded the blanket around the candle and drawings. The snap of the candle was not as painful to hear as the crumpling of the sweet illustrations. "You will remain in this room on minimal rations until you are told otherwise. Am I understood?"

Amelia could only bob her head in agreement; her eyes filled with tears, and she tried to focus on the floor before her. The punishment was extreme, but she had not heard Molly's name mentioned. She would take whatever was put upon her as bravely as she could as long as they did not involve her. Shuffling her family out of the room, the

Shephard slammed the door behind them. His chastising voice boomed from the other side.

Grabbing her pillow, she slipped her hand into the fabric and was grateful to feel the folded paper. She wrapped her arms around the feathered comfort and held it tightly as she fell to her bed. The flood of emotions building beyond containment finally found release with sobs she made silent by the pillow held firmly against her face. It could have been minutes, hours, or days that she screamed as far as she knew. One thought ran into the next as she pushed out all of the outrage and grief of what had happened and what was still to come. Eventually, her door slid open, and her father's voice cooed words of comfort to her as his calloused hand rubbed softly over her back.

"Why is she allowed to do the things she does, Papa? She is cruel for the sake of cruelty! How does everyone look away from her madness?" Amelia's body shook with another wave of tears.

Gavin Taylor, always gentle with his words, shocked Amelia out of her agony, "You're right, my girl. There is no excuse for her or how we let her away with it all. She's nothing more than the devil's whore."

She stared up at her father, whose tight lips closed into a frown. "Papa!" she exclaimed, a surprised laugh rising from her chest. That was language saved for the crasser members of the village and only out in the fields or after too much wine. He answered her only with a shrug and a small chuckle of his own.

"I know everything looks bleak right now. I'm well acquainted with the pain of the powerless after all these years – but we will get through this together, okay? We always do, and we always will." He gave her a quick peck on her cheek and was gone as quickly as he had arrived.

He was right that they stood by each other. She could always rely on her family when times were tough. Unfortunately to Amelia, it seemed that all of the troubles had been brought upon them by herself lately. She felt more of a burden than a support to them.

She wiped her cheeks dry and looked about her room. Her fingers traced the lines the sun had bleached around Sarah's drawings and the small nails that remained, trying to picture them still sitting proudly on her wall. All she had been left with was her pillow, bed, the unsteady, small table that once held her candle, and the few items of clothing she owned. Being held captive in her own room without her books was torturous. She hoped the

Shephard believed her about not knowing anything about them, if only so she did not know or take joy in the pain their absence was causing her.

Castigation could last for months if it were so decided. She would be fed only wet oats and water, not be allowed to partake in any social or religious gatherings, and no one would be allowed to visit her or her family until she was deemed forgiven. The one bright spot in that was that as long as she was being punished, her wedding would not occur. Every day away from Finley Ward was a prize.

If only she could be given the penance cast on Molly when her brothers had left. Her immediate family was gone, her blood relatives turned their backs on her to save their own skin, yet she landed in her personal oasis. Alone in the woods, she was reading books and sipping tea. It would be a perfect life. Amelia chose to ignore the fact that she did not know a mainlander who could bring her the spoils that Molly could enjoy. Being cast out would not have the safety net that Molly was blessed with.

No matter how good the fantasy of that was, bringing so much trouble onto her family gave her a shame that was too heavy to hold. She quieted the truth that shouted out to be heard. If she were to be the sweet, obedient girl she was expected to be, the life it would bring would change her into someone who was nothing more than dead inside. Could it be worth it to keep her family out of the eye of the Shephard? Stepping up and taking responsibility was one thing. Letting herself exist in a bottomless pit of despair for the rest of her life was entirely different. It was not something that she was ready to commit to.

Waiting to be ready for things was not a luxury she was afforded. Responsibility was the only word she would allow herself. It was the burden of being an adult, she decided. Crying herself silly would not change anyone's mind about what those responsibilities were. No matter how often she reminded herself that, she did not feel more mature, and the pit in her stomach did not lessen.

A conversation with Molly would have stilled the thoughts she could not silence. She always pointed Amelia in the direction of the answers she needed. Who knew how long it would be until she saw her again? She wondered if she would be told of Amelia's situation when her rations were brought. She would be sure to worry without knowing what had happened to her.

The only way that Molly would be told was if someone knew of their friendship, which only her mother, Ellie, and Adam were aware of. Molly knew better than even to mention her name to the few people tasked with her minimal care. The wrath of the Privy would rain down on everyone in the know if it became common knowledge of their time together.

Running away, taking a chance to live away from the island, seemed better by the day. She wished more than anything that she could ensure no harm would come to her family if she did. There was no plan she could imagine ending with happiness for all.

She allowed herself a moment inside a fool's paradise when she considered if her father truly meant they would always get through things together. Maybe her leaving would be the catalyst that helped them flee as well. Perhaps they would follow her. Maybe, just maybe, she needed to be the one to take the first step to lead them away from a life that was darkening more each moment.

None of that mattered because *maybe* was not the word that would make things better.

Responsibility, Amelia. Your responsibility is to keep your family safe.

'Responsibility,' she repeated in her head. Her chest skipped with the echo of the tears that had stopped.

Sarah's secret knock, a tiny scratch, and a quick rap on her door told her she was on the other side.

"Amelia?" she whispered, "Are you all right?"

She rose from her bed and sat against the door. "Don't worry about me. I'm just fine." She tried to keep the hoarseness from her upset out of her voice.

"I'm sorry they're being so mean to you." Sarah pushed her tiny fingers under the gap in the door. Amelia sniffled back fresh tears at the tender sight of her innocence. She reached out and touched her fingertips to hers when she sniffled as well. "I can stay here with you until they let you out. I won't let you get lonely, okay?"

Amelia pushed away the teardrop that broke free, "I appreciate that, Sarah. I don't want you to get in trouble like me, though. You just make sure to be good for Mama and Papa and do whatever they ask of you."

"Okay," Sarah replied glumly. She linked a finger with hers.

"Is Mama doing okay?"

Her mother had been so angry at Shephard Ward that Amelia worried that she would never calm herself and be forced to take to her bed with another agonizing headache.

"I don't know. She left with the Shephard and hasn't come back. Secret church stuff, I guess." She tightened her linked finger.

It had felt like a couple of hours since she had been shut away. A meeting that long about her could not be good. The wedding reception had to be long over by then. Hopefully, word of her castigation had not reached Ellie, and she could enjoy the rest of her celebration.

"If she's not home soon, I need you and Peter to get to bed. You need to be Papa's helper until she comes home."

"I can do that." A cheer rang in her voice at the chance to do some good. "Don't tell anyone, but I made you this." A piece of paper slid under the door. Sarah had created a new drawing to replace the ones that had been taken. The family stood hand in hand with a blazing sun shining down on their smiling faces. "I hope you like it."

"I love it, Sarah. Thank you so much." Amelia wanted to admonish her for breaking the rules. The last thing she wanted was for her little sister to find trouble for being kind. The drawing was too sweet for her to cast any shadows on to the moment, so she only thanked her again. "You go find Papa now and see if he needs help with anything."

They both did the scratch and rap on the door as a sign of goodbye, and Amelia moved back to her bed. Pushing the corner of the picture onto one of the nails, she admired her talented sister's work. As exhaustion started to overtake her, she carefully pulled the picture from the nail and tucked it away with the flower print. She did not need someone barging in and finding it while she slept.

Without a blanket, she tucked her legs into her skirts and did her best to fend off the night's cool air. Sleep was a blessing and came quickly. Unfortunately, it was not for long.

"Here, Shephard? This seems inappropriate." A voice outside of her window stirred her awake. The room was still dark.

"It is the perfect place if I declare it to be, Sister Emily. Do as you are told!" the Shephard commanded.

Sister Emily was the keeper of the Morrison seat on the Privy Assembly, a quiet woman with a stern hand for her children.

Amelia slipped from her bed to the window to see what reason she and the Shephard would have to be outside her bedroom window. The faces of all members of the Privy were clear in the light of the moon. Her mother stood in the group's center, her face as cold and still as stone.

"I think it would be best to sleep on this, Shephard. Let our prayers ask for guidance before we act too rashly," Sister Annie Miller proposed. Her faith was almost as strong as her obedience to the Shephard. Fear danced in her eyes when Shephard Ward turned to her.

"I will not be disobeyed! This woman is leading her family astray, and you believe we should let more time pass before we bring them back to salvation? You are the one being heartless if you can stand watching these good people fall!" Shephard Ward screamed the words into the night as she grabbed Jane by the hair to push her to her knees. "Prepare her for the cleansing."

Amelia gasped as two of the women pulled her mother's blouse to her waist. Shephard Ward locked eyes with the horrified girl peering through the window and grinned wickedly as she brought down the straps of her whip. She stared as if seeing into Amelia's soul each time she struck her, cries of brutalized pain ripping from her mother's gaping mouth. The whizz and crack of the leather against the air and then her back rang in her ears.

Her father rounded the corner just as Amelia could see the blood starting to stain the thin fabric of her mother's clothing. "My God! What are you doing? This is inhuman!" he bellowed and ran to his wife.

The Shephard released her to the ground and turned to walk the path back to the square without a word to Gavin. The others of the Privy followed at her heel when he gathered his wife into his arms.

Amelia's breath came in bursts that held her lungs tight. Jumping away from the window, she did not know if she should run for her mother or her siblings or chase after the wicked woman who could be so disturbingly vicious.

Making her way to the front door, she stumbled out into the night. They had to leave. There was no way that life on that island would ever be safe again. She wanted to pound on every door and scream for the others to join her. To warn them of the danger of the Shephard, a woman who was a virtual flame that would lick against each home, each family, until it was destroyed to ash. The woman who led them in faith had chosen violence and used it as if it were a holy verse to be revered. There was no forgiving such betrayal.

She wanted nothing more than to run to Molly's and have her tell her that all would be well. To tell her what path was correct and how to heal her family.

If she was caught at her cottage, there was no telling how violent the Shephard could become. Turning on her heel, she headed the opposite way into the forest, her chest burning with every step.

Over and over again, she begged in her mind for her family to follow her as if she could will them to read her mind as she moved further away from the smothering pressure of life under Shephard Ward's heel. They had to have had enough. She could not take any more of what her life had become.

Stumbling over roaming roots of trees, her legs were quickly scratched and bruised. Each time, she picked herself up and kept moving.

Getting past the woods, she fell onto the sharp rocks of the water's shore. Eruptions of sobs choked her, trembling every inch of her body. The inky darkness of the waves that lapped against her was cold and threatening. She was trapped between two endings that were each harrowingly uncharted.

She needed more time to choose.

Pulling herself up on her bloodied legs, she made her way to an overturned tree whose roots rose high above her head, creating a shelter from the night. She tucked herself underneath and focused on her breathing until her lungs unclenched. The nightmare of her reality eventually exhausted her enough for the nightmares in her mind to take over as she shivered asleep among the damp tree roots. It would be her first night she had ever spent alone.

Chapter Eight

She had not been aware that she had drifted off until the foreign sound of waves lapping against the rocky shore shocked her awake with a start. For an instant, she was confused as to where she was. The sting of the scratches that tore her skin had her rubbing her legs and remembering the horrid night that had passed merely hours before. She shivered against the cold early morning air that drifted in and around her. The tree's roots that had provided comfort in the darkness of night now revealed all sorts of creepy crawlies that slithered through its mud and over her body.

Scrambling out into the bright sunshine, she shook out her braid and the loose tendrils that had slipped, assuring herself that none of the bugs had taken up home in her hair. A tremor of discomfort raced up her spine at the thought, and she gave her skirts an extra toss. The smudge of soil on her clothing that had caused her such distress the day before was nothing compared to the state she found herself in. She finished off a rip in the fabric, pulling it loose. Soaking it in the water, the salt burned at the razor-thin slices across her legs and elbows.

The few hours of rest gave her body a modicum of energy but did nothing to appease her mind. Running away had been a mistake. It would bring nothing but trouble for her whole family. Crooking her ear towards the path to the village, she heard no one. There was no search party shouting her name nor any sign that her family had wisely packed up and followed her.

The sight of her mother's bloodied back flashed in her mind. Her heart ached and brought on sobs that she allowed to take over her body, and she slowly slipped down to her knees.

All because of a couple of books.

If the Shephard's cruelty could be that swift over something so small, what would her life be like under that woman's roof as her favorite son's wife? The uncertain future made her want to run further than she had already, yet she knew that would only bring more abuse to her innocent family. The punishment for her behavior would have to be her burden to carry.

Brushing herself off, she stood and stared out at the water that lapped cooly at her feet. She was desperately thirsty but knew better than to drink the salty temptation. Every warning that could be spoken of the sea that surrounded them had been pressed upon them as soon as they could walk. According to every tale she had been told, its dangers ran deeper than its waters. Watching the sunlight turn the tips of each wave into a magical sparkle that twinkled like the stars in the night sky, she could not imagine something so beautiful ever being dangerous. The few remnants of the rickety ship that had carried the founders lay just feet away as a reminder that things were not always what they seemed.

A few rusted pieces of metal were pressed into rocks, the only things left of the disastrous voyage. The storm had ripped apart the shattered ship and then further by the surviving passengers when they required the scrap to build their new lives. Amelia could not make herself step closer to what was now nothing more than a memorial. The thought of being near something that brought such devastation felt as if she would be standing within a freshly dug grave.

Flora Edgar's grave.

She turned her back to the melancholy relic and looked further across the water. Nothing appeared before the sea met the sky in any direction she looked. Shades of blue were the only thing outside of her island prison.

What seemed like her best option when fueled by fear and the adrenaline of escape now seemed foolhardy. It would be just as easy to grow wings and fly as it would cross to the next shore. Molly had said that John would travel on a boat. Nothing left of the ship on the shore could be useful to her. It would be called a skeleton more than a boat now.

She wondered where John would secretly arrive and imagined him sailing up to her with offers of help. The idea to put her rescue in his hands was quickly pushed away. He had done so much for everyone as it stood. If it were to be found out that he helped villagers cross to the mainland, not only would he be in peril, Molly would be done for. Even if it were an option, there was still the matter of her parents not wanting to leave.

Her stomach rolled at how much trouble she would be in if and when she returned. Her behavior had already gotten her mother horrifically beaten. If it was noticed that she was missing, especially during her castigation, it could mean punishment for many more people she cared for. Not to mention ruining the first days of her best friend's married life. If Ellie knew she was gone, she would be sick with worry.

Weighing the pros and cons of returning home with apologies as thick as oak, she grew more nervous. There had to be a way to fix what she had done. The retributions would continue until she returned. Her only hope was that no one would be in any shape to notice her absence, thanks to the wine-soaked night they had indulged in. If there were to be any semblance of peace, she would need to return and face the consequences sooner rather than later.

She paced back and forth along the rocky shore, demanding that her stubborn feet take her home. Leaving still seems a better choice, no matter how selfish. As if the universe had something to say about it all, the skies opened up with heavy rain that beat down upon her, soaking her to the bone. The rocks became slippery as she moved as quickly as she could toward home, and she found herself on her knees more than her feet. A crack of lightning that felt only a few paces away from her caused her to dive into an opening in the cliff wall just to the side of the forest's path. The electricity from the bolt lifted the hair on her arms.

The temperature inside the stone space still held the winter cold as it was veiled from all light, and she trembled in her drenched dress. The sky blackened with the heavy storm clouds, making the cave ominously dark. She strained her eyes to make out any shapes, praying that an animal did not make her sanctuary its home, and slipped her hands along the stone wall, making her way far enough inside to keep the sheets of rain at bay.

It was hard to ignore that the very thought of leaving the island had brought down the heavens upon her. If the waters around the island were not strong enough to hold her, the skies above would. The idea of a curse may not be as outlandish as she had thought.

Tripping over what she believed to be a rock, she landed hard on her bare hands and let out a curse of her own to the pain that electrified her palms. When she started to brace herself to rise to her feet, she felt something smooth, like a long, cold finger, and shot back, landing on her behind. Reaching out again, she patted along the stone ground. When she felt it again, she was relieved to recognize the texture of a candle. She could not help having a laugh at herself for being so shaken up by something so harmless. Reaching out further, she found a wooden crate that held more candles than she had ever seen, along with a stash of stone flints and candlestick holders. She did not give herself time to wonder who they belonged to or how they arrived within the cave before she moved to bring herself some light.

Setting a candle in place, she made a few attempts with the flint before the wick started to glow above the smooth lard. The safety of the light it brought allowed Amelia to take the first calming breath she had had in what felt like days. The flicker of the flame pushed along the cave's walls, and her eyes followed the dance of light and dark until she spotted a marking that drew her to its spot.

Right in front of her, painted on the stone, was a corpse flower.

It had faded with time but was easily recognizable as the bloom found on Molly's print and decorated the church's books. Stepping back from the wall, the light illuminated more of the cracked rock, and even more flowers haphazardly painted all over the space appeared before her.

Surprised by what had appeared, she dropped the candle, sending her back into a void that made her scream with fright when a flash of lightning and the boom of heavy thunder exploded outside, echoing against the hard walls. Timidly, she patted the ground until she found the flint and relit the candle. She lit a second and then a third for good measure.

Turning back to the paintings, she noticed a large leatherbound book propped up in a corner. A book just like the ones under lock and key in the church. This one had a weaving of delicate branches surrounding it along the floor. Tiny star-shaped white flowers with golden yellow rings in the center had been tucked into the half-moon-shaped wreath. Some were still fresh enough to look newly picked, while others had dried into the bark of the sticks over time. She carefully set a candle on the ground beside it and lifted the book.

Opening the worn cover, she found the corpse flower, precisely as it was on the print she had been given, drawn page after page until she stopped on a list of names written in faded ink. The few she could make out were all of early settlers of the island. As she flipped through each name, the ink became more precise, written in a different hand, and the names became more familiar. Everyone she recognized was long dead. Holding the candle closer, she noticed they started to have a thin strike through those listed, with the hue changing the further into the book she read. It was becoming brighter and, eventually, appeared to be deep slashes of red. Holding the page close to her face, a gag caught in her throat. Whoever wrote that book had been crossing out names in blood.

Closing the cover, she set it on the ground and stepped away. That book belonged to someone well-versed in her community's names. Someone who was sick enough to use blood as ink. As much as she hoped it was from an animal and not a human, the difference really didn't matter. There was something deeply troubling with whoever owned that book. More worrisome was whoever it was had stood where she currently found shelter.

Amelia walked to the cave entrance, wondering if it would be safer to wait out the storm or to make a run for it. She did not want to be in there when the book's keeper returned.

Questions poured down harder than the rain just outside. *Could it be the Shephard's book? What purpose did it serve? Why would she keep a list of villagers in a cave?* It did not make sense to her when she had the security of the church to keep whatever secrets she wanted.

If it wasn't her...

Amelia stood rigid with panic—the Watchers.

There had to be somewhere they went when they drifted away from the forest. Somewhere that they existed during the snowy winters and the months between sightings.

She rushed back for the book. If a Watcher's hands wrote it, she had to bring it back and show it to the Elders. This was much more dangerous than mysterious shadow people merely keeping tabs on them. The spirits of the island that she feared were keeping detailed lists of members who had died. Turning the pages, she reread the names. Each one had passed on. Name after name of villagers that had lost their lives had been struck across with blood. Her eyes stopped on a name that confused her.

Malcolm Clark.

Molly's younger brother's name was printed clearly and slashed in crimson. There had been no word of his life once he crossed to the mainland. Even Molly did not like to speak of him. How would the Watchers know that he had died? If he even had.

She turned more pages until another name popped out to her. Alice Stewart. The sweet little girl, Ellie's tiny cousin, who had wandered into the woods, never to be seen again. They had all been assured that the brutal cold and the hungry animals were to blame for her death.

The ink scratched in front of her told her that whoever owned this book knew more than the villagers. Her shaking hand turned to the last page that held names. Her fingers drew up to her throat as dread consumed her. Arthur Allen was crossed out with blood still so red it appeared fresh, and below that, one last name.

Peter Taylor.

Her brother's name, written in deep black ink, was the last entry in the book. Although a drop of blood from Arthur Allen's name had fallen to the side of it, Peter had not yet been crossed off. Amelia slammed the book shut and blew out the candles with one burst of breath. She may not understand what the book was nor who it belonged to, but as long as her brother's name lay inside, she would do whatever it took to protect him.

The rain had died down to a mist, and the clouds above had started to lighten when she exited the cave with the book tucked firmly under her arm. Whatever trouble awaited her meant nothing compared to getting that book to her mother. If anyone knew what to do with it, it would be her. This was bigger than anything she had been running away from, and it had her trying to pick up her pace back home.

The path had become slick and washed out in spots from the storm. The smell of wet pines and musty earth filled her nose as she moved at a frustratingly slow speed so as not to fall. Her legs ached from the scrapes and bruises that covered her.

Questions of who may already know of the book scattered her thoughts. *Why would the Watchers draw the corpse flower? What could they know of Flora Edgar? Could they have been the ones to curse the island?*

If they had powers of that strength, they could have caused the shipwreck and tragic deaths of the entire Edgar family. If the curse was real, the Shephard might actually be telling the truth of her visions. Nothing but mayhem had occurred since her last episode; that could not be denied. She may have been seeing more than Arthur Allen leaving. Something far more dangerous.

Amelia stopped to catch her breath and thought of Shephard Ward's words. She had said she knew he left for the mainland. She made no mention of him dying. Everyone listed in the book was known to be resting in the graveyard behind the church, all but Malcolm, Alice, Arthur, and, thankfully, Peter.

A snap ahead of her on the path startled her away from her confusing thoughts. Looking about for the cause, she found herself alone. Another breaking branch ahead held her in place and stopped her from continuing.

"Hello?" she called out, hoping it was just someone out looking for her or, better still, an animal small enough not to be a threat. The only reply was the caw of the crows above. She scolded herself for running off into the night, alone in the woods. If she had stayed put, she could have been helping her mother with her wounds instead of being a sitting duck in the woods and possibly causing more scandal. The book in her hand gave her courage, and she told herself it was meant to be. It would all be worth it in the end.

She stepped forward only to hear another loud snap from behind a cluster of low branches that rustled without wind.

"Who's there?" She hoped a harmless rabbit or squirrel would appear. Better to feel foolish than frightened. "Adam, if that's you, please just come out," she speculated hopefully. "I really need you to see something."

"Sorry. I didn't mean to scare you," a deep, unrecognized voice apologized from behind the trees, just out of sight. It was not Adam's voice. The shadow of whoever spoke stretched out onto the trail.

"Who is that? Come out from there," she insisted, attempting to sound firm. "I can explain where I was. I know I'm probably in a lot of trouble, but I need to show everyone something," she held the book tight and started to ramble about finding something of great importance. The shadow stretched out further in the post-storm sunshine that had begun to shimmer down through the trees. The branches from which the voice had appeared stilled while the shadow remained. "Please come out from there," her voice quaked.

The shadow moved slightly from side to side in front of her and started to pull back along the ground into the brush. She took her chances and darted past, heading as quickly as she could back to the shelter of her village. Whoever, or whatever, was in that forest was not one of her neighbors. She shrieked and jumped when a low-hanging branch opposite where he hid tangled with her skirts. She slapped it loose and continued to run up the path.

"Wait!" the voice called out to her as she turned down a fork in the trail, "Wait!" Amelia knew she would do no such thing and kept moving, glad to put space between them. "You dropped this!"

Amelia slipped, catching her footing at the last moment before she tumbled to the ground. She turned to see what he was speaking up as she brushed a wild tendril of hair from her face. That is when she realized her hands were empty.

He had the book.

Chapter Nine

Her chest heaved up and down from fear and fatigue. Her eyes stayed on the path stretching before her. The way home. The escape from whoever stood behind her. She could hear the shuffle of his feet when he took a few steps forward.

"It's okay. I'm not going to hurt you or anything. I just saw you running, and your legs are cut up pretty bad. I wanted to make sure you're all right." His voice was steady and low in a way that Amelia was surprised to find calming. "I'm sorry. I'll go. I'll leave your book here, okay? It's on this log, okay?"

She heard the thump of it being set down and braved turning around to face him. He stood about ten yards away, looking at her with as much curiosity as she did to him. His clothing was pristine, without a mark or sign of labor anywhere she could see. His oversized shirt, blue as the summer's sky, had a cloak's hood attached that her wore over a crisp, white brimmed hat. It was not the way she would imagine a Watcher to dress. He tugged down his hood and exposed a symbol she did not recognize across the front of his hat. He looked to be about her age, with piercing blue eyes and short dark curls that peeked out from the sides of the strange hat.

"Who are you?" she asked with a voice that held strength she did not feel.

He took a step forward and stopped when she took a step back. "I'm Cole. Cole Bennett," he offered, giving her a nervous smile and a half wave.

"Bennett," she repeated. The family name of her favorite Jane Austen character, Elizabeth. Her eyes narrowed on him, interest overtaking fear.

"Yeah. We, I mean my friends and I, came over for our senior challenge." He shifted in place and gestured randomly out into the woods. "They're around here somewhere. It's stupid, I know, but it's something everyone does."

She had no idea what he was talking about. It made her nervous that there were more people somewhere out of sight. She was as concerned for herself as much as what they may come upon within the dark of the forest.

The young man who stood awkwardly staring back at her did not look like he would be much of a threat to The Watchers.

"You're a mainlander?" she asked, crossing her arms to steady herself. She hoped it made her look casually unafraid. He was the only person from across the water, other than John, that she had ever seen. He was the very first one she had ever spoken to.

"A mainlander?" He breathed a short laugh with a quizzical twist on his face. "I'm from across the bay if that's what you mean. I live in Wellesley."

She frowned, and his brow creased when he laughed again. It made her feel foolish. "You shouldn't be here," she admonished.

"I know. I told them that it was a bad idea. They didn't want to break tradition, and I was too chicken shit to say no, I guess."

Amelia smothered her amusement at his use of the cussword.

His hand slid into a tight pocket of his pants and pulled out a shiny rectangle on which he tapped his fingers before holding it up to the sky. "There is no coverage here at all," he sighed.

She didn't know how he could say that with trees so dense that some parts of the forest stay as dim as dusk all day, with the land hidden from the sky. "What is that?" She moved steadily toward her book on the log, one small step at a time.

"What's what? This?" He looked from the object to the inquisitive look on her face and held it out to her. "It's my phone. It's a telephone," he added when she still seemed unsure.

There had been a telephone in a book that Molly had given her that she had enjoyed. The description was nothing like what Cole held in his hand. Holding it out to her as she picked up the book, she jumped back when he tapped the glass that covered the telephone. A picture of a scruffy black dog appeared.

"How did you do that?" she asked breathlessly.

"It's my screen saver," he answered as if that was all the information required. He held it up again, moving his finger across and changing the images that appeared. "I guess you guys really are living off the grid out here, huh?" He tucked the phone back in his pocket. "Are you guys Amish or something?"

"I..." Amelia didn't know what that meant and did not want to feel like a fool again. "We live simply. There's nothing wrong with that." It felt unnecessary to defend herself to a stranger who had no right to be standing in their forest. Her back stiffened anyway.

"I'm sorry. I didn't mean to offend you." He frowned and looked about him as if the words he needed would appear in the air around him. "Everyone is just so curious about you guys. Old man Clark is pretty serious about keeping us all off the island."

Old man Clark? "Do you mean John Clark?" she asked with a burgeoning excitement that he may know Molly's brother.

"Yeah, is he like your leader or something?"

Amelia held the book to her chest. "No. He's not one of us anymore. He chose to leave."

"He sure spends a lot of time over here for not being a part of your, uh, community."

"His sister lives here, and he helps us out from time to time," she informed him, unsure of how much she should allow him to know of their lives. The mainlanders were not to be trusted, after all. John was the only exception she would allow herself.

"It's got to be nice having his help. It can't be easy living out here." He pulled a leaf from the tree beside him and started to strip it nervously. "He'd be so mad if he knew we were out here. No one is allowed."

"Well, you shouldn't be out here, that's true. It's not a safe place to wonder about," she chided.

"I can tell," he said, pointing at her injured legs. She shuffled her skirts with one hand to pull them over as much as they could reach. "I'm sorry we came out and bothered you. When my buddy saw Old man Clark bringing over boatloads of supplies, he figured there was going to be a party, and, I don't know, I guess he thought that would be the perfect night to do the challenge."

"What is the challenge? To make it across the water?" Amelia could see how that could be a feat of accomplishment.

"Yeah, I guess. It's a stupid tradition for seniors at Wellesley High. Before graduation, we're supposed to come across without being caught. It's bonus points if you spend the night, like we did."

"You've been here all night?" she asked with shock. They spent the night milling about in the woods without knowing how much danger they could have been in. "Where are your friends?" Fear of the stranger was overtaken by the concern of what could have happened to his friends. She grabbed the edge of his shirt and started back toward the water. "You need to find them and get out of here! Anything could have happened to them!"

He stumbled a step with the force of her tug before he dug his heels in, "Whoa! It's okay. They're around here somewhere. Probably back at the tents at the beach."

She snatched her hand back from her grip on his sleeve, giving herself a mental reprimand for being so bold.

"I didn't see anyone when I was there. Are you sure they'll still be there?" Looking back and forth between the path's two directions, she weighed the importance of what lay at the end of each.

He pulled out a bundle of keys from the wide pocket in the front of his shirt and jangled them. "Unless they swam back," he laughed. "My boat isn't moving without me."

The idea that he could come and go from the island whenever he wanted was incomprehensible. John's back and forth to the island had never seemed as easy. It was still mainly under the direction of the Privy that he would be allowed to arrive. The contraband that he would secretly bring his sister was the only thing he appeared to do of his own volition. He would be in even more trouble if he had been found out than the young man who calmly stood beside her.

"You should get back to them now before someone sees you." She was just as concerned that someone would see her with him. That punishment would surely be the box, even if she had not already been under castigated. She was running out of time to sneak back without her night-long absence being noticed. "You need to go. Now."

"Are you sure you're okay? I can help you back if you want," he offered and started in the direction of the cottages.

"No!" she exclaimed, holding her hand out to stop him from approaching, nearly dropping the book. "You should go. Mainlanders are not supposed to be here."

Her heart felt like it had leaped into her throat when a crash of breaking branches echoed behind Cole. They both jumped at the sound. A group of two young men and three young ladies dressed in the same manner as Cole came into view along the trail. They laughed happily and let out a whoop when they saw him.

"Will you dummies keep it down?" he barked at them in a hushed voice. "You're gonna get us in shit!"

"Oh my god, Cole! Look at her! You found one of the weirdos in the wild! Did you find yourself a little cult girlfriend on your walk?" a girl with glossy blonde curls that bounced over her shoulders teased. She skipped the distance between them and linked her arm with his, looking at Amelia with pretentious wonder.

"Seriously, Aubrey? Are you even capable of not being a raging bitch?" Cole snapped at her, pulling his arm away. His face sunk with her appearance.

Amelia wished more than anything that they would turn around and leave without another word. She looked toward home, wondering if she should leave them to sneak back into the village. Worry that they would follow and the chaos that would cause held her in place. She tapped at the book she held tightly as she watched them argue among themselves and stood stiff as a board, willing them not to see her even as she stood a few feet away. It was overwhelming to be so close to strangers. The only new people she had ever met were the wrinkly-faced newborns of her neighbors and the characters in her novels. Six people she did not know felt like a crowd too large for her to handle.

"Ooo, someone's testy today. Still hungover from the festivities last night?" Aubrey sneered, patting Cole on the behind. Amelia looked away with embarrassment.

"Aubrey, can you even attempt chill? You always ruin everything," a second girl, slender with large, friendly pale green eyes, said before elbowing the abrasive girl's side. "I'm sorry. She can't help herself," she added to Amelia. "I'm Greta." She paused, waiting for Amelia to introduce herself, and continued when she didn't, "This is Madison, Jax, and Nathan." They all gave a quick wave when their name was called. "You live out here, huh?" She waited again for Amelia to speak. "It's really cool over here."

Amelia stared at each of them for a blink and then back to Cole, "You need to take them home. You cannot be here."

"We're still on a rush from that wedding last night. Were they first cousins or brother and sister?" Aubrey sneered and laughed too loudly with a mouth opened as wide as a goat's.

"Okay. That's enough. Let's go," the boy introduced as Jax ordered, pulling her back down the trail. He was taller than the group, with broad shoulders that easily dragged the rude girl along. "You're a real piece of work, Brey."

The one Greta had called Madison had hair similar to Aubrey's, except not as long or glossy, and twirled a curl as she followed behind them without a word when her abrasive friend snapped her name.

"What? It's not my fault she lives on a creepy cult island!" she laughed again, louder. The grating sound slowly disappeared down the narrow path with them.

"I am so sorry," Cole blustered. "She is...I am so sorry, Amelia. There is no excuse for her."

"Amelia, is it?" Greta asked and received a slight nod. "That's a pretty name."

"Thank you," she replied softly. Greta seemed to be much kinder than the explosion that was Aubrey, and she gave her a face-splitting smile in return for Amelia speaking. The boy introduced as Nathan stood silently, watching the conversation without looking like he cared to join. He had the same shy eyes as her father. That did not change the fact that they needed to leave.

"I'm sorry for Aubrey. There is something seriously wrong with that girl," Greta called out in the direction where she had left. "It was dumb of us to be out here anyways, I guess, so sorry for that, too," Greta admitted. She looked down at Amelia's legs. "Oh damn! Are you okay? Those scrapes look nasty."

"I'm fine. Thank you. I really need to get home, and you all need to get back to where you belong." She flicked her hand at them, shooing them like her mother did when the children got underfoot in the kitchen.

"She's right. We should have been gone by sun up if we don't wanna get caught. My dad won't let us near the boat again if he knows we were out here," Cole lamented. "I'm sorry for all the trouble, Amelia. We'll get going before we get you in trouble."

She nodded stiffly and turned before they did to hustle home. If she ever saw them again, it would be too soon. Aubrey especially. The nasty streak in that one would rival Finley's. That would be a perfect pairing, she thought, imagining what a wedding of the two would look like.

She stopped and spun on her heel. "Wait!" she called out to their backs. "Did she say you were at the wedding last night?"

The three turned back to her, sheepish embarrassment coloring their faces.

"We just watched for a bit. I'm sure no one saw us," Cole answered.

"You're lucky no one did!" Amelia hollered. She felt so exposed and violated that strangers had been milling about in the woods, watching their private, joyful moment. "How long have you been watching us?" she asked slowly, a realization creeping in.

"We've come this one time. I promise. It was just for the senior challenge," Greta insisted. "I'm really sorry."

Cole peered up at her momentarily before his eyes returned to his feet like a scolded child.

"How many of you are there?" Amelia pressed. "How many of you come out here?"

"I don't know. A few of the class have. It's not as popular as it used to be years ago. Old Man Clark kinda cracked down on it. A few of us thought it would be fun to start it up again," Greta said, clamping her mouth shut when she saw the anger in Amelia's eyes.

Without another word, Amelia broke into a sprint home. She did not turn back or acknowledge the trespassers when they shouted out more apologies.

The unseen eyes watching her had been the young mainlanders, not Watchers. It was foolish young folks from across the water that had scared her so, not Watcher's, who had suddenly started to appear during the day. The idea that there was no such thing as Watcher's and that it had been the curious mainlanders all along brought relief for only a breath.

That did not explain the purpose of the book she held nor the reason for Arthur and Peter's names on the list.

Even though Mainlanders were considered awful and spiteful people, the few she had just met did not seem as though they would be killers. Aubrey had a sword for a tongue, for certain, but did not seem as if she would genuinely harm someone. They were kids, just as she and her friends were, even though Ellie was now a wife. The thought still brought her surprise that her dearest friend had been married the night before. For an existence that rarely saw change, it had started to come far too quickly as of late.

As she approached the edge of the cottages, she stopped by a large divot in the ground by an overturned tree. Being caught with the book could mean serious trouble, on top of being outside during her castigation. She wanted to speak with her mother as soon as she could, and there was no way she would risk putting the book in her hands before they knew what to do with it. Setting it in the divot and tossing some leaves over top, she looked over the hiding spot and then added some more leaves for good measure.

She pulled out her braid, redid it in a smooth plait, and rubbed the dirt from her arms and legs as best as she could manage. The sun above told her it was approaching lunchtime, which meant many of her neighbors would be making their way to their homes for a midday meal. It would be difficult to sneak back unseen.

Hopping the short fence at the back of the garden, she shimmied along as low as she could manage until she could jump over the opposite side beside the shed. She put her head down and headed home, tucked along the tree line, desperate to see the state of her mother. Her heart dropped as she passed the rear of the church and heard voices from within. Moving tightly along the wall so as not to be spotted, she risked a peek around to the front. The single white candle was set on the porch. They were cloistered again, and she hoped it was not because they knew she had left. She would have to wait to speak with her mother, but more importantly, she needed to return to her room.

When she reached the rear of her cottage, she peered across the square to see her father making his way home. Moving swiftly, she scurried inside and was in the shelter of her room before anyone could set eyes on her. She was still catching her breath when her father knocked on her door to tell her it would be alright to join them at the table for lunch.

"Amelia!" Sarah called out to her. "You better get a wiggle on! Peter already has his eyes on your bowl!" She giggled and bounced to her seat when Amelia opened her door. From the lighthearted mood of her sister, she could tell that she was none the wiser of what had transpired the night before just outside of their home. There was no sign that anyone had any idea of her absence.

Her father and brother were already tucked into their broth when she and Sarah joined them. Her father kept his red-rimmed eyes on his bowl, not braving a look at his children. Amelia's spirit was crushed to see her sweet father suffering. It would be of no use to ask him how her mother was once the children had set off again. He looked to be on the edge of tears as it was and did not want to set him off.

"Ellie looked so pretty last night, didn't she?" Sarah exclaimed, an innocent smile dancing on her lips.

"Yes, she did. Very pretty," Amelia agreed. Her voice did not carry the singsong merriment of her sister. It felt like the wedding had been days ago with the exhaustion that burned through her body.

"And that pork roast was so yummy! I thought Peter was going to grow a snout himself if he had another serving!" Sarah teased and fell into a fit of giggles when he snorted like a pig and gulped his broth.

"It was all wonderful. Ellie is blessed," Amelia agreed again. She sipped from her bowl even though she did not have an appetite.

"Your wedding will be even better, I'm sure of it." Sarah did not notice her older sister glowering at the notion. "I'm going to wear flowers in my hair, just like Ellie did, even though I won't be the bride."

"Uh–huh," was all Amelia offered, her mind taking her from the room around her.

Just that morning, she had her feet in the water with eyes on the horizon, with hopes of life far from their island dancing in her heart. It had been a mistake to run away, and she was deeply thankful that no further harm had come to her loved ones for her rash decision. It was time to accept that the village was all she would have outside of her fantasies, and that would have to do.

Even if that meant marrying Finley Ward.

When his smug face appeared in her thoughts, she transformed it into a fresh, fruity-smelling teabag that sunk into a warmed teapot. Turning to speak with Ellie about her wedding, she was surprised that her mind showed Cole sitting at her side instead. Splendid trousers and billowing cotton shirt replaced his strange clothing, and he smiled gladly at her before sipping his tea.

Amelia shook herself from the scene that played out and stood from the table, her bowl in hand.

"I should get back to my room. I don't want to cause any more trouble," she mumbled as she put her dish in the wash basin.

"With Ellie on her wedding break, I don't see them keeping you from the garden for long," her father predicted, his eyes remaining on his lunch. "Should be back to the usual soon. Don't let yourself worry."

She gave a quick nod to his words and excused herself. Sitting on her bed, with nothing but her thoughts, she hoped he was right. A crack against her window pane had her on her feet. A second crack had her looking outside to find Adam with a hand full of pebbles. She opened the window the slight slice that it allowed.

"Hey!" Adam called out to her, looking much less green than the night before. "How are you holding up?"

"You shouldn't be here, Adam. Didn't you hear about my castigation?" she said quietly, looking about to make sure he was not being spotted.

"Of course I have. I'm not going to leave you here to suffer alone," he gave a smile that turned to a frown as he watched her. "Something else has happened, hasn't it? You look like you've seen a ghost."

"I met the Watchers!" Amelia blurted. Adam tilted his head with confusion. "Well, not *the* Watchers. Mainlanders! They were watching us yesterday." She was furious with herself for not keeping it to herself, yet she had to share what had transpired with someone. Of everyone she knew, Adam would be the one who would be able to handle such shocking events the best.

"What are you talking about?" he whispered, worried eyes scanning the fence line.

Amelia wondered how much she should divulge to him. With the little she had already admitted, her excitement returned to worry. If he were to possess knowledge of what had happened, she would be passing on the risk for him to shoulder, as well. He stared impatiently at her as she silently argued with herself. He knew nothing of John nor the secrets she kept with Molly. She wished it was Molly she was confessing to. It would be much easier to be completely truthful. With how much trouble she had caused, she doubted that she would be able to risk a visit to her anytime soon.

A big secret had already been spilled, and he was one of her best friends, after all. He was now the only friend she had left who was living outside of marriage, and she knew well that Adam was a faithful secret keeper.

"I was in the woods earlier," she said, thinning the story for his protection, "and I saw some Mainlanders." Her lips tightened, holding in the whole story.

"Are you serious? Where?" he demanded with awe, looking along the tree line as if they would be standing there, waiting to greet him.

"They were down the trail," she answered quickly, hoping he would assume she had been sneaking to see Molly. "There were six of them – three girls and three boys. They all looked to be around our age."

"Hallelujah to the universe above!" Adam shrieked, holding his hands up to the sky. "Please tell me they're coming back! You have to introduce me. I knew it. I knew someone would save me from this mundane purgatory."

"Adam, have you gone mad? Do you know how much trouble it would be for everyone if they were to come back? I told them to leave and never look back," she whispered in a raspy hush. She was right that he would not be shocked, but she did not expect him to be so ecstatic.

"Why? They must be more interesting than the potatoes that live on this island! I can't believe you got to meet them, and I didn't," he sulked, clearly not as perturbed by their appearance as she had been. "What did they look like? Charlie said he heard they wear metal clothes and have shaved heads. The guys and the ladies!"

Amelia had to laugh at the excitement in his voice. "They didn't look like that. They all wore trousers, though. Even the girls," she gushed quietly. "They were loud, as well. I don't know how we did not all hear them last night."

"Last night?!" Adam shouted. "They were here last night? Wait...when did you meet them? I was with you almost all night until they locked you away in your room."

"Shh...keep your voice down. We don't need anyone else hearing about this," she ordered. "They said they watched the wedding."

"You met them at the wedding? How? Why didn't you introduce me?" Adam marveled. "How did no one notice them?"

"I think everyone was pretty busy with the event at hand, Adam. But I didn't meet them there. I think that's who I saw, though, during the day. I don't think it was the Watchers. I think it was them."

The memory of hiding behind the church and hearing the hushed voices in the woods trickled into her head. A heat rushed over her cheeks when she remembered cleaning her skirts and lifting them to her hips. The giggles that had followed. Her mouth went dry at the thought that Cole may have seen her undergarments.

"As crazy as that all is, it does make more sense than Watcher's appearing during the day." His eyes were distant, lost in thought. "What if it is just Mainlanders? What if they're the Watchers?"

Amelia was glad he had come to the same conclusion, yet did not feel comfortable sharing her thoughts on it. Especially mentioning the book she had found. "It could be," was all she said.

"So, where did you meet them?" he pressed.

"After the Shephard left, I broke castigation and went into the woods...to collect my thoughts for a few minutes," she lied.

"Whoa! Are you serious? You could have ended up in the box, Amelia. What were you thinking?"

She did not want to lie to him any further and only replied with a lift of her shoulder. She would come clean about everything she had been through and discovered once she spoke to her mother.

"I'm glad you didn't get caught," he said quietly, looking around as if he was suddenly aware he, too, was breaking the rules just by speaking with her. "Everything is getting so upside down so fast. First, Ellie's married, then you're engaged to Finley, then you're stowed away like a prisoner, and now this! More has happened in the past couple of days than in years!" Adam said with wonder. "Speaking of which, how are you doing with the Finley situation?" His face tightened with disgust. The opinion of the Shephard's golden child was universal among the villagers.

Amelia sighed heavily, "As best I can, I suppose. It was bound to be someone. I never imagined it would be this bad, though."

The change in subject sat heavy in the air between them, and no one spoke for a spell.

"At least you get to live in the big house," Adam finally added.

"I do," she nodded.

"Well, listen to that! You're already quoting your wedding," he teased with a laugh. "Now we just need your new friends to come and save me from this wakeless hell before you leave me for the wives pew."

Amelia laughed weakly at his jesting, ignoring that her heart wished for the same rescue for herself. One that she knew was impossible. She reminded herself to keep her head down, do what was best for her family, and not give the day's visitors a second thought. The image of Cole pouring her tea in the garden of a grand estate was drowned away with the reminder of newfound responsibility. Dreams were now only for Sarah and Peter, not her.

The weighty slam of the church's door and the footfalls of the Privy Assembly across the porch had Adam away in a flash. Amelia pulled her window closed and latched it. There was nothing left to do except wait for her mother's arrival.

Chapter Ten

Jane did not join Amelia as soon as she arrived home, much to Amelia's chagrin. Listening at the door, she could hear the voices of other members of the Assembly speaking quietly in the common area. There was no way she would dare breach the threshold of her room while they were milling about. She could only make out murmurs of voices until her father's erupted, ringing out against every surface.

"I will not have it! No, Jane. This is too much!" he bellowed. A shuffling of feet and the click of the front door told Amelia that the other members had taken their leave at his outburst.

She braved opening her door silently, just an inch, to better hear what had enraged her father so. She had never heard him so angry or so vocal to the Privy.

"It will be rushed, I know," her mother faltered. "She'll manage, Gavin. She will be prepared, and I know she will do well."

"It is not about being prepared, Jane! Not only is my Amelia too good for that man, but I take offense to her threatening us! Sarah is only seven years old. To even speak of her marrying a thirty-three-year-old man is beyond repugnant!" he roared. Amelia held her breath when he continued. "She has gone mad with power, Jane! Something has to be done. To say that Amelia would be an outcast if she did anything to disrupt the marriage? How are you not terrified at the idea of Amelia living under that roof with those monsters?"

"Of course I am!" Jane bleated. "How dare you suggest otherwise? I have been doing my best to keep our children safe, Gavin! For the love of God, I was beaten for all that I've done, and even still, I would do more. I would do anything for my family!"

The house went silent except for the smothered cries that Jane covered. The absence of her brother and sister reacting to the scene told her they had been sent outside when the group arrived. She gave thanks for small miracles yet wanted nothing more than to rush out and hug her, to do whatever she could to comfort her weary mother. Amelia had begun to feel like the bane of their family's present and future.

"I'm sorry, Jane. I'm sorry, you're right," her father affirmed gently. "It's the shock of it all." There was a calming moment of silence before he managed to speak again. "How is your back, my love? Would you like me to get you a cool cloth?"

"No, I'm fine. Thank you," she sniffled. "I hate how she turns us against each other. I hate how powerless she makes me feel."

"We will manage like we always do. Amelia won't scoff at the wedding being moved up so soon. Thankfully, she is strong like you," Gavin added with a tired laugh. "I still don't understand the thinking that Sarah would inherit the Taylor seat if Amelia were banished. It doesn't make sense. If anything, Peter would. An obscene union of a child and her son would not change any of that."

"I agree. Her threats are too large to comprehend anymore. The members were all stunned into silence when she started her rants," Jane lamented. A clink of glass told Amelia that her father had wisely gotten his wife a glass of wine. "All she would say was that there were other plans for Peter. She refused to say more."

"What could possibly be more important for Peter than taking a rightful seat on the Privy if they were to overstep Amelia?" Gavin queried with disbelief. "It wouldn't be a Cleric's position. Cleric Gordon has already selected Andrew Stewart to mentor."

"Other plans was all she would say," Jane repeated, defeat heavy in her voice. Her glass rattled on the table. "I'm going to speak with Amelia. Keep Peter and Sarah occupied outside, will you?"

Amelia shut her door before her mother could see she had been eavesdropping.

Whatever Shephard Ward meant of Peter's place among them, she believed all would be well if she kept good and minded the rules—the time of fun and rule-breaking had caught up to her, causing pain and suffering for not just herself, but for her family. There was no way she would allow her young sister to be married, and she would do anything to keep Peter safe. His name scratched in the book carried much more weight with the ominous threat of his future.

Everything would be fine if she could find a way to do as she was told. She was sure of it. It had to be. The idea of telling her mother about the book suddenly seemed like the worst next move she could make. She had brought about enough trouble. If she left the book where she had hidden it, maybe the earth would swallow it whole, and it would be as if it never existed. Whoever was its rightful owner would forget all about it, and no more harm would befall them all. Adam had been right. There had been too much change too quickly. Normalcy needed to return.

Hopefully, that would calm the Shephard as well. Her displeasure always left everyone unsettled.

"Amelia! Your legs!" her mother cried out when she entered the room.

She tugged her blanket over the injuries, "Please don't be angry."

"Angry? Who did this to you? What has happened?" she demanded, pulling the blanket from her lap. "My grace! You're ripped apart!"

"It's nothing. I fell. I swear, I'm alright," Amelia fibbed, knowing she would not be believed. "I'm sorry. I was trying to go out my window last night, but then I told myself better. I won't try it again, I swear."

Jane looked from her daughter's wounded legs to her pleading face. The slight opening in her window would barely allow her arm to pass, let alone her body. Only a fool would believe that lie, and her lips tightened into a resigned frown. "Look me in the eye and tell me that more trouble will not come from whatever it is that you're hiding."

Nothing she did ever remained hidden from her mother for long. "I made a mistake. I'm sorry. I won't do it again."

Her mother turned out of the room and returned with a dish of water and a soft rag. She cleaned her scrapes thoroughly without a word and then set the bowl on the floor. "I'm sure you heard your father and I." She leveled a knowing stare at her daughter.

"I heard you shouting, yes." Amelia looked to the floor, ashamed of yet another broken rule to add to her list.

"The Shephard has decided that there will not be a traditional engagement for you and Findley," She swallowed deeply, pushing down emotion. "You will be married in three days."

"Three days?" Amelia balked. "The marriage lessons alone are at least a week, not to mention getting things together." The longer it took to prepare, the longer she was not his wife. Three days of freedom was too little to imagine.

"Shephard Ward has decided that since you will be in the care of her home, your lessons can take place after the wedding. She will carry out the task herself." Jane looked straight ahead at a spot on the wall, keeping her voice tight. "I know you will make us all proud."

Amelia would not allow herself to cry. Findley did not deserve the energy. Just as her mother had made sacrifices her entire life, so would she. The Shephard wanted the marriage for reasons she could not comprehend, but that did not matter. It would keep her family safe and in the church's good graces. She mirrored her mother, staring straight ahead, a comforting numbness taking root.

"It will be hard not to live under this roof, but I will make you proud, Mama. I'll behave. Things will be good again." Jane coughed as she smothered a sob, pulling her daughter to her and grimacing when Amelia wrapped her arms around to her back. "Does it hurt terribly?" she asked quietly, regretting causing her the pain in more ways than one.

"Probably just as much as your legs," she answered with a half smile. "We'll all heal and move on. Good times are ahead of us. The universe will provide as long as we keep good and do as we should." Her body was tight as she stood from Amelia.

A knock on the front door caused them to share a curious look. Soon, Findley's booming voice was heard, shouting at her father.

"She is my bride. I can see her whenever I want, Gavin," he barked with condescension.

Both ladies balked at the nerve of him calling his elder by his first name. Amelia was hardly on her feet before he was through her bedroom door as if he owned all he had stepped upon.

"Findley, what are you doing here? This is highly inappropriate," Jane spoke as she stepped between her daughter and the intrusion.

"I don't think it's for you to decide when I see my bride, Jane. My mother has asked for you to join her in the Clerics cottage. Wedding plans, I'm sure," he said dismissively, patronizing arrogance oozing through every word.

Jane gave her daughter a hug and a strength-giving squeeze on her shoulder before she left without another word, rage-filled eyes locked on Findley.

He removed the leather bag he wore slung across his chest and dropped it with a thump on her floor. Moving past her, he tossed himself on her bed, his ankles crossed and his hands behind his head. Amelia tried to ignore that he was only inches away from the corpse flower print she had hidden.

"So, I assume you've heard the news? Our big day is coming up soon," he crowed with a wide grin cracking across his face. "You must be so excited."

"Please get off of my bed. This is highly inappropriate," was all she replied.

"You Taylor's seem to have a lot to say about others' behavior, don't you?" he sneered as he sat up, yet remained perched on the side of her bed. "I would think with all the sneaking around you do, you would not have the nerve to judge others."

Amelia kept her eyes on her door, willing him to leave. He replied with a snort and stood. She backed herself against the wall to keep him away when he moved slowly toward her. He did not stop until her nose nearly touched his chest.

"Please, you need to leave." Her nerves betrayed the strength she tried to exude when her voice shook nearly as much as her body. His breath was hot on her face, turning her stomach.

He kept his eyes steady on her when he stepped back to retrieve his bag. Lifting it, he slid his hand inside. The devious grin, which twisted his lips, gave him a look of menace that nearly made Amelia call out for help.

Keep good, do as we should. Keep good, do as we should.

She repeated the phrase until she had steeled herself to hold her head high and return his stare.

"I think my little bride has been naughty, hasn't she?" he accused with a sickening playfulness. Amelia said nothing. "I think you dropped this?"

He pulled his hand from his bag to reveal the leather book she had buried, a few leaves still stuck to the cover.

Amelia nearly retched. Locking her knees to stay upright, she glared back at him. "I have no idea what that is."

"Oh, so you choose to take me as a fool, do you, dear bride? That will not do." Amelia stopped herself from reaching out and snatching it away when he flipped open the cover, eyes scanning the pages. "Is this your little friend Molly's doing? Looks like something a witch would have," he asked with a disgusted sneer. "It will not do for you to be sneaking off into the woods to spend time with a decrepit old enchantress, Amelia." He turned the page. "The only question I have is whether or not I should tell our Shephard about this flagrant transgression or if I should handle it myself as my first husbandly duty?"

"Findley, it's not my book. I promise you I did not get it from Molly," Amelia pleaded for him to believe her. More trouble did not need to arise. More people did not need to come to harm. She cursed herself for bringing the damned book so near the village.

He shut the book with a bang and returned it to his bag. "I suppose if I were able to decide what my first husbandly duty was to be, I wouldn't choose for it to be tattling on you to my mother." He moved toward again. "I can think of something that would be much more pleasant for both of us."

"Time to go, Findley," Gavin announced with the danger in his voice filling the room. "There is much to be done in the next few days. It would be best if you left us to it. Now." He stepped between the two and pointed to the door.

The novelty of being spoken to in such a manner danced in Findley's eyes for several blinks. He licked his lips and turned his attention back to Amelia. "I suppose he's right, my darling one. You'll want to make sure everything is perfect for me." He patted the bag and lifted a knowing brow to her. Gavin followed him out all the way to the door and slammed it furiously behind him.

Amelia curled up on the bed, allowing the shaking to overtake her body as the tears flowed relentlessly down her cheeks. Her mother was by her side in an instant, whispering soft words of nurturing and rubbing her back. It would take every inch of her being to survive a marriage with that man, and even then, she did not know it would be enough. She had never felt so powerless. It felt as if she were falling to a cold, hard ground that she could not see but knew would soon arrive to shatter her very being.

Eventually, after her eyes ran dry, the strain of the past day lulled her to sleep. Instead of finding a moment of peace within dreams that took her far away from her troubles, she found herself awash in a vengeful sea. One by one, each member of her family called out to her, screaming her name from a ship that violently broke apart and launched them into the deep waters around her. Findley stood proudly on shore with the leather-bound book held high over his head. His laughter snared around the shrieks of her family as they struggled to stay afloat, unseen hands pulling them into the icy depths. Just as she lost the last of her will to remain above the waves, a heart-piercing cry ripped through the stormy skies.

"Amelia! No!" the voice screamed. "NO!"

She knew the voice in an instant. It was Molly.

She awoke with a start, her dress soaked in the sweat the nightmare had brought. She gasped for breath as she struggled to free herself from the tangle of her blankets.

"NO!" the voice called out once more. "Please, help me! Don't do this!"

It sounded as if it was coming from the square. Amelia's eyes widened as her heart seemed to stop. The nightmare had come to life. Molly really was calling out for help.

CHAPTER ELEVEN

HER FEET WERE POUNDING out of her bedroom, wanting out of the cottage and toward the square before her mind could decide what was happening. Molly's fearful cries were so heinous Amelia's soul shook to the very core with every devastating sound that poured from the panicked woman. Never in her life had she heard something so eerily raw.

There was no quick way to her side when Cleric Gordon and the Shephard darkened her doorstep, blocking her exit before she even reached the door. With the shock that burned through her veins, she unwisely tried to shove them aside, only to have the Shephard twist her braid in her bony fist and force her to her knees.

"My goodness, Amelia. I believe you have caused enough trouble for one day, have you not?" She looped another length of her hair, causing Amelia to yelp in pain. "You should be thanking us for learning the truth behind your misdeeds instead of further disobeying me. It would be a shame for such a bright young woman, my future daughter at that, to fall from grace due to the influence of a sad old woman who has no issue with dancing with the devil."

"Please, Shephard. Let her go. You're hurting her!" Jane begged. Gavin held her back when the Shephard gripped Amelia's hair, lifting her by her scalp. Amelia screamed from the strain, her neck stretching to compensate.

"This one needs to learn some respect, Jane. It seems I will be forced to do what you have not." She pointed to Sarah and Peter, who were wrapped around their mother's legs, their faces contorted from the hysterical wails that ripped from each of them. "All of the children of this village have been coddled long enough. Enough!" she repeated, causing the children to smother their cries into their mother's skirt.

"Shephard, if I may," the Cleric began and snapped his mouth shut when the Shephard's expression told him he may not.

She closed her eyes, taking deep, ragged breaths until her chest settled peacefully. Opening her eyes, a pleasant grin had replaced the rage that had turned her face crimson. "It has certainly been an emotional few days, has it not? My visions had warned us that dark times were coming, did they not?" She smiled proudly at her assumed feat. Looking down at Amelia, she shook the braid free from her hand as if she were surprised to find it there in the first place.

Gavin moved to help his daughter to her feet and away from the deranged woman. "What is it that's happened, Shephard? Why have you brought Molly to the square?" he asked gently, not wanting another shift in her mood to turn violent.

"Once again, the blessing of Amelia's betrothed has come to aid in the matter of her soul," she proudly declared and turned out the door. "and once again, I am tasked with protecting my flock from the malignant evils that conceal themselves among us."

The group followed behind, the Cleric at her heel like a hungry dog. Molly's screams grew louder the closer they made it to the square. When they rounded the corner, the horrific scene came into full view. Amelia fell to her knees with distress when she took in the state of Molly.

A long wooden pole had been set to stand in the middle of the square. Molly had been tied against it, the rough ropes causing her neck and wrists to redden from the friction. Amelia howled a cry when she saw a spittle of blood had traced its way down her chin.

"What are you doing? She's harmed no one! How can you be so vile as to hurt a powerless old woman?" Amelia erupted, desperately trying to find the will to rise to her feet again. "Let her go!"

The Assembly, with the exception of Jane, formed a line between Amelia and the place where they held Molly captive. Their faces did not have the certainty that steeled the Shephard's face, yet they held their ground. Most were unable to look her in the eye or take in the pain that exploded from every pore in Amelia's body as they stood with their backs to the violent scene that had been created behind them. The rest of the village had been filing into the small area of the square, attempting to sort out why the woman was being held in the center of the commotion. Some raised their voices with concern; most stood jaws agape. None of them understood what was happening or how far the Shephard had now gone.

"Vile? You dare declare me vile, little girl?" the Shephard balked and snapped her fingers. Findley appeared at her side holding the leatherbound book. The audacious pride he wore the last time she saw him had been eaten up by newfound apprehension. He handed the book to her and stepped back into the crowd as if attempting to be swept away from the holy mess his mother had created. "Do you recognize this?" she asked, holding the book for the gathered to observe.

"That is not mine!" Amelia hollered with a strained voice. "And it's not Molly's either! You need to let her go! You're hurting her!"

Molly said nothing in her own defense. Her terrified screams wore thin with the strain of the attack, and tears streaked her face as she held herself as tall and defiantly as she could, her eyes turned up to the sky, which blazed with the late-day sun.

Ellie pushed her way through the crowd and rushed to Amelia's side when she locked her desperate expression on her. Helping her to her feet, she looked around, attempting to sort out what was happening and, more importantly – why. Walter, who was joined at her hip, assisted in steadying Amelia once she rose. They were just as bewildered by what they were witnessing as their neighbors.

The Shephard turned to the crowd, who were raising their voices to what they realized was taking place. "This woman has been given the grace of our protection, of our kindness, for more years than I care to mention." She held the book out for each one of them to see. "In return for our attempts at forgiveness and to give her a better life – even after her family turned their backs on all of us – she continues to show the poor moral character that has been the curse of the Clark family since they stepped foot on this island with our founders."

"Shephard, what has she done?" a man called out, receiving a ripple of murmured questions throughout the crowd.

"Our sweet Amelia has been spellbound! This hag has corrupted her mind, spirit, and soul with the darkness she practices. She has attempted to turn her against us, just as she would certainly try the same with you if she had the chance." The Shephard pointed her long, crooked finger at Molly, disgust dripping from her words. "We have all lived with the scourge this woman has brought down upon our land for too long. I would have failed in my duty to you all if I allowed her to continue. Who knows what travesties she would bring to us cloaked under the innocence of my Findley's bride?"

Amelia clung to Ellie as if she was the only thing that could keep the ground from opening below her and pulling her into the bowels of Hell. The madness of it all seemed impossible. Once again, someone was being harmed for her choices. Molly had never even set eyes on the book that was being used as proof of her poison. The poor woman had not even dared to step outside of her own cottage since before Amelia had known her.

"What's in the book?" another voice questioned.

"I will not corrupt you, my flock. I will not give voice to the evil contained in these pages. I care too deeply for you all," she preached with her hand over her heart. The Cleric stepped forward and took the book when she held it out to him. He turned swiftly for the church, holding it against his tunic so as not to allow any curious observer to see more than they already had. "I am so very grateful that this hold over her was discovered before any true harm could be done. My wonderful son has not only exposed the danger his bride had found herself in, but he has selflessly insisted that the wedding will still occur. Taking on such a challenge may tarnish his soul, but I know he will carry them both into salvation with the strength and resolve he demonstrates to you all each day."

Amelia found Findley in the crowd and was glad he retained enough humanity not to revel in what he had caused. His attention stayed on his feet while an uneasiness appeared to dry his mouth and twist his brow. The glares from those around him did not match the praise being bestowed by his mother.

"You've made your point, Shephard. Please let Molly return to her cottage now. The shame is quite plain for us all to see now. I so greatly appreciate all you have done for my daughter," Jane said convincingly enough to have some shout-out in agreement. "You have shown us the path to light once more, and we all thank you."

Amelia felt sick at the recognition her mother was passing on, even as she knew it was simply to appease her. Whatever it took to lessen the time that they would abuse poor Molly in her name was what they needed to attempt. She struggled to settle the painful sobs that seized her chest. She stepped forward once she had pulled herself together enough to stand on her own.

"My mother is right," she lied. "I apologize for all the disruption and heartache I have caused you all." She spoke with her eyes set firmly on Molly. "It is not fair that you all have the burden of what I could have caused with senseless actions." Her voice hitched. She paused to compose herself.

"Shephard Ward, you have done us all a great deed in bringing this wickedness forward and shielding it from us further," her father added when Amelia could not continue. "I think a lesson in compassion should be your next offering to us all. We should let Molly go home."

"A wonderful act of kindness in honor of the upcoming nuptials," Jane suggested.

The villagers mused in agreement. A few stepped forward in hopes of assisting in the act. They were shunned back into the crowd by Shephard Ward before they could approach the woman's bindings. Rage began to fill Amelia when she realized how powerless they all were to one woman.

If only John had convinced Molly to join him years before, none of this would be happening. When he found out what they had done, he would surely insist that she leave for good. The weak-minded fools that kowtowed to every word and demand of the Shephard would have a rude awakening when he no longer worked in the shadows to sustain them all. The thought of their hungry, filthy faces looking to their savior for help and finding empty hands was exactly the penance they all deserved.

"I think the best way to honor their union is to have a guarantee that this woman's sorcery is no longer able to reach us," Shephard Ward replied. Amelia found hope in the thought that a complete banishment would take the decision to leave from Molly's hands. It would break her heart to no longer have her near. It would be more painful to watch the Privy find more reasons to scapegoat the poor, peaceful woman in the future.

"That could be for the best," Jane concurred and approached the center of the square. "Let's take these bindings off and prepare for her departure." She jumped when her hand was slapped away by the Shephard's swift hand.

"We will do no such thing." Her stony glare made its way around those circled. "I will not risk my flock for one more moment." Her attention snapped to the Cleric when he returned. His hands were held tightly around an object he had concealed. Stress wore on his face when he focused on his beloved leader. "Now is the time to prove our purity," she declared, raising one finger high above her. "We will be the harvest that feeds from this land, not the tide that bleeds from it. An uneasiness to the severity of her tone washed over those gathered. The brief moment of wishful hope that had spurned Amelia on drained away. "Know that I will always remove a threat to our Good Land."

The Cleric opened his hands to reveal a cloth-wrapped parcel. The Shephard flipped open the loose sides of the fabric and plucked up the sharp dagger she exposed. She held it on her outstretched palm, presenting it for all to see. Molly's cries for help rang out again when the setting sun glinted on the polished blade. Pleas for mercy erupted around them, the horror of what was being threatened too much to bear.

"It is with a heavy heart that I find myself in such a grave situation. The weight I carry for you all is something I do out of responsibility and with the deepest love," she testified to those who begged her to stop. With a twitch of her head to the Privy members, they dutifully moved to circle Molly, creating a wall between her and those who could be her salvation.

"Ellen, you have lost your senses!" Jane shrieked. She was tossed to the ground by her fellow Assembly when she ran to assist. "You have all lost your minds!"

A man stepped forward in an attempt to grab the dagger, shouting for others to join him.

The threat against Shephard Ward snapped the Cleric back to her side, crazed madness turning his dead eyes fiery. "To go against the Shephard is to go against us all!" he bellowed and shoved the man to the ground. "You shall not question or speak, or you find yourselves at the same end of that dagger!"

The crowd went silent as if the words had a gale wind's strength to freeze all in its path. The rustle of leaves in the forest surrounding them was the only noise that joined Molly's screams.

The Shephard, clearly pleased with the stunned compliance, lifted her chin with pride and closed the distance to Molly. "You have presented yourself as a menace and danger to us all. Your dark doings will no longer be tolerated, and your punishment has been decided."

Without as much as another breath, she plunged the dagger deep into Molly's chest, straining to give it a twist for good measure. Blood pumped in spurts from her heart, saturating her dress of rags in bright, wet crimson. Her eyes widened at the attack before her head fell to her shoulder, and her newly empty gaze turned downward.

Amelia's heart felt as if it had stopped at the same time as her dear friend's. Air refused to enter her lungs after a scream tore through her like a lightning strike. The earth seemed to reach up and pull her down as her head slammed to the ground, her body awash in a pain she did not know was physically possible, contorting her on the dusty ground.

The world around her spun as she tried to make out the villagers' words that had risen up around her before everything went mercifully black.

Chapter Twelve

Amelia had witnessed death before. Too many times to count for her young life. Living as they did, there was always an expectation of it that walked alongside their solitude. Her parents had both lost their own when Amelia was as fresh to the world as Sarah. Family or peer, child or adult, no one could hide from the inevitability of death's reach. It was merely seen as familiar to Amelia. A tragedy locked in a moment that would soon be over as if it were nothing more than a passing storm they would suffer together.

It was not until she lost Molly that she *knew* death. It was no longer something that happened. It was a storm that appeared above and refused to budge, drowning everything it could reach. It was something that changed the world. Her world. Amelia knew she would never be the same.

She rubbed at eyes when they opened, unable to focus in the dim light. Quickly, she recognized her cramped space to be the box. Her hands traced along the worn wooden interior, shuffling her hips until she was more comfortable. Standing was impossible. She settled for curling into a comforting ball, her arms wrapped tightly around her knees. Outside her newfound prison, she could hear no sign of anyone nearby. The slight breaks between the boards gave little view of what was left of the devastating dissonance that had erupted around her. There was no way to know how long she had been out cold or how long she had been in the box. The setting sun had already left the evening's chilled breeze to envelop the air that slipped in around her.

Molly's voice, her heart-wrenching cries, still echoed in her ears. She rocked her body, trying to soothe away the horror of what had happened. Everything that she touched had started to wilt. Her mother had been beaten, and now her dearest friend was dead. A knot tightened within her stomach when she thought how it had all just been allowed to happen. An innocent woman was dragged from her home, the only place she felt safe, and had her life snuffed out in a flash. They had all done nothing more than watch. She let out a wail of angry grief and pounded her fist on the heavy lid above her.

"Cowards! You are all cowards!" she called out to the empty square around her. Repeatedly, she shouted her condemnations of the villagers; each time, her throat became more hoarse until she had no more strength to protest their sins.

The cold took hold of her, and she shivered and wept until her mind could cope no longer and dragged her away to a night of fitful dreams.

In the following days, she continued to rage against anyone who dared pass by. Villagers had gone about their daily routines as if they had not witnessed a thing. The word of the Shephard was even more potent than Amelia could have ever imagined. Her demands for them all to acknowledge their mortification remained ignored. Her meals of broth and bread were slipped through a thin opening that was quickly shut closed.

So many times, when the condemned had spent time within the judgment of the box, they were left in their own filth until released. Amelia did not know why or by whose sympathy, but she was allowed escorted trips to the outhouse. Twice, she struggled and shouted as soon as the box was opened, and twice, the box had been re-sealed above her. On the third attempt, she knew better than to upset the ones assisting her in order to maintain some dignity. She glowered at the few who dared to me-ander while she was going to and from, silently cursing them all. Her heart crushed in on itself when she would pass the spot in the square that had held Molly's last breath. No sign of her existence remained. Not a shuffle in the dirt or drop of blood could be seen. The inhumanity of wiping away any sign of her life and death made Amelia wonder if she had merely lost her mind and imagined it all. The memory of Molly's screams told her she was not so lucky.

Without setting eyes on her family or friends, distress for their safety ate away at her. She would be unable to go on if any more harm had come upon those she cared for. Her thoughts went from planning an escape to knowing that no passage across the imprisoning waters would await her.

The sun's heat beat down on her during the day, melting reality and fantasy into one. The cold of the night snapped her into a hyperawareness that held onto her anger as if it were the weapon that would save her. Something that could save them all. She would go from being betrayed and broken by her parents' absence during her punishment to guilt and concern that her actions were most likely being brought down on the shoulders of anyone who would dare speak out in her favor.

When sleep mercifully would grant her momentary reprieve from the never-ending solitude and a heart so heavy she was at times sure it had rotted away altogether, she had dreams of Cole whisking her from the box and across the choppy water, away from everything she had known and grown to hate.

After what she imagined had been about five days, the lack of substantial food and the ability to move her body started to bring about a forced calm that stole away the anger and, thankfully, the energy to grieve. As she grew more docile, the fight slipping from her spirit, a few more kindnesses were allowed.

When her mother was finally allowed to approach her, her familiar and solacing voice whispered in through the cracks as if they were a light that would glow among angels. She assured her broken daughter that it would all be over soon, and they would be reunited. The idea of going about life as if nothing had happened became easier to digest the more her mind slivered and her body weakened.

The strength to fight had transformed into a need to survive.

Several more days passed until the heavy wooden slats of the lid creaked open to reveal the sunlight framing her father's face. He helped her up over the edge of the box and quietly escorted her home. Peter and Sarah watched silently as he helped into her bedroom and onto the soft embrace of her bed. Her mother came in briefly to help her out of her soiled clothes and clean her up with a basin of warm water before pulling a fresh nightshirt over her head and tucking her under her quilt. She hugged her gently as soon as she was done and instructed her to rest as she slipped out the door. It all felt like a fevered dream when she allowed her body to sink into the mattress below her.

A pitcher of water and a plate of cornmeal biscuits with an entire jar of her favorite strawberry preserves sat on the low table beside her bed. Even though the smell was divine, her stomach wanted none of it. She stretched her arms and then her legs as far as her joints would allow, the space she now enjoyed seeming much more significant than she remembered.

It was clear Sarah had spent her time hard at work with her charcoal while Amelia was being held. New drawings nearly covered the wall that her bed was set against. She rolled to her side, taking in the happy scenes that her sister had created. Her family was drawn, hold-ing hands under a giant smiling black and white sun. A bird was sketched as it perched happily on a tree branch with musical notes dancing from its beak, and her favorite: Sarah with a broad smile riding a goat- images Amelia would treasure forever.

All of her furniture and candles had been returned, and the meager belongings seemed extravagant after living with nothing but her thoughts in the box. She rolled onto her back and looked about, wondering how long she would be allowed to remain. With all that had happened, she could not be sure if the marriage to Findley would go forward. The unshakable numbness that had settled into her soul caused her not to care either way.

Her attention landed on a tall glass filled with tiny white flowers that had been set on her dresser. Fresh flowers were not commonplace in their homes, so the special touch was even more meaningful. She smelled the air deeply, wondering if she could pick up their scent. When she only found the warm scent of biscuits, she pushed herself up from the bed to get a better look.

Her toes did not touch the floor before her back became frigid. They were flowers she had seen before; not in the forest or the small patches among the weeds. It had been in the cave. The yellow stars that sat in the center of the white petals like a golden iris were unforgettable. They had been among the branches that circled the book.

There was no doubt in her mind that they were put there as a threat. It was frightening to realize that she could be sure from who.

Voices from within the cottage startled her from the speculation.

"I know, Ellie. She wants to see you too, I'm sure. What is best for her now is rest," her mother said with polite insistence, "Come back tomorrow, and we'll see how she's doing."

Soon after, the door could be heard closing. Her mother was right. As much as she wanted to see them all, she was too exhausted to have her room filled with the anxious energy of her friend. She stood at her window, wondering if she would find Adam waiting to visit, and found no one.

Sliding the window open, she deeply inhaled the freshest air she could have imagined during the past smothering days. Moving across the room, she snatched the flowers from the glass and swiftly back to the open window to toss them to the ground below and then shut the glass as if it would protect her from whatever the flowers meant.

She poured some water from the pitcher into the mug that sat beside it and dragged it down in one gulp. The smell of the biscuits still held no temptation, so she gulped a second glass and crawled into bed. She found against the weight of her eyelids to look at every detail of Sarah's drawings for as long as she could. When sleep claimed victory, it was for many hours of dreamless rest well into the next day's afternoon.

Her body ached from the dead state it had been left in overnight. She had been so still, her fingers still rested against the wall. Charcoal from the painting stained her hand. Rising for whatever the day would hold, she slipped out to their outhouse. It was nice to use the family's latrine again, rather than the public one, and it was especially lovely to be able to go alone.

When she had finished, she dared a look to the ground below her window. The flowers no longer sat in a clump below.

Had they been a dream?

Amelia could not decide if they had ever been in her room at all. Who would have found the bunch and disposed of them if they had? Her tired mind could not sort out the possibilities.

"Amelia!" Ellie exclaimed, closing the space between them quickly and pulling her into a hug that shot bolts of tenderness into every joint and muscle she touched. "My poor friend! How are you? I'm so proud of how strong you were! If it were me? Oh, my goodness, I could not even imagine," she said quickly, as if all the words needed to be said at once. Amelia stepped out of her embrace, overwhelmed by the outburst. "So much has happened," Ellie continued, looking between Amelia's cottage and her neighbors, "and I don't know how much you know, but we need to talk. Walter has told me things that have my brain spinning. I don't know up from down anymore, and it has been torture without you." She stopped herself, and shame melted over her face. "How awful of me. I'm so sorry. What you've been through." She pulled her against her again.

"Ellie, please, you're crushing me," Amelia pleaded, taking an extra step back when Ellie released her.

"I'm sorry. It's all so much. After all you've been through, and I haven't even given you a chance to dress for the day before demanding your attention." Ellie wrung her hands with a frown.

"It's alright. I understand," Amelia said with as much affection as her empty heart could muster.

"I've just...Walter...," Ellie took a deep breath, in and then out, to calm her racing thoughts, "There are things you need to know about the Allens, Amelia. I know you need to rest, and I know it all may be too much for you, but what Walter has told me..." she insisted, speaking with stressed hush.

Before she could expand on whatever news she held that had worked her into a fit, Jane Taylor called out to her with displeasure.

"Elsbeth! What are you doing milling about back there? Let my Amelia relieve herself in peace, for goodness sake!"

Amelia followed along back into the cottage when her mother tugged at her sleeve. Ellie called out mountains of apologies in their wake until the door closed behind them.

"How are you feeling today, Poppet?" She held her at arm's length, hands on her shoulders, looking her over. "Were you able to sleep?"

"I did, Mama. I slept well, thank you." Amelia took in every inch of her mother, overwhelmed with love and gratitude to have her standing before her. She was glad to see she now moved freely from the pain her beating had caused, although she rubbed at her temple to soothe her head.

"Now, now, dry your tears," Jane began, "We've gotten to the other side, and with more rest, you'll see the world in beautiful colors again."

Amelia sniffled back more tears that insisted themselves upon her and dragged her sleeve across her face. They had begun to fall without the shudders of tears as if her spirit was attempting to release the pain she held that she could no longer feel. "Yes, ma'am," was all she said.

"You are to rest more today, Poppet. That is an order, understood?" her mother lovingly declared. "Would you like to spend more time in bed, or would the chair be more comfortable?"

The commotion of Ellie's appearance and the open space of the common room made her head spin. "I think I'd like to stay in my room for a while more if that's alright. I might try to sleep some more." The silence of the box had brought a stillness to her mind that kept her from falling into the pit of madness that lay in wait below her. Even just a chat with her mother was too much to handle, with every word seeming too loud and too close.

"That's fine, my love. You go and get yourself settled in bed. I'll bring you in some porridge in a bit." She kissed her head lightly and stepped away, allowing Amelia to compose herself.

"Mama? Where did they..." She wanted to ask where Molly was, even though she knew she did not have the strength to withstand the answer. "Is she...," she tried and again had to swallow the lump that grew in her throat.

"Go get some rest, my love. All will be well," Jane answered when Amelia could not continue. She could only nod to her mother and obey her wishes.

The calm returned as soon as she was behind her closed door. She slipped down to the floor and sat with her back to the wall, trying to quiet her thoughts. Ellie's words had taken root and refused to be ignored, no matter how hard Amelia tried to clear her mind.

What had she been going on about? What would Walter have told that was so important that it needed to be the first thing Amelia heard? The secrets were never-ending on that island, and she wished she could hide away from all of them. They never brought her anything but suffering.

The thought of secrets reminded her of the last book Molly had given her and the treasured paper she had asked her to safeguard. A quick peek under her mattress found the book still safely squirreled away. If her room had been searched after she was put in the box, they had not thought enough to check there. Lifting her pillow, her hand slipped into the cover until she felt the flower print. She held it in both hands in front of her, reading every word and then rereading them as if the answers to all of her problems were miraculously laid bare for her.

There was nothing of help, and there would be none to be found because it was just another quill in her skin. Another secret that had been added to the pile. She gripped it in her hands, willing herself to rip it into pieces so small it would be carried away like dust. The memory of Molly would not allow her even to tear an edge. She returned it to its hiding place. The frustration that still ate away at her caused her to throw the pillow at the wall, bouncing off of Sarah's artwork and landing on the floor. Hurrying to her bed, she bounded across it to ensure she had not damaged any of the precious drawings. One corner of the depiction of her family had suffered a bent corner that she immediately smoothed.

When she moved to retrieve the pillow, she noticed the glass that had held the tiny white flowers was gone. Had whoever had placed it there and taken the bundle she had tossed outside taken the vase as well? Paranoia was finding a comfortable home in her mind.

The food her mother had set out for her the night before was also gone. She told herself her mother had simply cleared away the dishes and took the glass along with them. That did not answer the question of who had put the flowers there.

The crack of a pebble against her window made her jump with a start. Peeking outside, she knew it would be Adam before she laid eyes on him.

"How are you holding up?" he asked with concern when she opened the window.

"As best as I can, considering. One minute I'm crying, the next I'm," she searched for the word, "numb, I suppose? If I'm to keep any sanity, I want to focus on moving on. The what-ifs are not for right now. I'm out and ready to get things back as they were." She did not admit that Molly's screams were still constant in the back of her mind. That would be something she would forever keep to herself. The punishment she demanded of herself for letting it all happen.

"I thought you were trying to show off to everyone with the longest stay in the box," he jested and smiled when she gave a tired laugh.

"Well, you know me. I always try to impress." The comfortable banter she shared with Adam came as easily as always, and she felt a tension in her shoulder that she did not realize had lingered slowly loosened. Friends like he and Ellie were to be valued, and that she still had them to rely on brought her a comfort that relaxed her even more. "How is Ellie doing? I hope all of this did not ruin the glow of her new marriage."

"Oh, that glow is quite present, if you ask me!" he gave her a conspiratory giggle that flushed Amelia's cheeks.

"Adam! That is no way to speak of our friend," she playfully admonished. "More importantly, she was just here saying that she had something to tell me. Something about the Allens that seemed very urgent. Do you have any idea of what she could have meant?"

"Not a clue. I've barely seen that one for days, other than the back of her head sitting in the wives pew." He shrugged. "I have news that will top anything she could give you, anyway."

Amelia turned to her door, ear cocked, to make sure her mother was not near with the porridge she had promised. The tune she whistled was clearly still in the kitchen. "Well, go on. Out with it," she demanded when she turned back to him. She stretched and leaned her elbows on the windowsill, her back still aching from her time in the box.

"Your friend Cole returned!" he gushed. "Don't worry, no one saw him but me. I spotted him when I was out checking my rabbit traps."

Amelia's calm sank into her stomach. "Are you sure no one saw him? Did you speak with him?"

"I'm sure. He was only there for a minute or two to inquire about you."

"You didn't tell him where I was, did you?" she blurted, unsure if it was the embarrassment of being punished by the Privy or worry that another person could be pulled into the mess she so desperately wanted to bury away.

"I know better than to speak to a mainlander about village going's ons," he replied proudly, as if it were common for him to chat with people from across the water, and Cole was not the first one he had ever met.

"What did you tell him?" she asked with urgency. Her mother's footsteps could be heard.

"Just that we were all very busy from the wedding, and he'd have to come another time if he wanted to see you again."

"What? No! If you ever see him again, you make it clear that he is never to come back here. Not one foot on this island!" she ordered with a rushed growl and quickly shut the small opening to her window.

She was on the bed, catching her breath, when her mother knocked and popped her head inside. She sat the tray, holding a bowl of porridge and a glass of milk on the side table with a smile.

"Thank you, Mama."

"No worries at all, my Poppet. You eat what you can and then get some more rest. Tomorrow is another day, and Lord willing, you will be back on your feet and in the garden again."

Amelia did not watch her as she left, the humming returning to her mother's lips. She was too consumed with looking at the milk. It was the glass that had held the flowers just the day before.

Chapter Thirteen

An uncomfortable calm fell over the village as some tried to understand what had happened, and others tried to forget. Amelia did her best to keep her head down and press on in the following days. Her mother encouraged her to keep her chin up and have faith that all would be well again. Words she spoke as if they were enough to hold them all up. Even as she saw the fire in her mother's eyes had smothered away with the trauma they had all witnessed and suffered, Amelia still took her lead and trusted her to get them through.

The Shephard had made few appearances since carrying out her judgment on Molly, apart from holding her seat in the front pew during services. The visions had returned with a fury that kept her cloistered away in order to sort out their meanings for the sake of her flock. Jane had confided in her daughter that Shephard Ward had been seeing the deathly flowers bloom tall at the doorsteps of many different cottages, and the smell of them overtook her attention when she would brave to step out in their midst. Amelia kept her feelings on the matter and the madness she saw in their leader to herself. She had shown her teeth and proven that she would bare them to anyone who crossed her.

It had been decided that her wedding to Findley would be carried out as planned; however, not until the Shephard had worked through whatever it was she believed the visions were trying to tell her. As long as she was shut away working through the insanity she believed to be sacred, life in the village went on as it had. Amelia was happy to go along in that manner forever.

Every day that Amelia stood alongside Ellie in the garden, and not sitting beside her in the wives' pew was a reprieve. She would stick to the promise she had silently made – there would be no more arguments from her, but even in her complacency, she made sure she would find joy in the small victories.

When she returned to the now burgeoning garden, Ellie had been desperate to divulge whatever it was that Walter had shared with her. Amelia, not wanting to engage in anything that could bring further trouble, made a point to remind Ellie of the church passages that she herself so loved to use to keep her friends in line. A reminder to *keep good and be the harvest that feeds* helped keep her lips tight. The apathy for her life that she had cloaked herself in left little interest in conversation. She now preferred silence. Silence did not bring trouble to her path.

As the days began to have the appearance of a return to normalcy, Amelia gave further thought to the possibility of a curse. Not one that comes in visions or through the waters that surrounded them, but from within themselves and the outsiders that made it their business to invade their private space. The rules had been set out for a reason, and it had carried them for six and soon to be seven generations on the Good Land. It had been foolish, arrogant even to think she would know better. The very idea that it was acceptable for her to set her own life, to pick and choose what she decided was right or wrong. With enough time to think of the options, she decided the curse was among them; that was certain. It rested in the hearts of every member of the Shephard's flock and would slip out of any crack it could fit and rot everything it touched. It possibly spread from whatever haunted Shephard Ward's mind, although she would never say those words out loud.

Bringing peace had started to feel as simple as being aware and cautious of that threat until a few weeks had passed, and she found herself harvesting mushrooms in the forest. She was thinking of how happy her father would be when he saw the basket overflowing with his favorite chanterelles and the bounty of soup they would bring when the voice behind her nearly frightened her enough to drop them.

"Hey," Cole greeted, approaching her slowly. "Sorry, I didn't mean to scare you."

Amelia started back for the village at first sight of him. "You should not be here. You're going to get everyone in trouble."

"I just wanted to make sure you were okay," He stayed rooted in place on the trail behind her. "I was talking with your friend Adam and wanted to make sure you were all right."

She turned at the mention of Adam, "Whatever he said, he spoke out of turn and had no right to speak for me in the first place."

"He told me that he wants to leave this place," he shared and braved a few steps toward her when he saw she was suddenly not in such a hurry to leave, "He said a lot of people do. What worried me is that he said you do and that they're going to make you marry some douchebag."

Amelia did not understand what the word meant, not that it mattered. She was too caught up in the fact that Adam had done precisely the opposite of what she had requested of him and made Cole feel encouraged to return. Worse than that, he had the nerve to talk about her private matters with him.

"Well, Adam can say what he wants about himself, but I have never wanted to leave here," she lied. "What I can say is that I want you to leave. Now."

"So you can honestly say that you like living here?" he asked her with a twinge of anger in his tone that Amelia found out of place. "You're seriously going to marry someone just because they tell you to? You're eighteen years old, Amelia." She glowered when he said her age. Adam had been having more than a passing conversation if such details of herself had come up. "You're still a kid. Just like me! You should be hanging out with your friends and getting ready for college. Adam is right. You all should have a choice if you stay or not."

The anger, frustration, and grief she had been swallowing erupted in his direction. The space between them closed quickly as she shouted, "Choice? Do you think anyone has a choice? Not that it is any of your business; my life here is just fine. I have my family, I have my friends, and I have a good life. I don't need to live the way you do to have a life worth any value."

"I'm not saying you have to live like me, Amelia! I'm saying you deserve to live like *you* want," he roughly pushed his hands through his dark tangle of short curls, closing his eyes with frustration. "I know it's not my place to say any of this, but I just...," he sighed and lowered his voice, "I just want to see you happy."

"And how do you know I'm not? You know nothing about me," she spat, enraged that he would make any assumptions about her, yet a curiosity as to why he would bother to at all started to tickle her thoughts.

He started to speak and looked away. His feet shuffled in the dirt. He paced the pathway around Amelia and stopped between her and the direction of her home. "I know it's creepy as hell, but I've seen you before I met you. That day wasn't our first time out here. I know it's wrong, and we should never have come at all, but I can't change that now. When we first saw you guys, you used to smile so much," his lips upturned as he shared the memory. "You were always laughing and had this sort of spark in you." His face blazed red with his bare honesty. "That's not you anymore, Amelia. Adam says so, too. You're just a shell of that girl now, and I want to help you find her again. To help you and Adam – and anyone else that I can," he added with pleading in his eyes.

Amelia had to tighten her grip on the basket to stop it from falling from her shaking hands. He had been watching her? He and his friends had been sneaking about and peeping on them as if they were a novelty set out for their entertainment. They had probably been laughing at their simple ways, judging them for not living as the mainlanders do. As if they had a life any better.

Now, he stood there, telling her he knew what was best for her?

"How dare you!" she shouted. She raised her finger to point her judgment into his face, stumbling the basket to her feet. She knelt down to retrieve the spilled mushrooms and continued her outage when he bent to help. "I don't need you to save me, Cole! The arrogance you must possess to think you know better than we do!" She slapped his hand away when he attempted to put one of the loose mushrooms back in the basket.

"I'm sorry. I don't think I know better. I only know what I see and what Adam has told me." He rose from her side, taking a few backward steps toward the direction he had arrived from, looking down with a remorseful bend in his brow.

"You don't know a thing about anything! Life seems mighty easy for you people. Always going where you please, even when you have no right to be there. Doing whatever you please whenever you please, but you know what, Cole? If I leave, my little sister has to marry that man! My seven-year-old sister, Cole." Tears erupted as she crumpled over the basket's handle. She was mortified that she admitted to something that was not known outside of her home or the Privy. The reality of honestly having no choices of her own struck her deeply, choking her as tightly as the sobs she could no longer contain. The sudden concern for her that he showed felt like the time she spent with Molly when she would remind Amelia that there was life outside of the world that held them captive. It made her feel too raw, too dejected.

In less than a month since she had lost her, she had slipped in line with the flock and turned her back on the courage that Molly had spent so much time building within her. Her cowardice was as disrespectful to her dear friends as anything else the villagers had done while she had been alive.

"What?" Cole fell to his knees in front of her. "You have got to be joking! That's illegal, Amelia! They can't force a child to marry a grown man! You need the police! You need help with everything that is happening here. There are laws to protect people for a reason!"

The thought of the trouble that would bring, the danger, horrified Amelia. "NO! No one else can come here! You don't understand how things work here, Cole! You can't just walk into our church and tell them all they're wrong."

"You have to believe that I don't want to make trouble for you. I want to help you. You deserve so much more than this," he said with defeat quieting his upset. He reached out and took her hand.

Amelia started to pull away but allowed the comforting gesture for a second longer than she should have before she slipped her fingers away to roughly put the rest of the mushrooms in the basket and then stood away from him. "Please, Cole. If you want to do something to help me, just leave. Please leave and never come back."

She ran past him, away from the direction of the village, as quickly as she could. There was only one place that would bring her any sense of peace. As painful as it would be to see Molly's cottage without her inside, it was exactly where she needed to be.

The further away she got from the strangle of the church and the fear and confusion of Cole, the easier it was to breathe. The world made sense from inside those cracked walls that had become a part of her being. Molly would not be there to share new wisdom, but the memory of her would refresh her spirit. Shame pressed down on her when she allowed herself to admit she had cast Molly from her thoughts to ease her selfish pain. It was easier to ignore the loss than to treasure her memory. She would never recover from losing such an incredible part of her life, but she was ready to allow the happy moments they shared back into her heart. She needed to sit by Molly's chair and clear her mind.

The basket dropped again to the forest floor without Amelia noticing, and she walked over its contents, crushing them all under her heel when she arrived at the clearing to Molly's cottage.

The door hung open on only one hinge, and the small window that had been her only source of light had been smashed. Before she could reach the entrance, she could see the small table that held their prized sugar dish on its side. The crystal bowl, which had been so lovingly filled for their beloved hummingbirds, lay shattered on the ground beside it. No sweet birds were there, buzzing about to welcome her. There was nothing left for them now.

She ran to the entrance and screamed when she saw what remained. The few belongings that Molly had retained had all been destroyed and tossed about her home.

Her prized books were shredded, and the pieces settled across the broken dishes and furniture that littered the sad dirt floor. Her few dresses and aprons had been torn apart as if a savage animal had been let loose within the hallowed space.

It was no animal of the forest that had desecrated that home. Amelia's teeth clenched, and every muscle in her body tightened. On the walls, just as she saw in the cave, were corpse flowers that covered the chipped plaster. She slammed her hand against one, crying out for the injustice and indignation that had come to the poor woman who had done nothing wrong to anyone in all her years of life. She looked at the paint that stained her hand

and felt the room spin around her. The same chalk paint that was used in the church's murals. The chalk paint that was made with supplies John Clark brought to them in exchange for the paltry care they provided for his sister. There was no doubt in her mind now who was behind it all. Not Flora, not a curse, not the shadowed Watchers in the woods. It was someone who possessed more evil within her body than any soul suffering in Hell. Shephard Ellen Ward was never going to stop.

Chapter Fourteen

Amelia attempted to clear away some of the mess. Molly had hated her home to be untidy. There was very little she could do other than pile the destruction that was once the whole of Molly's universe as neatly as she could. Finding one book left mostly untouched, she wondered if she should risk taking it. She flipped through the pages and read the most explicit scenes she had ever seen. It was obviously one that Molly had kept to herself, and even through her shock at the words, she smiled at the reminder of her friend's scandalous ways.

As a declaration of her dissent, the book was tucked into her pocket before she left. There was no way she could detach her mind and soul from her life any longer. She would be damned if Ellen Ward was allowed to cause harm to one more person. There was no way to know what her first move should be, but no matter what, she would move against the Shephard. She would be stopped.

"Oh, Amelia! I am so sorry," Adam, who stood at the trailhead, said to her when she could finally step out of the cottage.

"What are you doing here?" she said with surprise. Adam had never been to visit Molly as far as she knew.

"I heard shouting in the woods and came to see what was wrong. I caught Cole as he was leaving. He said you headed this way, and I knew there was only one place you would go if you were upset." He stepped past her into the cottage's remains, "Damn it," he cursed, shaking his head in disgust. "This is worse than I had heard."

"You knew about this?" Amelia demanded, pulling him out of Molly's private nest.

"I had heard word of some of the elders coming up here. I didn't think they would go so far." He looked over her shoulder at the mess that remained.

"Why didn't you tell me? Why didn't anyone stop them?" Amelia tried to shut the door as if it could keep what was left safe from another attack.

"I didn't want to upset you anymore after all you've been through," he said earnestly. "I didn't know how much more you could take, especially since you seemed to shut us all away lately. When you see your friend as a shell of what they once were, you do what you can to keep that shell from cracking."

Amelia could appreciate what he said and found it thoughtful to concern himself with her even as she tried to be less of a burden to everyone around her. It was wrong to take her anger out on someone who was just as powerless as she was. She let out a frustrated sigh, "I hate how they turned on her. She had nothing to do with that book."

"So, it's true? You know what that book is?" he asked. She could tell he was trying to quell the excitement in his voice. As usual, his eyes gave him away. "You've seen it before?"

"Yes, I have seen it, and no, I don't know what it is," she said, not knowing how much she should say at all. She decided to continue when his face crumpled with confusion. "I'm the one who found it. Molly had never even seen it as far as I know."

"Well, I'll be dicked in the nob!" he shouted at the revelation.

"Adam! Watch your tongue," she shot back.

"I think it's called for, Amelia," Adam countered. He stared at her, taking in her confirmation of what he believed to be bitter gossip. She offered no more until he spoke again. "Well, out with it! What was in it? Where did you find it? Why didn't you tell me?" The questions came too quickly to answer, and Amelia had to hold up her hands to stop the barrage of inquiries.

"I found it out past the woods," she admitted sheepishly.

"*Past* the woods?" he repeated. "As in at the waters?" She nodded. "Amelia Taylor! I knew you were a wild horse, but I didn't think you had it in you to be so rebellious!" he gushed with praise. "Does anyone else know that you've gone there?"

"We do now," Ellie replied, stepping around the trail's bend into view with Walter.

"Ellie! What's happened? Why are you here?" Amelia quizzed with building panic. The last time she had seen her friend near Molly's cottage, she had been awash in desperate tears.

"The chatterbox told me you were headed up here before he took off after you," Walter answered with a tease, yet his face remained creased with the serious thoughts he carried. "and I told Ellie."

"It's despicable what they've done here. That poor woman," Ellie mourned, tears already starting. "They do nothing but destroy everything anymore. That woman is nothing more than a villain." She spoke the word as if it were the dirtiest one ever spoken.

"We should get out of here. All of us gathered out here will surely be noticed by someone," Amelia directed, trying to herd them back down onto the trail. "We can all talk about this another time when we know it's safe."

"That's just it, Amelia," Ellie said, stopping and refusing to return to the village as she wished. "There isn't a safe time for anything anymore. We need to talk now."

Amelia was taken aback by the sternness in her friend's words. The timid and agreeable Ellie was nowhere to be found in her eyes. Instead, she saw the fire that not so long ago ignited her mother's.

"She's right. We cannot go one more day like this," Adam agreed. "The elders are too blinded by tradition to do anything to help themselves, let alone us."

"What are you getting at?" Amelia was at once glad to have allies with eyes as open as hers and terrified at how real the danger became when they admitted it existed.

"We all need to leave, Amelia," Walter spoke the words to the ground in front of him and then met her eyes. "As soon as possible. We need to find a way to get off of this island."

"No, what we need to do is take a stand! We can't run away and leave the troubles for everyone else to suffer. There is no way we will convince everyone to abandon the only life they have ever known and risk everything to leave. We'll be the ones they go after next if we even suggest it. No, we need to stay and fix things." Amelia crossed her arms and looked each one in the eye.

"How do you propose to do that? We don't even know how many snakes have twisted themselves in with the Shephard. Not to mention those that blindly follow her word," Walter argued. "She has become too mad to fight, and we are too outnumbered to try."

"I can't leave my family behind. You have no idea what could happen to my sister." Amelia's voice shook with frustration and fear.

"We will take them with us! At the very least, we'll take Sarah," Adam offered with his hands clenched in a plead of agreement.

Having a group to stand with felt good as she tried to find her legs again. It was less so to have entirely opposite ideas of what needed to be done. Leaving was always the easy answer that would be tossed around in times of youthful rebellion. Seeing what could happen to those who made that choice, what would befall their families left behind, became far more treacherous with the eye and mind of a maturing adult.

"If not me, if not Sarah, it will be someone else," Amelia lamented. "These people are our people. Not all of them carry the evil blood that Ellen Ward does." She stood proudly when she saw their faces light up, impressed that she dared not call her the Shephard. "Most are too scared to speak up."

"Tell them, Walter," Ellie spoke quietly at first. When he did nothing more than look at her, sharing an unspoken conversation, she repeated it loudly, "Tell them!"

He pressed his lips, kicking at the rocky soil below him, and nodded before he began, "My father did not leave for the Mainland. He never wanted to leave here or our family." He stopped and looked to Ellie, who took his hand. "It was me. I wanted to leave."

"What? Are you serious?" Adam interrupted.

"For the love of all that is holy, Adam. For once, can you keep your trap shut and listen!" Ellie roared. Ellie had never shouted at him before. Adam's head tucked into his shoulders, and he snapped his mouth shut at the outburst. "I'm so sorry. You must...I'm sorry. But please do keep quiet. This is very hard for him to say."

Walter frowned, his face downturned, and continued, "I'd had enough of it here. I saw my sister married to a man she detested, Shephard Ward was having crazy visions that did not make sense to me, I was tired of breaking my back day in and day out to go to bed with an empty stomach."

It was not hard to accept his feelings. They were silently shared with most of the villagers even as they were told it was all for the sake of a holy life to feed the Good Land.

"If it was you," Adam started, biting his lip shut with one look from Ellie.

"My first mistake was telling my father. I had had a particularly hard day, and I was already frustrated when I heard a couple of members of the Privy gossiping about a possible decision for Ellie's pairing." He gave her a tight smile that she returned, squeezing his hand in hers. "Hearing that she may be married to that weasel Freddy Morrison was enough to break me."

Amelia had always thought she had caught Walter giving Ellie sweet glances when she wasn't looking, but she had never considered he had such strong feelings for her. Emotions so strong they had pushed him to choose to exile himself?

The thought of that moment in time had Walter stewing inside, his face tense with emotion. Amelia wanted to pepper him with questions in the silence he created. Knowing it would be best to let him tell it all in his time, she stood closed-lipped beside Adam, anxiously waiting for more.

"It's okay, Walt. You need to tell them everything," Ellie gently pushed.

"Enough was enough, and I wanted to leave. I told my father, and he begged to never speak of it again. I told him there was no changing my mind. As soon as I figured out how to get off the island, I would," he looked away, containing the resentment building inside him. "My father told the cleric. He wanted him to counsel me. To change my mind. All he did was tell the Shephard. When she came to us, she said only one of two things would be allowed. Either we all left in shame, or my father left on his own. Penance for raising an unruly man." His entire face twisted, fiercely attempting to hold in the feelings that dampened his eyes. "He refused to allow everyone, including my sister's new family, to be punished for what I said and what he did with it."

"Arthur was a wonderful man who cared so deeply," Ellie interjected, giving Walter a second to compose himself.

Walter nodded in agreement and turned to wipe his face. "She told him she would not banish us if he left without a word, not telling my mother or anyone else. That the punishment would be lessened."

"Oh, Walter. I'm so sorry," Amelia said in a quick breath. She had known in her heart that Arthur would not leave his family by choice. Banishment was heartbreaking, but at least it made more sense. Why he had to do it in secret was what she could not comprehend. The Shephard never missed a chance to make an example of someone.

"The thing is, I couldn't understand how he left, how anyone managed to get off the island. It was the one thing I could not sort out when I was planning to leave," Walter continued. "I asked Ian Miller in passing one day when we were working in the pens – how would it ever be possible? That's when he told me about John Clark."

"John?" Amelia repeated. "Molly's John?"

"Yes," Walter assured. "Ian said he had heard he sometimes comes to the island and brings the Privy things. That he had a boat."

"Wait – Molly's John? Who is that?" Adam asked quizzically.

"Molly's brother. He would come here from time to time and bring things from the Mainland," Amelia confessed, her hand automatically reaching to cover her pocket that held her new book.

"What?!" Adam balked.

"Shush, now," Ellie ordered.

"I couldn't shake the guilt of my father all alone over there. He knew no one and had nowhere to go. I went to the Shephard and told her I wanted to join him. I begged her not to punish my family further and to let me go to him. Let me help him find a new life over there. She, of course, refused to allow it. It is impossible for her to live with anyone in her flock turning their back on her," Walter said with disgust. "I told her I knew about John. At the very least, I would find him and ask him to look in on my father's situation. I was sure she would be enraged by my mentioning John, or at least she would have denied that he existed. Instead, she flipped her mood like a leaf in the wind. She told me there was no need to bother John with their personal troubles. That she had told Arthur he could send word when he was settled and that it would make the situation much more complicated if it all came out to the other villagers. She reminded me how kind she had been in her treatment of my mother. If the Privy knew I was still making problems, they may no longer support her decision. She has that way. She knows how to double the weight of guilt and press it down on you until you can't breathe. You've all witnessed it."

"Did you ever get to speak to John?" Amelia braved, interrupting to ask. It had just occurred to her that she did not know if he knew what had come of his sister.

"No," he replied quietly. "The Shephard told me it would be a shame to lose an able-bodied man to the mainland and that my responsibilities would be a strain on another. She said if I would vow to keep good and spend more time listening to the word, she would do her best to improve my life here. She asked me," he paused, looking to Ellie for encouragement, "She asked what it was that would make it worth staying, and I said, Ellie."

"That sounds unbelievable! The Shephard doesn't have a kind bone in her body," Adam exclaimed. "How did you get her to do such a thing for you?"

Walter shook his head, "It was not kindness, Adam. She was trading me for my silence. I was to make no mention of John and ask no more questions about my father. In exchange, she announced our engagement."

"The secrets are far too deep within that church," Amelia observed. "At least this one seems to have a sort of happy ending."

"He's not finished," Ellie said quietly, her emotional upset twitching her lip.

"I took her word. I knew I shouldn't, but I took her damn word. I told myself that everything would work out. I'd be married, we would receive word from my father, and maybe one day, if I worked hard enough, was a good enough man, he would be allowed to return." Walter took his hand from Ellie's and rubbed roughly at his face, pacing the ground around him. "But he's not coming back. Ever."

"How do you know that? You need to keep faith," Amelia attempted to console.

Walter stopped, his eyes wild. "NO! I have no faith! I know because it was his dagger that monster plunged into Molly's heart!" Birds above them launched out of the trees, frightened by the loud boom of his voice. Their wings flapped through the leaves, escaping to the sky above. "He never went anywhere without that knife, Amelia."

"We don't think Molly was the first person the Shephard has killed," Ellie murmured, the words too hard to speak.

Amelia immediately thought of Arthur Allen's name crossed out in blood. "Oh dear, God. The book!" The trio all looked to her at once.

"What book?" Ellie asked. "*The* book?"

Adam gasped, "The book they said was Molly's? What was in it, Amelia? You need to tell us."

She avoided meeting Walter's eyes. There was no reason to keep it a secret any longer. He trusted her enough to share his family's secrets. It was his father's name that was written in the book, after all. Her heart hitched – Peter's name was next. If Arthur had, in fact, been murdered, and there had been other killings in the past, there could be more in the future. Her sweet little songbird of a brother could be in grave danger.

"Amelia," Ellie pushed. "Does that book have something to do with all of this? Have you seen inside of it?"

"Not only have I read it, I was the one who found it." She wondered where the Shephard had hidden it away, most likely within the church. They would have to get it back if anyone were to begin to believe them.

"You found it? Was it at Molly's like they said?" Ellie asked, looking astounded at her friend's secret.

"No, I found it by the shore. It was in a cave there," she admitted, still torn whether or not to put the weight of her knowledge onto them. "Walter, your father's name was in it."

"What do you mean? What did it say?" Walter stood tall, anger reemerging.

"That's just it. Just his name." Amelia pinched at her lip, trying to remember each name she had read. "A list of names, actually. All villagers that had been crossed off on the paper, including your cousin Alice." She could not bring herself to say what she believed to have been used.

"Alice? What does she have to do with all of this?" Ellie asked with wonder.

"I don't know, but what scares me is that Peter is the last name on the list, and it had not been crossed out yet." Amelia was now resolved to tell them everything she knew. They would have to work together to get support to remove Ellen Ward from the Privy Assembly.

"My father's name was written in that book?" Walter asked Amelia, who nodded. "What is it? Whose is it?"

"A secret book that is tied to missing or murdered folks? I'm pretty sure we can say it belongs to the Privy!" Adam said in a burst of acknowledgment. "Do you think your mother knows anything about it?"

"I don't know, I never got to show her before...," Amelia's words choked in her throat when she looked back to Molly's cottage. If she ever got her hands on that book again, she would have to resist the urge to tear it to pieces just as they had done to Molly's life.

"This just proves my point more! We need to get out of here. We need to find a way off of this island and get help," Walter implored. "Staying here to try and fix it ourselves is nothing more than begging to have our names put in that book. Think of Peter, Amelia! We need to help him, and we can't do that on our own."

Amelia shook her head. There was no way she would leave her family. "No, Walter. I won't. I can't leave without trying to make a difference. I won't leave my brother and sister."

"Your parents are more than capable of looking after them. Your mother is on the Privy, for God's sake! If anyone is to know what is happening, it would be a member, would it not?" Walter argued desperately.

"How did his name end up in the book then?" she retorted and then conceded, "I understand what you're saying. I don't know. All of this is so much larger than us. I cannot imagine leaving without telling them what is happening below their noses."

"There is not one person we can trust in that village," Adam sneered with a glare toward the path that led back to a home that had become anything but. "Walter is right. We need to get help."

"I trust my mother. She will be able to help," Amelia insisted. "I know if we tell her all of this, she will know what to do."

"You know I love you, and you know I love your mother, but I'm sorry, Amelia. I don't trust anyone on that Assembly anymore." Ellie took her friend's hand to soften the blow of her words.

It was something that she never believed she would hear. Ellie was taking a stand against the makers of the rules, the leaders of the church, and those who made up the world as she knew it.

Amelia felt in her heart that they were right. She was not ready for it to be true, but she knew. Regardless, she dug in her heels and told herself they must stay. "Even if no one can help us with what we've learned, they won't be able to help you get to the mainland, anyways."

"Cole said he would help," Adam announced to Amelia. "He told me he would do whatever he could."

Amelia started for the trail, "No, Adam. It's not right to get him involved more than he already is. It's not his fight."

"Who is Cole?" Walter interrupted.

"One of Amelia's mainlander friends," Adam smiled slyly.

Her jaw dropped at the very idea. "He is not my friend. I barely know him. You've probably spoken more with him than I have."

Walter and Ellie shared a perplexed look with each other.

"Either way, Amelia, he said he wanted to. It is his choice," Adam pushed on.

"Fine, if you want to put him in danger, go ahead. I want no part of it," Amelia said with her fight dying as she began to feel alone once more. There was no fighting against them when their minds were as made up as hers.

"He's a mainlander?" Walter asked, trying to understand the newest mystery set before him.

"He is. He and his friends have been out here snooping around. It was part of a dare or something. I don't understand a lot of what he goes on about. I know he means it when he says he wants to help, though," Adam explained with an irksome look at Amelia's stubbornness.

"Do you know when he will be back?" Walter asked Adam.

"He was here just before we came up here. There's a chance he's still here."

"Did he say where he accessed the island?" Ellie asked, looking at Amelia and then Adam. As twisted up as Amelia was with not having them side with her, she was impressed with the grit that had sprouted up within her timid friend.

"I just know it was near the cave. I didn't see his boat, but when I first met him, it was on the trail right by the shore," she answered. "He had pointed past there as where his friends were."

"Can you show us where that is?" Walter asked Amelia, who stood tight-lipped in the circle. "Please, Amelia. Show us where you were, and I won't ask any more of you. I can wait for him, and you can all return to the village."

Amelia knew there was no stopping him. It would be of no use to anyone if she stood in their way. With a defeated groan, she agreed and started down the pathway that started out within the twisted branches behind Molly's defaced home.

Questions about the book, the cave, and the mysterious mainlanders peppered Amelia as they made their way to the water. The more she shared, the more they seemed to speak of helping rather than running. They knew they had to get the book back from the Shephard, and it was decided that getting it to John would be the best option. Amelia was convinced that as much as they needed to do their part, they would need support beyond their capabilities. She was adamant that she would not leave her family, but she promised to help those who wanted to seek help outside of themselves.

When they walked through the clearing to the rocky shore, they all stood in silent awe at the view. If they chose to leave, the rest of their lives may exist across the waters they would have never imagined crossing. If they remained, the perilous evil that had been overtaking their village could snuff out their lives before they even wet their toes.

Amelia pointed to the cave she had found shelter in. No one stepped toward it.

"I will wait here until someone comes. You all head back and act as if everything is as it should be," Walter directed. "Make no mention of me, and hopefully, no one will notice I'm gone. Ellie, you should head home and stay inside. Seeing you may cause questions about me." Ellie nodded and hugged him tightly.

"I'll stay with you," Adam said to Walter, "You shouldn't have to do this alone."

"No. The more of us missing, the more suspicion we'll bring. I'm fine on my own," Walter insisted. "These people are responsible for my father's death – I know it. I am going to do whatever it takes to make them pay."

The book was the closest they had to proof of that being true. They did not need anything more to know it happened after seeing what they had done to Molly, and something had to be done before that fate befell another member of their community.

"As God as my witness, they will not spill another drop of blood in that village," Walter vowed.

Ellie stood close at his side. "We'll do it for Arthur," she said softly.

"And for Molly," Amelia added.

They turned when Adam started to wave and found Cole standing just feet away at the head of the trail. His blanched face made it clear that he had heard what they had said.

CHAPTER FIFETEEN

"Cole!" Adam exclaimed and started toward him. "I'm so glad you're still here." Cole remained rooted in place, staring at the group on the beach. "We need your help."

"They've been killing people? Is that what you said?" Cole asked, disbelief worrying his face. "Like, actually killing people?" Somehow, he was able to find the strength to start across the pebbled ground to them. Walter and Ellie looked at him as if he were a strange animal that had wandered into the village square. Everything from his clothing to his haircut caught them off guard.

"I told you this was all too much for you to involve yourself in, Cole," Amelia said quietly. She was embarrassed by how he must see them now. Savages locked away on an island kept away from the civility of the mainlanders that she read about in her novels. More so, she feared the danger they had placed him in. He had made it clear that he was a kind soul, and she felt horrible to have him fall into the middle of their living nightmare.

"Adam is right. You guys need to get out of here – now!" Cole proclaimed, rooting through his pocket for his boat keys that he held up to them. "I can take you now."

"Wait," Amelia called out when he started along the shore with Walter right behind him. "We can't all go, and we need to decide exactly what we'll do. Walter can't just appear out of nowhere and start yelling about murder." She knew there was a better chance of whoever they spoke to thinking they were crazy if that was their approach. If it was John they spoke to, he needed to hear about what had happened to his sister in a gentler manner. If he had any of Molly's spirit, he would most likely erupt with the news.

"I know Walter needs to go with Cole and at least talk to John. He's our best hope, I think," Adam suggested. "Ellie should go home and not be seen like he had suggested. It wouldn't be strange for the newlyweds to be locked away together, and that stops anyone from looking for Walter." All but Cole nodded in agreement, with Cole simply trying to take in all that was being said. "You and I need to get that book back so we have it when John comes," he said to Amelia.

"What book?" Cole asked.

"Amelia found it in that cave over there. We think it has something to do with all of this," Adam said and pointed.

Cole moved quickly to the entrance, with the foursome following slowly and unsurely along. When they entered, he pulled out his phone and clicked on the flashlight.

"What in the...." Walter leaned in with awe. "What is that?"

"It's my phone. There's a flashlight app," Cole answered, quickly realizing they would have no idea what they were talking about. "It's...uh...," he stammered and looked to Amelia for help.

"It's mainlander stuff. Not anything we need to get distracted by right now," Amelia ordered, trying to hide her own amazed wonder at the bright light in his hand. "I found the book over here." She walked further into the now well-lit cave to the tangle of branches and flowers that had circled it. They all looked up at the corpse flowers painted on the stone walls. There were many more that could be seen in the clear light projected from Cole's phone.

"What the hell is all of that?" Cole asked with growing fear in his voice. "This place is beyond creepy."

"They're the cursed flowers," Ellie advised him, "The church says they represent a curse brought down on our founders." She spoke the words as if it was easily understood and turned bashful when Cole looked at her as if she had two heads. "That's what they say," she added quietly.

They stood over the twisted branches and tiny white flowers as if they would be able to give them a clue as to what to do.

"We need to get that book back," Adam said, "and whatever else they have hidden away with it. If we can get into the church without being seen, who knows what we will be able to find."

"What is this book you keep talking about?" Cole asked, shining his light over the top of the cave and back down to the corner.

"We don't exactly know," Amelia answered with a crooked frown. There was so much to explain to Cole, and not only was there no time, but she was not sure he would understand or even believe her. "We think it will be proof of the evil that has been attacking our community for some time now."

"Evil? Like *evil*, evil?" Cole asked, turning his light back to the flowers on the walls. "Are you guys talking about the devil or something?"

"There are many forms of evil that are always at the ready if you don't pay attention," Walter said almost as if to himself.

"Whatever has taken charge of our village is evil; I know that much," Adam added. "And the only devil I'm sure of anymore is Shephard Ward."

Amelia went quiet as the others discussed what they knew of Ellen Ward. The most troubling thing to her was that her mother sat at that woman's table. There was no way to know what she was aware of and what the Shephard had kept hidden all to herself. Evil would never find a home in her mother's heart; she would bet her life on that. If any of the dark doings were known to Jane Taylor, she would have already started to move against it all.

"What is this?" Cole asked, illuminating a wooden box that Amelia had not noticed before. On the side was written the Shephard's favorite phrase:

Be the harvest that feeds from the earth, not the tide that bleeds from it.

"That has to be hers," Ellie whispered and bent to look inside. She reached in and pulled out what looked like a long, thin stone. She held it to Cole's light.

He took it from her and laid it on his palm to get a better look. His eyes bulged, "Oh fuck!" he shouted as he tossed it to the ground. "That's a bone!" He wiped his hand quickly on his sweatshirt.

Walter bent to pick it up, turning it over and looked into the box. He pulled out another bone and compared it. "Not just any bones." He held one up and repeated the Shephard's phrase scribbled on the box, reminding them all of the long, ghoulish finger she would hold in their faces when it was said. "These are human fingers." He set them back in the box and took another look. His face twisted into a horror-struck snarl, and he stepped away, nearly tumbling to the ground, pointing inside.

Amelia pushed forward to see what had caused such a visceral reaction. Set on top of what looked to be several dozen bones was one that still retained a small amount of flesh. A gold band was still held in place. She gagged and stumbled back.

"What is it?" Ellie demanded as she attempted to comfort her husband.

"It's my father's wedding ring." Walter's pain overcame him as he staggered out into the fresh air outside of the cave. Ellie chased after him, her shock from the find the only thing stopping her own tears. Adam, who himself had turned green, followed them out.

"That is his father's finger?" Cole questioned, stepping even further away from the box. "What the fuck is going on around here?" He grabbed Amelia by the hand and dragged her along behind him and out onto the beach.

Ellie and Walter had walked to the water's edge. She rubbed his back as he worked to contain the forceful emotions that had taken control. Adam had made it to the treeline beside the cave before he lost his lunch. He continued to wretch even when he had emptied his stomach. Amelia offered him her handkerchief and got him settled on a fallen tree's log once he caught his breath.

"Why would she do that? What is a reason to be so sinister?" he asked, handing her back the hankie he had used to wipe his brow with before pulling out his own and swiping it across his mouth.

"I think anything that woman does is well beyond reason at this point," Amelia decided, sitting beside him. They watched Cole walk up and down the beach, holding his phone to the sky, an explosion of curse words pouring from his mouth.

"What in the world is he doing?" Adam asked, the sight nearly causing him to laugh in the midst of the chaos.

"I have no idea." Amelia watched him curiously.

"Do you think he'll still have it in him to go across with Cole?" Adam asked, gesturing to Walter, who was slowly gaining his composure in Ellie's arms.

"I think there is no stopping him now," she replied, knowing that Walter would not let such an abuse of his father go unpunished.

"There's no bars here at all," Cole griped when he joined them again, holding up his phone. They saved their questions, knowing it was not the time to learn of the mainlander's modern lives. "Do you think he's good to go still, or should I go on my own."

"I'm fine," Walter shouted over to him. "Let's go." He quickly kissed Ellie's cheek and started in the direction he and Cole had started in earlier.

Cole looked between him and Amelia. "Please come with us. I can't leave you here with all of this," he begged. "Any of you," he added, looking to Adam and Ellie.

"We'll be fine. Don't worry about us. You get him to John, and he'll do the rest," Adam promised. "You go with Walter, and we'll look after each other. Don't worry," he repeated.

"I'll be back as soon as I can, okay? Stay here and wait for us. Do not go back to those people, Amelia. Please stay here," Cole insisted.

She responded with a tight smile, knowing she could not promise that. Cole started running to catch up with Walter, who was marching along the shore, now a driven man. He looked back at her uneasily before they disappeared around the corner of the beach.

"We're not really going to wait here, are we?" Adam questioned.

"No," Amelia announced and started for the trail. "We're going to get that book." She stopped when she saw Ellie had not moved, her eyes still locked in the direction Walter had taken. Amelia walked to her and took her hand. "He'll be alright, Ellie. He'll be back before you know it."

Ellie looked over the vast water that framed the landscape before she gave a nod and started back to the village with Amelia and Adam. The nervous energy and exchange of information that had carried them to shore was replaced with fretful silence on their return.

When they arrived back within the village's border, Ellie did as she had been instructed and headed straight for the Allen's cottage.

Amelia and Adam followed along the treeline until they reached the church. They listened at the rear window until they were sure they heard no voices or movement from within. As nonchalantly as their pounding hearts would allow, they strolled to the front porch, relieved not to find the white candle lit. They made small talk with each other and gave friendly waves to the few people who passed by until they could slip up the porch and through the church door without any prying eyes upon them.

"Where do you think she would hide it?" Adam whispered, eyes scanning every inch of the church.

Amelia remembered that her mother once mentioned a cupboard behind the Privy Assembly's table that held all the marriage papers. It was as good a place to start as any. She told Adam to follow her when she hustled behind the altar and choral benches to the enshrined room that lay beyond.

She had only dared peek in the Privy Assembly's gathering room once as a child, and the reprimand she received from her mother turned her off from ever attempting it again until that moment. Their power was so great that there was not even a lock on the door to keep others out. The threat of their displeasure was enough to repel curious eyes. Unfortunately, the same could not be said of the cupboard doors that lined the wall. Amelia jiggled the heavy metal locks that sealed the secrets away from them.

"What are we going to do now?" Amelia moaned. "There is no way the Shephard would leave the keys lying around for us to find."

Adam raised a finger to his lips to shush her and disappeared back into the church's main hall. Amelia tried to loosen the locks with a wiggle and felt hopeless.

"This should do the trick," Adam announced with a heavy broken handle from a lantern in hand.

"Adam, that's not going to work," Amelia said doubtfully.

He ignored her misgivings and slipped one end between the wall and the door. The wood that held the lock's latch gave a loud crack. They froze, waiting to see if they had been heard. When no one rushed in to accost them, Adam pulled open the door and rifled through the contents. Handwritten books of scripture, notes on past and future pairing, and rough drafts of hymns filled the first. Not finding what they needed, they tried the next cupboard and then the next, stopping each time the crack of the wood echoed around them, praying they had not been heard.

Luck was on their side on their third try. Amelia recognized the leather corner of the book that peeked out from the linen cloth it had been wrapped in. She slid it from the shelf slowly and screamed when something slipped from the fabric and clanged at her feet against the polished wood floor.

Adam quickly swooped down to grab it. He held up the dagger that had been used to kill Molly, the same knife that Walter said his father was never without. Amelia nearly lost her strength when she saw that it had not been wiped clean of Molly's blood. Seeing her visible pain, Adam took the book from her, set the dagger inside the pages, and re-wrapped it all in the cloth.

"We need to get this to your mother," he directed, his eyes holding hers, keeping her focused on what must be done. After it was all over, she could fall apart for as long as she needed. "If there is anyone that has been in this room that we can trust, it's your mother."

"The new hymns should become quite popular," the cleric's voice rang out as the front door clanged open. Andrew Stewart, his cleric-in-training's voice could be heard agreeing.

They looked at the cupboard that held the hymn papers with the lock snapped away, and panic set in. They both shimmied under the heavy Assembly table with no escape other than the door the cleric had entered through. Being caught in that room would be punished far more severely than spending more time in the box. With the state of the Shephard since her attack on Molly, their lives were on the line.

"It will one day be your job to care for these and compose new melodies to lift spirits and inspire these cretins to keep their hearts pure," Cleric Gordon said with arrogance. Their footsteps clacked along the pews, getting closer to the Assembly room. "It will be some time until you can access our cupboard, however. Shephard Ward has trust in me that she would not dare put in you yet."

The smug slither in his voice made Amelia's skin crawl even as her heart threatened to stop with the fear of being found. She slid herself in further under the table. Adam held the linen-wrapped bundle tightly in his arms as if it were a shield from the cleric's eyes.

"Fredrick!" The Shephard's shrill bellow bounced from every surface of the church. Amelia held her breath.

"Yes, my Shephard. What can I do for you? I was gathering the hymns to work on with Andrew for this evening's service," he said with an overly sugared inflection. "He has been doing well with..."

"You can fuss about with that later. I need your assistance now," she barked, and his feet picked up pace when he shuffled back to the door. "Now, Fredrick!"

Adam and Amelia remained unmoved from under the table well after the door had shut. They took an extra minute to turn their ears to any slight sound that could be a new threat to their exposure. When they had as much certainty as they believed they would get, they got themselves up and away from the Privy's room as fast as they could. A quick pause to listen at the front door was the most they would allow themselves, wanting to be out and away from the church.

Adam kept the book and dagger covered well even though they hurried along, hidden by the back of the buildings. Barging through the Taylor's front door, they slammed it behind them. Amelia called out to her mother, who emerged from the back room when she heard the commotion.

"Mama! Please, please don't be cross with me. We need your help," Amelia panted, pulling Adam along to the privacy of her bedroom.

"What has happened?" Jane asked, following behind the wind storm of her daughter, "Poppet! What has happened?"

Amelia tugged her mother the rest of the way through her doorway and shut the door. She pointed to the bundle in Adam's hands, unsure of how to begin. Adam set it down on the bed and stepped to the side to allow Jane space to inspect what they had presented her with.

She flipped over one flap of the linen and then the next, exposing the leatherbound tome. "What is this? What has you so upset?" She blanched when she saw what lay in front of her.

"Do you recognize that, Mama?" Amelia asked, hoping with all of her might that she was not involved with whatever that book represented. "Do you know what it is?

"Is this..." Jane opened the pages to the spot that concealed the dagger. "Oh, my word! Is that...?"

"The dagger that was used to kill Molly," Adam finished.

"Where did you find this?" Jane demanded and turned to the two. "Answer me right now, Amelia. Where did you find this?"

The anger in her mother's eyes frightened her. She was not sure if it was because of what she had been shown or because she had been the one to bring it to her. She stammered, unable to answer.

"Do you know what it is?" Adam asked when Amelia could not continue. "What the book is for?"

Jane looked down to turn another page, covering the blood-stained dagger, and read the names listed. "The Shephard would not let us see it. She said it was Molly's book of revenge." Jane turned another page. "How did you get this?"

"Mama, I know it was wrong," Amelia started, forcing herself to find her voice, "We took it from the church."

"Were you seen?" Jane centered her attention on her daughter.

"I don't think so. There's more that you need to see, Mama." Amelia turned the page to the last with ink and pointed to Peter's name. Jane's hand trembled as it lifted to her face, covering her gaping mouth. "Do you know what it means, Mama?"

Jane shook her head slowly, her fingertips tracing her son's name.

"Mrs. Taylor, I think it's time we all realize that the Shephard is no longer fit to lead us," Adam put a hand on her slumped back, silent tears tracing down to her chin. "We're all in danger now. If that book means what we think it means, Peter is in the most danger of all."

Jane slammed the book shut. She shoved it further on the bed and then, filling with anger, picked it up and threw it at the wall. The dagger tumbled out and landed with a clang. "Gavin!" she hollered for her husband as she flew from the room. "Gavin!"

Amelia's father appeared from the back room; his brow twisted with the bewilderment of seeing his wife in such a state. "What? What's wrong?" He held her as she collapsed into his arms. He looked to Amelia and Adam for answers.

"I was right, Gavin." Her body shook against his. "I was right all this time. She is a monster."

"Who?" Gavin held her out from his chest to look into her eyes. "Who, Jane?"

"The Shephard," she spat. "It's been her all along. Her preaching about sacrifice was not just words. No one would listen to me. How many have we lost because no one would listen to me?"

The revelation felt like a lightning strike to the cottage. It was clear to Amelia that her mother knew the printed and stroked names represented death that Ellen Ward had brought down on to whom she claimed to be her flock. If no one was to stop her, Peter would be next.

Gavin demanded to see what had made her have such an outburst. When they brought him to the book that lay open on Amelia's bedroom floor, he stared at his son's name printed neatly on the now wrinkled page. He picked up the book, set it on the bed, and gently ran his palm over the folds, flattening the crease that bent Peter's name as if caring for the letters protected the child in life.

"She said she had special plans for him," Jane said hardly above a whisper. "I did not want to believe what my heart was telling me."

"Where is he?" Gavin burst from the room and out the front door. "Peter!" He paced, his eyes wildly searching for his son. Amelia, her mother, and Adam ran after him when he headed to the square, his voice becoming louder and more frantic as he called out to his son.

"My goodness, Gavin," the Shephard sneered. She stood beside the well with one hand on the bucket and the other on Peter's shoulder. "Screeching like that will wake the dead."

Chapter Sixteen

THE FEW PEOPLE WHO had been milling about with their daily duties had stopped to watch the exchange. The Shephard smiled pleasantly at them as they held their shovels and baskets, the late afternoon sunshine bright on their tired faces. Peter squirmed against her hold, his scared eyes begging his father for help.

"Peter, come here, please," Gavin requested, his voice as calm and even as he could manage. The boy started toward his father until Shephard Ward tightened her grip on his small shoulder. "Please take your hand off of my son, Shephard."

"You seem upset. Is there something I can do to ease your burden today?" Shephard Ward pulled Peter closer as she spoke. "Your family has been through so many troubles."

"Take your hand off of my son, Shephard," he repeated, his voice beginning to rise again.

"I would think you would have learned your place through the lessons given with love to your dear, Amelia. I would think twice before using that tone with me, Gavin." Her eyes grew dark, transforming her friendly grin into that of a predator's sneer. "Jane, do keep him in order."

Amelia stood tight to her mother, who held her hand as if the Shephard could steal her away even from a distance. They did not notice Adam return to the cottage to retrieve the book. The more Gavin and the Shephard held their standoff, the more villagers gathered to see what was happening. Amelia became lightheaded and shook with the memory of the last time she had witnessed everyone coming together in the square. Molly's screams filled her head as she pictured the empty stare that filled her lifeless face. There was no way she would allow that to happen to even one more person, let alone her brother.

"Let him go!" she cried out as she tore away from her mother. Her pace quickened when the Shephard began to laugh. "Let him go!" Amelia erupted and cracked her hand across the Shephard's cheek. The laughter was replaced with silent surprise. Her hand released Peter when she reached to touch the spot of the hard slap, and he ran as fast as he could to his parents, confused and afraid. The

Shephard stared at Amelia, her resentment smoldering from within.

"This is what the Shephard used to convince us all that what she did to Molly, what she did to Amelia, was for our safety. For our souls!" Adam called out to those gathered. The Shephard looked to see him holding up the stolen book. He stepped forward when she grabbed Amelia's braid and yanked her back to her as her new barrier against what may come. "Look at her! She has no soul! She is cruel and deranged and will be the downfall of all of us."

He started to open the book to explain what it held when the Shephard lifted her leg and drove her boot into the side of Amelia's knee. Her leg bent at an impossible angle as she tumbled to the ground, a wail of agony ripping from deep within. The Shephard tightened her grip on her braid, holding her limp body up for the crowd to see.

"How dare you!" Jane roared at the woman who held her eldest daughter captive. She grabbed the book from Adam and held it open. "This is the work of who we call our leader! Look!" she insisted as she walked along the peering eyes. "You will all see names here that you know, people you loved. They are all gone now. Dead and buried because of that woman's actions!"

"Yes! Everyone look!" the Shephard agreed with a cackle. "Cleric Fredrick, assist this poor woman. Please ring the bell to gather the rest of our flock. Let them see the evidence of the Taylor's evil that Jane is so thoughtfully presenting for us."

The crowd pushed forward to see what the book held as the Cleric retrieved the heavy bell and rattled it as a call to assemble in the square.

"She has been fooling us all. She does not live by the good word any longer! She has been taken by something darker than anything I have ever known," Jane insisted, turning the pages. "I beg of you, do not listen to the lies she spreads."

The Shephard laughed harder, the more emotional Jane became. "So, they should listen to you? Do you present my flock with the book that the witch possessed as proof? The witch that held your own daughter's soul so tightly that she nearly corrupted her beyond redemption?" She held Amelia's head higher with a yank on her braid. "My actions have saved this child. You all have been saved by my hand against the power of that malevolent woman who was allowed to live on our Good Land. I took the lives of one to prevent more names from being added to that damnable book. Do not now grow weak against what I fight so hard to protect us all from. You know to listen to my words! I speak only the truth."

The looks of puzzlement turned to judgment that was directed to Jane, who continued to plead with them all to listen to what they did not want to hear. "It is her book! It is written in her hand! If you will only look at what is written. Please, you must believe us. My own son's name is here. Arthur Allen's name is here!"

"Jane, I beg of you. Do not make the Taylor name become as unwelcome as the Clark's. If the hag's power still bubbles within your blood, we can help you. I will do everything in my power to bring you back to righteousness. What I will not allow is you or your cursed daughter to harm another member of my flock," Shephard Ward stressed with compassionate concern slipping over her face. "Do not make this harder than it has to be."

"Don't you dare accuse my mother! You all have to listen! She has lost her mind and will come after all of you next!" Amelia screamed against the pain. "A woman of kindness would not treat us like this!"

"You are correct in that, my dear. I am not treating you like this. I am treating the evil you have yet to shed." She snapped her fingers to two men who stood nearest. "The box. Now," she directed them, releasing her hair once they had her to her feet. "I will do whatever it takes to rid you of the curse that Molly has put upon you as punishment to us all for our pure hearts." She wiped the hand that had held her on her apron as if she had been touching goat manure.

"No!" Gavin exclaimed, trying to fight his way through to his daughter. Amelia watched the crowd hold him back as she was lowered into the now familiar cage, nearly losing consciousness when her crooked leg folded beneath her.

"I shall always help my flock be the harvest that feeds this Good Land and never the tide that bleeds," Shephard Ward announced.

Amelia cried out in anger when the crowd erupted in cheers for the Shephard's words. There was no hope to cling to when it was so few against so many. Her parents' voices trailed off as they were moved from the square, allowing a paralyzing alarm to take control of Amelia. She called out for them, and for her brother, for her sister, for anyone who would dare help. The only reply was the drone of the Cleric's voice calling out words of worship from what they had deemed the good book. The ripping ache that shot up and down her leg twisted the contents of her stomach and brought darkness to and from her vision. The verses Cleric Fredrick called out blurred into a buzz that hummed her mind into a daze. It seemed so near ago that books had been her blessed escape. The world within the world that held her. Now, a book had helped to lock her into a world more heinous than anything she could have imagined. From dream to nightmare with the turn of simple pages. She felt foolish, allowing herself to think that she could have the strength that Molly held proudly for so many years, that she would be someone whom those ensconced in the power of the Shephard would listen to.

"Ellen Ward!" a man's voice boomed, silencing the square. "Ellen Ward, you show yourself now, you wicked bitch!"

A murmur rippled around the box, bringing Amelia back into the present. She did not recognize the voice of the man who had the fearlessness to shout out a challenge to the Shephard. She tried to move herself enough to glimpse through a crack between the boards until the pain forced her still.

"Behold my flock! The tide has begun to bleed!" Shephard Ward had the audacity to allow an edge of humor to tickle her tongue. "John Clark has returned to strengthen the curse of his family. How much more proof could there be that Flora has returned in spirit to punish those who care for the Good Land?"

"Cut the shit, Ellen. Where is my sister?"

A tiny spark of hope started to glow within Amelia. Walter and Cole had gotten to John. His appearance was baffling to the majority of the villagers, who had no idea of John's visits to the island.

"She is where she needs to be for the good of us all," the Shephard said boldly. "Can you smell it, my flock? Do you smell the death that blooms from the cursed flowers? I can see them bursting from the soil below his every step!"

Amelia coward when the box's lid above opened.

"Come on!" Adam urged. He and Ellie stood above her, taking advantage of the attention on John and the Shephard to free their broken friend. Amelia pushed on her lame leg, ignoring the hurt that begged her to stay in place. With an arm over each of her friends' shoulders, she staggered to the side of a cottage out of view.

"Are Cole and Walter here?" she mumbled, words becoming hard to form through her weakness.

"I haven't seen them yet," Ellie replied, helping her get settled on the ground.

"Where did they take my parents?" She looked about for any sign of them. Ellie and Adam could only shrug, with sadness shadowing their faces.

"After all I have done for you," John shouted. The crowd parted out of his way as he moved to the center of the square. He was in his eighties, yet still appeared just as strong as any young man in the village. His towering height matched the deep thunder in his voice. "You better pray that what I have been told is a cruel lie. So help me God, if you have harmed one hair on her head, I will end you today. I saw what you did to her home! You all have a cruelty in your hearts that I could never have imagined!" The hitch in his voice betrayed him. It was clear he knew she was gone, whether he was ready to admit it or not. The heartache and furor over the loss battled for control of him.

Amelia watched a few people better grip their tools with his threat. John would be a sitting duck if they decided to act. She knew it would only take one crazed word from the Shephard for it to happen. The only thing working in his favor was his size. The closer he got, the more Amelia could see that he was even taller and thicker than he had looked when she saw him slip through the woods, and his booming voice took them by surprise.

"John Clark, you have already turned your back on us. You chose to leave us. You have no right to step on our Good Land," Cleric Fredrick sniveled. He took his place beside the Shephard when he saw the villagers starting to look defensive toward the loud interloper's threats.

"Hog shit, Fredrick. This Good Land of yours is my goddamn land, and you know it! Tell these fools the truth for once," he roared. "If it weren't for me, you all would have been chased off this island years ago!"

Amelia was as confused as the rest of the crowd with that revelation. Molly had never said anything about it all being her brother's land. When it came down to it, Amelia had never considered that anyone owned the land. It was ruled by the word of the Privy, and in turn, it was their possession.

"You may not step foot in this village with your lies, John. My flock will not stand for your disrespect," the Shephard said flatly.

"It's over, Ellen," John growled. He stepped further into the square and stopped when a few villagers stood their ground, tools in hand. "I almost wish I hadn't called the law on you fools. It would be mighty satisfying to show you all exactly what I think of you."

"There is no law on this island that stands above me," she retorted, her voice stronger when she saw her burgeoning support building through the crowd. "You would be wise to turn tail and head back to your shameful life across our waters."

"How can you listen to this woman's lies? I know you all are stupid, but I didn't know it was possible to be this stupid," he shouted at the crowd, who stood at attention until another growl rumbled from him. He stomped ahead when he saw they faltered, a hitch in his hip not stopping him. "I have spent my life trying to protect this damned place. Working my ass off to purchase it, fending off the rumors in town that you're nothing but a crazy cult. I've kept the law away, thinking that you may not be livin' the life I wanted, but you were livin' a life rooted in the good of our founders. Molly never told me that you all had turned batshit crazy! I'm gonna make sure each and every one of you pays for what you've done to her. She had more goodness in her finger than you all have all together!"

They watched him tremble, his aged face red beneath his short white whiskers. He took a step and stopped, catching his breath. Amelia worried that if he did not find a way to calm himself, his heart might up and stop, and he would drop right before their eyes. Not the ending she would ever wish on the man who was a true hero to them all, whether they knew it or not.

"He's telling the truth! You have to listen to him," Amelia implored. She tried to pull herself up with the help of her friends. The damage to her knee kept her on the dusty ground. "I know some of you already know it! Please tell them all that he is the one who has been providing for us. John Clark and Molly are the ones who made sure we were cared for, not Ellen Ward!"

Many gasped at Amelia's brazen use of her given name. She didn't care. There was no reverence for the woman left in her. Ellen Ward had destroyed the Good Land with the nerve of her own selfish desire for power over those who toiled day and night. Those who stood around the young woman looked down on her injured body with a mix of pity and indecision.

The Shephard pushed her way to where she lay. Disgust contorted her face, and she wretched when she reached her. "My flock! I am so thankful that you are not cursed with my visions. The cursed flowers are drawn to her like a moth to a flame. They want to consume her, to feed on the evil that has been passed on from the hag!" She held out her arms, ushering those near away from the injured young lady. "Stay back from her. She is more dangerous than Molly Clark had ever been!"

"You shut your mouth, Ward! You have no right to speak her name!" John could be heard, but those gathered blocked Amelia's view of him. A gasp waved across the crowd from where he stood and back to Amelia. It made her fearful that he succumbed to the stress. Another life stolen because of their blind obedience to the Shephard.

"Who are you? Walter, who do you dare bring to our land?" a man called out.

"Dammit, Cole, I told you to stay put! This ain't no place for you to be right now!" John railed. "Get back to your boat and back home. The law will be here soon enough, and you don't need to be caught up in all of this."

Amelia strained to see through the legs of the villagers crowded around. She did not hear another word from Cole and Walter. She hoped Cole had obeyed John's order and left as quickly as he could. There was no telling what could happen to him with the heated energy that had filled the square.

"Can you see them?" she asked Ellie, who herself was straining to see what was happening. She shook her head when, even on tip-toes, she failed.

"I'll be back," Adam whispered. He was gone before anyone could beg him to stay.

"Shephard, I think we should take a moment to calm down," Clark Ward said, approaching her. "If the law from the mainland really is coming out here, I think it best if we don't do anything to cause them alarm."

"What do you know of the law over there?" another unseen man in the crowd balked.

"Some of us have more knowledge than you can handle. Some of us are more faithful," Clark retorted with a sneer.

One by one, the villagers started to bicker among themselves. Some knew of John, some knew of the life-saving supplies he brought, and some even stated they knew of the leather-bound book. One woman claimed she knew her neighbors had a secret life on the mainland.

Amelia knew others had to have known of John's existence. He had been the backbone of their lives for longer than Amelia had lived. With the claims and accusations being thrown around, she could not sort out who was truthful and who was simply caught up in the moment.

The Shephard raised her voice as loudly as she could. She did nothing more than add to the cacophony of arguments that exploded throughout the square.

"Come on, we need to move you." Adam appeared behind the girls, Walter and Cole at his side.

Ellie leaped to her feet to embrace her young husband, a cry of relief slipping from her lips.

"Cole, John is right. You shouldn't be here," Amelia managed through gritted teeth as they slowly lifted her. They were able to get her to her balanced on one foot before she begged for them to stop. Even the tap of her toes on the ground would send a blaze of sharp torture up her leg.

"Either should you, Amelia. None of you should be," he retorted, wrapping her arm around his shoulder. Adam did the same with her other arm. "We need to get you somewhere safe before the cops get here. I have a feeling it's going to be messy."

Unable to walk and paralyzed by pain, Amelia started to feel the panic of entrapment. "You're going to need to leave me here."

"That is not going to happen," Cole objected. She yowled in pain when he tried to adjust her in their arms.

"I need to find Sarah and Peter. I have no idea where they are. I have no idea where my parents are. I'm not leaving without them. I'll be ok. Just leave me here. Go to Cole's boat. John said help is coming," she panted, trying to sit herself down again,

They ignored her directions and held tight. Walter and Ellie attempted to lift her legs to carry her more swiftly, only to have her wail out as soon as her twisted knee moved.

The Shephard turned back to where Amelia had laid, and her glare rose to where her friends were now holding her up. Fear slipped over her frustration when she saw the young men who had appeared at her side. She raised her finger, pointing to them, and turned back to address the crowd. "Do you see the damage done? Outsiders feel free to walk our land as if it were their own. The world we have spent generations protecting is crumbling, just as our founders knew it would if we did not stand strong!" She pointed to Amelia, "This is the future we stand to burn within if we allow this evil to spread! I have warned you and warned you and warned you, my dear people. How much more proof of my gifts do you need?"

"You leave them alone, Ward!" John shouted as he forced his way through to the other side of the square. "You have spilled your last drop of blood, woman!" He pushed roughly at any man who dared stand in his way.

"Not a step further." Cleric Fredrick stepped in his path; his chin held high with a confidence that he fed on from the crowd, even though the rest of his being could not follow. The dagger was in his hand and pointed up to John's face. "You have insulted our Shephard long enough. It is time for you to leave our land." He waved the dagger in the air to show he meant business.

"You damned fool. I'm not going anywhere." John moved again only to have the cleric hold the dagger out further, only a few inches from the man's face. "What are you going to do? Stab me in front of all these people?"

"Why not? It was good enough for Molly?" he sneered. John's fist was up and thrown before Fredrick could complete his smile. He launched backward, blood quickly flowing from his nose when he reached the ground.

"You son of a bitch!" John attempted a second attack only to be held back by the crowd, who looked more disgusted with Fredrick's words than John's assault on him. John struggled against their restraint, trying to finish what he had started.

"Who is spilling blood now, John Clark?" the Shephard accused. She snatched up the knife and moved in on him, grinning wickedly at the man trapped in the arms of her flock. She faltered when the crowd began to swallow John away, pushing him back into the safety of their numbers.

"Enough!" Ellen's husband Andrew shouted, holding his hands to her in peace. "Please, I beg of you, no more. This is madness." He held his hand out for the dagger.

Ellen Ward's eyes went crazed as she bared her teeth, "How dare you! How dare you all! You do not decide when I have had enough!" She held the dagger out to anyone near. "After all I have done for you, this is how you thank me? You allow the evil to consume you right before my very eyes?" She spurted and coughed. "The stench of death has bloomed below each one of your feet. There is nothing I can do to save you anymore." She looked around with chastisement for those who were now turning against her and then to Cleric Fredrick. "Get up, you fool!" she screamed, kicking his leg. He answered with a moan, curling up into a ball at her feet.

"Please, Ellen. Give me the knife," Andrew repeated. "Let's go home and calm down. We can sort all of this out. Just give me the knife."

Agreement spread among those gathered, begging for it all to end. What had been would never be again with all that had been revealed. The cracks that had been forming were now a chasm that held the flock on one side and the Shephard on the other. The villagers stood as one with the heavy tools of their labor tight in their fists.

The tide of favor was turning on her. She turned to Amelia, her ragged breathing making her pant like a wild animal. Cole, Adam, Walter, and Ellie stood firmly around her, with a look of challenge on each of their faces. She turned back to the villagers. They all shared a look of pitied disgust.

She shrieked up to the sky and turned to charge behind her. Ellie was the nearest to her attack and helpless when the Shephard pulled her against her body and set the knife to her throat. "I will decide when this is over."

Chapter Seventeen

Seeing the fear in Ellie's innocent eyes was the line drawn in the sand for the few villagers still willing to listen to the Shephard. They demanded she release the petrified girl before more damage was done. In response, the anger within Ellen Ward began to bubble and boil; her words became more hateful and cruel as she deemed each and every one of them sinners and the reason for all of the suffering that had come upon them.

"Ellen, please. Do not do this. This is madness," Andrew Ward timidly approached her. All eyes turned to him when he spoke. The man had been virtually silent for most of their marriage, and seeing him take a stand against his wife was almost as shocking as the attack she was mounting against them all. "Please, love. This is not what our maker wants of us. Show mercy. Please."

His attempt to calm the storm that she had become only enraged her further. One glare from her wrapped him once again in silence. He looked heavenward with a tight sigh that caught in his chest before he slipped back into the crowd, his head held down with the heft of his fearful shame.

Francis Miller stepped forward, his shovel at his side. "None of this is necessary, Shephard. We will listen to what you say. I know I speak for everyone when I say we are sorry that we have let you down." His words sounded devoted, yet his crumpled brow that narrowed his eyes spoke to his doubt. The voices around them rose up in agreement with what they all knew to be a lie.

Ellen looked around, wild-eyed, deeply taking in the scent only she could smell of the cursed flowers engulfing her mind in a mania she could not escape. Ellie squeezed her eyes shut, fighting to keep her body as still as stone, the blade pressed dangerously to her neck.

"To go against your Shepherd is to go against you all!" she bellowed. "You will be your own downfall if you continue to ignore my warning! I am the one that has had to get my hands dirty. I am the one who has made the sacrifices required to keep evil from slipping over our land! All the while, you were all letting it grow and blossom in your hearts and minds. I alone am trying to redeem your souls, and you ungrateful heathens dare to turn on me?" The Shephard gripped Ellie tighter, pressing the dagger harder against her porcelain skin, causing a whimper to slip from her lips.

"Let her go!" Walter implored as he shot forward to his wife. Grabbing the Shephard's arm, he spun her off of Ellie and down to the ground with a thud, her face ablaze in scarlet when she looked up at him. A scream that began deep in her gut exploded from within at the man who had the nerve to lay a finger on her. She held the dagger in her fist as she lunged upward, sinking it into Walter's stomach, tearing through his flesh, and darkening his shirt with blood. He doubled over, his mouth twitching with his hitched breath. The dusty earth around their feet lifted and fell like a fog from the quick strike.

"NO!" Ellie struggled against those that held her back, trying to get to Walter when he crumpled down to his knees, holding his hand to the wound. She pulled as hard as she could manage, unable to get to his side. She cried out for him as he stared at the ground before him, crumpled at their deranged leader's feet.

The Shephard wiped the dagger on her skirt and held it out for all to see, thrusting it toward anyone who stepped near her or the injured young man. "Look around you! How can you not see them? They bloom from your sin! They are ripping through our soil and poisoning us with their petals! I can see your devious minds helping them along, stinking of the death that will come for you all! Even as you choose to fight me, I will always fight *for* you. I will not let your weakness be our downfall!"

No one stepped forward to raise their hands to their leader, but the tools in their hands became weaponized the more she spun into the lunacy that pushed her. A few of the women gathered their children and fled for the safety of their homes. Those of the remaining broken flock were clear that they would not allow her to harm anyone else. They would do what they had to to stop her. Amelia prayed that her family was together and safe. The riotous crowd was becoming as unhinged as the Shephard, which would put everyone at risk for harm. The chaos was contagious and spreading quickly.

John urged the crowd to settle themselves. The riotous energy building among them was only fuel for the wildfire that Ellen Ward had become. "Ellen, please. These homes were built in the name of peace. You have taken the words of our founders and twisted them into what you have created here. Let's take a breath and calm down. I know you don't want to hurt anyone else."

With her attention now on John, Walter took the chance to crawl off to the side. Ellie and her mother helped him to his feet, bringing him away from the clearing where the standoff was intensifying. His mother joined them as they reached the wall that Amelia rested against, sitting him down and looking over the slash that still bled.

Ellie ripped her apron from her skirts and held it against him. "You'll be alright. It's okay," she cooed repeatedly to him as his eyes scanned her for injury. Only a reddened scratch on her neck from the dagger remained. He assured her he was not severely injured, even as the blood dripping from him onto the ground said otherwise. His mother kneeled behind him and wrapped him in her arms, cursing the Shephard.

"Put down the knife. Show your flock that you are here to save them, not harm them. Look how scared everyone is. This is not right," John continued. "Put it down, and we'll sort this all out."

"They are not in fear of me! They are in fear of you and the blight you have put on all of us by bringing your wretched world into ours!" Ellen spat. "Do not listen to this man! He feeds on the corruption he brings us."

Amelia looked to a commotion in the crowd and held her breath when she saw Sarah pushing her way through until she made it safely to her side, collapsing in tears. "I can't find Mama and Papa! Peter is gone too!" Amelia tried to hold in the squelch of pain with the weight of her young sister against her twisted leg. "I'm sorry!" the young girl yelped and fell into a fit of tears when she saw her sister's face twisted with suffering. "Why is she doing this to us? We've been good. Why is she so angry with us? I don't want anyone else hurting anymore." The tears overcame her again.

Amelia could only nod and affectionately press her head to Sarah's until the pain lessened. She wished there was an answer she could give her frightened young sister. Nothing made sense to Amelia any longer. Fear and pain were the only things left on the Good Land. It was clear that more blood would be shed if the Shephard had her way, drowning the only world she had known. She knew the end was near the night she lost Molly. Now, she could see the ruins that surrounded them. All that was left was her family – she hoped.

"We need to get you all out of here," Cole said, scanning the woods behind them. "Help will be here any minute. If we wait in the trees, we should be okay until they get here."

"I'm not going to be able to go anywhere – and I'm not leaving until I find my parents," Amelia replied. She tried to push herself up and gave up instantly. "I need to find Peter and make sure he is okay. Take Sarah and get her out of here. Please, Cole. Get her somewhere safe."

"No! I'm not leaving you," Sarah cried, holding Amelia's hand as tightly as she could. She hid her face in her shoulder, hiding away from the spectacle around her.

Amelia knew she meant it. She grabbed onto Cole's wrist with her free hand and heaved herself up, fighting the blackness that tried to swallow her away from the pain ripping through her with the slightest movements. Once she steadied herself, she looked between the trees and the crowded square. "Come on, we need to find my parents and my brother." She hobbled a few steps and had to stop, her stomach rising in response. Sarah stayed at her side, buried in her skirts. She set her palm on the wall as she dry-heaved.

"Where do you think you're going?" Ellen demanded as she spun around to see Amelia unsuccessfully attempting to flee. "After all you have caused, you think you can just slip away without a word? Who is this sinner you have called upon us?" She pointed the dagger in Cole's direction. "Do you all see what our Amelia has become?

She has the gull to sneak around with a mainlander like a whore, even after she has been gifted to my son."

"You've done enough, now. Leave that girl be," John said, trying to get her attention back on him. "Your quarrel is with me, Ellen."

"My name is Shephard Ward, you godless pig, and you will respect my position on the land you left. Don't dare take me so lightly, John Clark," she snarled, her eyes still on Amelia. "Finley, come and gather your bride. I'll allow you to decide her penance." She looked back through the crowd when he did not present himself. "Finley? Finley, do as I say and get this wretched girl out of my sight!" The deep indignation in her eyes faltered when she saw she remained alone. She squared her shoulders when her lip gave a slight quiver. "What have you done with my son?"

"We haven't done a thing to him, I promise," John said, risking a step forward. "Put the knife down, and we'll go find him."

She swept her eyes over the mass of her newfound enemies, finding none of her family remained. "I do all of this for you and turn your backs on me." Defeat softened her voice for just a moment before raising the dagger to her own throat. "I will not allow you to corrupt my soul as you have done to yourselves! If a sacrifice is required, as always, I will make sure it happens. How can you not see how much I do for you? I am not your enemy!" The blade remained at her throat as she implored the scattered flock around her. A hush slipped over the square. Shephard Ward's chest heaved up and down, watching them all with a fearful frenzy glowing in her eyes. "All I have asked of you is to live your lives as the harvest that feeds from the earth, not the tide that bleeds from it!' she hollered, spinning to lock eyes with all who braved to return her stare. "Be the harvest that feeds from the earth, not the tide that bleeds from it, you heathens! Is that what you want? My blood spilled for your sins?"

"The woman has lost her damned mind!" Adam exclaimed. "We need to get out of here."

"You all need to go," Amelia whispered and leaned her shoulder on the wall. "You need to get Walter bandaged, and Sarah needs to get away from all of this." She tried to release Sarah's hand from hers only to have her wrap herself tighter around her arm. "You need to go with them. I'll stay and find Mama, Papa, and Peter, and then we'll come and find you."

Sarah shook her head fiercely, refusing to leave her side. Time slowed down around them, every decision seeming impossible or wrong. Amelia did not know what would happen when the law arrived from the mainland. There was little she knew of them. Molly had once let it slip that her brother had befriended some of the higher-ups of the local law, and that was one of the reasons Shephard Ward kept him in her pocket. She also said they had guns. The villagers had not had a functioning gun in their hands in years. Not that she had seen, at least. Their simple tools would be no match to gunfire, and if they could not talk the Shephard down, there would be no choice but violence. If Sarah were to become caught up in it all, she would never forgive herself.

Walter shifted the bloody cloth he held to his stomach with a groan. "We're not going to leave you here, Amelia. We should try to get us all to the edge of the woods, like he said. There's no saying what that demon of a woman is going to do."

"He's right," Cole agreed, and Ellie gave a quick bob of her head, not taking her eyes from the Shephard.

John continued to try to persuade Ellen to hand over the blade. The only responses she would grant were verses from the good book that became more unhinged as she paced. The dagger remained at her neck just firmly enough to keep everyone at a distance. Her eyes had become cloudy with the delusions that filled her mind, and it was unclear if she could even see those around her anymore. She had transcended into her madness, leaving the others unsure how to stop the spiral from worsening.

"If she's acting like that when the law gets here, we're all in for a rough turn. We have to get that knife from her, John," Francis Miller pushed.

Amelia was confused that he would know anything about the law, let alone be so casual with John's name.

"You think I don't know that, Francis? There's a reason I kept them away," he replied, clearly knowing the villager. "I think it's best if everyone got out of here, and we'll try to settle her down."

"I was the harvest that feeds!" Ellen's voice ripped through the others who were all talking at once around her. "You have made me the tide that bleeds!" She raised the dagger above her head, her eyes pinched tight and her mouth hanging open with a soundless scream. Her arms swung the blade down toward her chest.

"Shit!" John cursed and launched himself forward, tackling her to the ground. The dagger fell from her hands, and he kicked it away. "Stop Ellen! Stop. It's over," he held her arms to her sides, his weight pinning her body to the ground.

Relief flooded the square in an instant. Amelia slipped down the wall, the exhaustion overtaking her. Sarah stayed clinging to her skirts, still frightened. The threat of the Shephard harming anyone else was gone, just as her mind was. The shell of their leader was splayed out on the dirt, her lips mouthing psalms that only she could hear. John held her firmly in place even as she seemed to have gone so far into her mind no one else existed.

"Let's get the women and children back to their cottages. We'll deal with her and the law best we can," Ellie's father, Gilbert, said, with a look to his wife and daughter.

A few others agreed, shuffling some of the wives and younger children away from the square. Most of the men gathered around John, some addressing him by name as if they had known them for years.

"If Sheriff Boyd gets a look at this, we're done. Either way, those two are going to need to go ashore," Gilbert said, rubbing at his salt and pepper scruff. "They're going to need more help than we can give."

Ellie looked at Amelia with the same confused expression that sat plainly on her face. As quickly as everything they knew was being torn away, another layer of secrets and deceit was revealed.

How many of them knew of John and his life on the mainland? How could they have allowed harm to come to Molly if they knew he existed? That he was providing for them and owned the very land they lived on?

Amelia had thought herself on the outside of her community for all that she knew. She had struggled with keeping secrets, worried about harming others with what she knew to be sinful and unacceptable.

The world as she knew it did not exist. The village around her may as well have been letters on the pages of her books. The Good Land was a false land of lies that she had been so frightened to leave. It made little sense to her that they would take anything the Shephard said as gospel when they were keeping the truth of themselves hidden. They were not living a pure life of goodness. They were nothing more than hypocrites.

Mary Allen looked over her son's wound, replaced the cloth, and walked briskly to those who remained in the square. She spoke in a hushed voice, looking back and forth between her son and those she spoke to.

"How are you doing?" Ellie asked Walter.

"It's not as bad as it looks," he replied with a crooked grin that did not reach his eyes. "I've had worse."

"We need to get you both up and cleaned up," Ellie's mother, Florence, stated, her hands still shaking like leaves.

"Did you know about John?" Amelia asked her.

"Now is not the time, dear," Florence murmured, avoiding her eyes.

"How much more don't we know?" she asked as she watched the woman help Walter to his feet. Ellie slipped under his arm and started to guide him into the cottage beside them.

"Amelia, no, it is not the time," Florence snapped. "Not everything that happens around us is our concern. All that matters now is that we get you and Walter fixed up."

"Fixed up?" Amelia exclaimed. "A mad woman snapped my leg and plunged a dagger into your daughter's husband! We didn't have a fall in the woods. We were attacked – by the same woman who murdered Molly Clark!"

"Keep your voice down," she scolded in a low voice. "We don't need Mr. Clark getting worked up again. Come now. We need to get you inside."

Amelia had no chance for another word before Florence grasped her beneath her arms and tugged up in one swift pull. She howled with pain, leaning on the wall beside her.

"Be careful!" Sarah shouted, pushing the woman away. "You're hurting her."

Cole held her weight when her body started to slide. He grimaced along with her, seeing the agony she was in.

Florence's hands twisted each other with worry, just as her daughter did in times of stress. "I'm sorry. I did not mean...," she stopped, overcome with it all.

"It's fine, Mrs. Stewart. I'm fine. I just need a minute," Amelia insisted. The woman who stood before her was not someone who hid the truth with purpose. She was just as overwhelmed watching their lives implode in an instant as she was. "Sarah, go with Mrs. Stewart. I'll be with you as soon as I catch my breath."

"It's okay, Sarah. We'll stay with her and help her inside," Adam said, bending to look the young girl in the eye. He started to pry her hands from Amelia's skirts gently.

Sarah started to argue, stopping when Amelia gave her a pleading look of exhaustion and allowed Florence to whisk her inside the safety of the cottage. There was no telling what would happen next, and she wanted her sister as far away from it as possible.

If she had convinced her family to leave, if Walter had not returned, if Molly had followed her brothers – what would be happening in that moment? The different outcomes of each question all seemed more ideal than the choices that had led them to that day.

She held her hip as stiffly as she could, supporting her weight on Adam and Cole as she hobbled out from between the cottages.

"Do you need to stop?" Cole asked when her chest gasped for air. Every step she took felt like twenty. "Don't rush, we've got you."

She allowed herself a minute to gain a slight burst of strength. She stared at what was left of their Shephard, still immobilized by John. It was a wonder that she had been an immeasurable force that ruled their every second just hours before. The woman she saw now was as frightening as a baby mouse, not the eagle that would have swooped down and consumed it. Ellen Ward, as they knew her, was dead and gone, irreparably broken by the demons that haunted her mind. It was difficult to remain angry at the pathetic soul she looked down on.

"Sheriff's Department!" a deep voice called out from the trail.

"We're over here, Dale," John responded, raising a hand to alert him. "We have a few injured that are going to need some help." He slowly rose from Ellen until he was sure she would remain on the ground. Her eyes stared through the reality she had slipped away from, taking no notice of her restraint being removed.

"What in God's name is going on out here, John?" the man asked, approaching the square. He wore a billed cap like Cole had worn but with a gold star on the front. They could clearly see the weapon at his hip. "Jesus Christ, what happened to her?" He stood over the Shephard, watching her twitch and pray. He pulled a heavy black block from his hip and spoke into it. He fussed with a switch on the side and spoke again. "Looks like no signal out here. Hey, Malone!" he shouted to one of the three similarly dressed men who appeared at the trail path. "Go back to the boat and see if you can get dispatch. We're gonna need medical, and they'll need to look into a psych room for this one." He pointed the black block at the Shephard. The man nodded and disappeared back into the woods.

"There's a young man that's been stabbed pretty nasty in the gut in that one there," John advised, pointing to the cottage that Walter had been brought into, "and this young lady here has a pretty nasty leg injury," he added, pointing to Amelia. One man moved toward the cottage, and the other jogged swiftly to Amelia. She was taken aback when she realized the lawman who approached her was a woman dressed in the same garb as the men. She spoke softly to her, asking her what had happened and where all she was injured. Cole and Adam continued to hold her up, with Adam sharing the same surprise as Amelia.

"You guys try and keep her as comfortable as you can. I'm going to get the first aid kit from the boat to help with what I can until EMS gets here," she told the boys and left as quickly as she had arrived.

"Can you make it to the house?" Cole asked her.

The space between where they stood and the door appeared to stretch further away the more Amelia looked. The burst of excited energy that had fueled her was draining. She shook her head no and motioned for the well in the square just a few feet from where they stood. She propped herself on the edge, glad to be off of her feet.

They watched as two more capped people appeared from the forest and approached the man John had called Dale. They gathered in a circle, speaking in quiet voices.

"Stay down, Shephard," Francis Miller said gently.

Amelia, Cole, and Adam turned from the officers to see what was happening. Shephard Ward had sat up, staring at the sky. Her mumbled words became louder.

"I mean it. Stay down, Shephard. We're getting you help," Francis said a little more firmly.

She slowly leaned forward until her legs pulled up beneath her, and she crouched like a feral animal waiting to pounce. "I am the harvest," she hissed.

"Uh, John. I think we need some help over here," he called out, stepping a few feet from where she had locked her eyes on him.

"I am the harvest!" she bellowed, launching from the ground across to where the dagger still lay.

"Knife! Knife!" one of the lawmen called out, causing them all to turn to the Shephard, who was now on her feet. "She has a weapon!"

"You will be the tide that bleeds!" Ellen screamed the words so loud they seemed to tear through her throat. She welded the blade above her head and ran for John.

The fright of the scene caused Amelia to jump up, pain shooting from her knee. Stumbling to gain her balance, three loud booms rang out around her, and a burning fire erupted in her shoulder that spun her around in place. As she fell to the ground, the crack of her head on the well was the last thing she heard before everything around her was swallowed in darkness.

Chapter Eighteen

The noise around her was too loud, too foreign. Opening her eyes, the sky was too bright. Her body moved on its own, bouncing rhythmically. She was unable to move her leg even though she could feel the throb that had taken root in it. A searing pain shot across her back from her shoulder each time she attempted to.

"I told them that damn fool should only be given a whistle," a muffled voice cursed. "That moron should be behind a desk."

Amelia tried to turn her head to see who was talking. A dull thump pulsated on the front of her head, making everything spin around her. Through blurry eyes, she saw a woman with one of the gold-starred caps sitting to her side. She recognized her as the woman who had checked on her when she was sitting on the well. Everything around her was bright white against her black clothing. Too bright. A gold bar across her chest read Deputy K. Raven. She continued to spout her anger to someone Amelia could not see, not noticing she was being watched.

As her eyes began to sharpen the bleary shapes surrounding the woman, the white above her became an overcast sky. The clouds moved quickly across the sky, faster than she had ever seen. The space above her was too vast. There were no trees to be seen, no cottages, no one she knew: only the clouds above and the newcomer to her world.

"Try and keep still. I know it hurts," Deputy Raven said with a softer tone when Amelia tried to lift her head. "It won't be too long."

Her body lifted from the ground and slammed back down. The pain nearly sent her back into the darkness. When she wretched, the considerate woman gently helped her turn to her side before her stomach's contents could lodge in her throat.

The ground below her was not dirt. It was pristine white beneath red splatters. It did not take her long to recognize it as blood. Lifting her hand in front of her face, she knew it was her blood. Panic started to spread quickly through her veins. She fought to sit up.

"Where...where...," was all she could manage.

The Deputy helped her settle herself a little higher on the bench where she lay, repeating her instructions to try and stay still. The trees finally appeared in front of her, although they were moving further away by the second. Turning her head to the side, she could see the chopping white-capped waves they were slipping up and over, the cause of the painful slamming of her body.

Realizing she was being taken to the mainland, she struggled against her own body and the restraint of the Deputy. Even if she were to get herself up and free, she was trapped by a body of water that surrounded them. A man appeared above her. His clothing was similar to the lawmen, but the letters on his hat and the symbol on his shirt were different. She narrowed her eyes at the snake wrapped around a stick stitched onto his pocket as he took her arm in his hand. She struggled against him when she felt a pinch in her arm until the intense pain of her body melted away, and she became dizzy with relief. Their conversation started to drift further and further away until only a hum remained.

She tried to move her fingers and found her arms to be limp. Same for her legs. She knew she should worry, that she should fight to free herself, to find her family, but her mind felt as soft as the gray clouds above. Shapes appeared and drifted away with the warm breeze that tickled her face.

A hummingbird, first colorless in the clouds, twittered down toward her, its iridescent green feathers becoming bolder as it approached. It hovered just above her, close enough that she could see its shining black eyes looking down at her. Its wings whirred, adding to the buzz that lulled her, the feathers blending into a soft blur of comfort.

She wondered if it was looking for Molly; if it had been one of the ones who had savored the sweet water that had been lovingly left out before everything had been destroyed. Her lips mouthed apologies to the tiny bird, unable to speak the words. She apologized to Molly for not being able to help her. She apologized to John for how her people had taken advantage of his kindness. She apologized to Walter for not leaving when he wanted to. She begged for atonement from everyone she felt she had harmed, purging her soul silently to the small bird that stayed to listen.

The well-being of her family was unknown, as was the state of their formally omnipotent Shephard. Guilt lay heavy on her chest for all that had happened. She had not even had the courage to visit Molly in whatever grave they had graced her with. If she were not permitted to return, or if her last breath were between the water and the mainland, she would lose all that was Molly forever. The poor woman would forever be in the Good Land, her only company being those who lay in the graves around her. The further away from home she traveled, the less sure she became of what life would now be. Even through the numb haze she found herself in, she knew there was no way to tell what her own body would be left as. Amelia shared a prayer with the curious bird and then watched as it slipped back into the clouds. She wondered if it would return to the island; if it did, what would it find?

She called out to it in her mind, 'Go to Molly. *Tell her I love her. Tell her I'm sorry.'*

Straining against the sleep that attempted to steal her away from the present, she listened to the distant voices around her.

Going to need a lot of backup to sort out that mess.

Has the abdominal trauma made it to the marina yet?

Boyd is pissed.

Old Man Clark is in for it, for sure.

Amelia watched another boat speed past them in a white blaze toward her home. The man with the snake on his shirt pocket appeared above her again, lifting her eyelids one by one and then fussing about with blood-stained cloth she could see on her shoulder.

"You're going to be fine..." he turned to the woman sitting across from them, "What's her name?"

Amelia's eyes trailed slowly over to her to see her shrug with a tight frown. "Not a clue. We grabbed and ran."

"What's your name, sweetheart?" he asked, leveling his gaze to hers.

She liked how kind his eyes were. They were a beautiful bright green like the hummingbird's feathers. She smiled when he asked her again, unable to answer. Her eyes grew heavy as her body felt chilled against the summer air.

Blackness crept in from the corners of her eyes, washing over her consciousness and then slipping her back onto the water. It became impossible for her to tell if her eyes were opened or closed - if she was awake, dreaming, or dead. The moments when the agony of her injuries would become the most intense sensation, she prayed for the darkness to return, the suffering seeming unending.

The time to get across the water was immeasurable to her until the purr of the boat beneath her quieted, and deafening noise started to build. By the time she felt the forward motion cease, the noise was entirely consuming. The sky above her was lit with flashes of red and blue light that swirled below the clouds. More faces appeared in her sightline, all speaking at once, none of them saying a single thing she understood.

Her body was lifted abruptly from where she lay and set on a more comfortable surface. Tears slipped from the corners of her eyes down into her hair. Confusion had overtaken the pain. Horror was keen to slip in next. The shock of it all made her lungs gasp; the quick sips of air they would allow were not enough to keep her chest from aching for more.

The sky moved quickly above her again when she was moved further into the screeching sounds of the main-land. She called out for her mother as best she could, the sound more of a garbled plea. New faces appeared above her, asking questions she did not understand and that she did not even attempt to answer. She begged to go home and to see her mother. The pain held her in place, not allowing her back to the life she knew. Her spirit started to ache more than her broken body with how alone she felt even as she was swallowed by the enormous mass of strangers that filled every inch of her vision.

The activity around her became as frantic as the buzz of the hummingbird's wings. Faces all blurred into one, and her ears rang like bells from the constant confounding clammer. A low ceiling above her replaced the clouds, and the slamming of a door softened the explosions in her ears.

When the vibrations of the movement started again, her body was jostled less than it had been on the boat. The windowless cage she was now held in was tight. The smell of the space was strange to her: bitter, yet almost without any scent at all. It made her nose twitch with a tickle. Her hand would not reach up to scratch it. Her mouth felt dry.

The man with the snake shirt continued to ask questions. He spoke into a black box like the lawman had done when she did not answer.

Amelia's mind had closed itself off from any more sensory assaults. The mainland had swept her up in its furious spiral of colors, uproar, and pain, whisking her away from any semblance of what she knew to be reality.

Her eyes closed it all off and brought her to her favorite meadow. Everyone who was dear to her was there, including her beloved Molly, who no longer hunched over with the weight of her years and could walk freely among the gardens. There was no blood, no fear, no noise other than the joyful laughter of her loved ones that blended in chorus with the rustling of the leaves. The scent of the hot cup of tea in her hands was even more comforting than the sweet blooms that circled their table. She traced her fingers over the vines that had been delicately carved for the Taylor family so many decades before, each polished sliver of wood familiar.

Molly held the crystal bowl, which now did not even have a chip, out for a hummingbird smaller than she had ever seen. The flicker of its wings was almost too soft to hear. Another appeared, followed by another, until they were so thick in the air that Molly became obscured by their beautiful little faces, swarming the dish for their treat. Their agile bodies flitted about, charming everyone with the flurry of their speedy wings. There were so many she could practically hear the quick beats of their minuscule hearts over the buzz of their wings.

Adam stepped forward to watch beside her. "She's going into shock," he said in a voice that did not belong to him.

"Who is? What's happened?" she asked, confused by the look of concern that creased his face.

She tried to run when the birds turned their attention to her, flying far too close to her. Pricks of their beaks pinched at her arms, and they pressed against her chest, pushing her back away from the manor garden she loved until they finally picked her up in the whirlwind of their flight, and she was powerless against their strength.

Her hands lashed out, slapping them all away as she fought to return her feet to the ground. The drone of their wings turned high-pitched as they flitted away, growing louder the further they got. The sound pushed her to the ground. She held her hands protectively over her ears and tried to roll herself into a ball, wanting nothing more than to escape the attack.

Voices began to overpower the sounds of the birds, pulling Amelia back to the real terrors she was fleeing. The chaos returned as quickly as it had departed. The ceiling was much higher now, with lines of bright lights that burned her eyes and slipped along above her. More strangers invaded her space with questions and shouts to each other of things she could not begin to fathom.

A hand with a tight, bizarre-looking glove covered her face, and the darkness slipped over her mind once more. It had never been more welcome. The dreams of the manor house did not return.

CHAPTER NINETEEN

During the next few days, Amelia was exposed to more new things and stranger's faces than she had encountered in her entire eighteen years alive. The closest person to a doctor she had known was Duncan Allen, who relied on herbal remedies and prayer. Amelia now lay in a hospital bed on the mainland with a barrage of different medical professionals fixing this part and that. She had surgeries on her shoulder and knee, which now had a tight wrap that held her entire leg still. Medicines had taken away her pain, and a lovely woman they called a councilor had sat with her and listened to her worries.

Everything she experienced from the time her eyes opened until they wearily closed was different from every day she had lived before. The electricity that ran through the walls of the building caused the lights above to be as bright as the noon sun. Foods she had never tasted and sat uncomfortably in her stomach. Right down to the textures of the fabrics, the walls, the dishes, and the furniture, it was all new to her. There was too much to see and smell from the bed that she lay immobilized in.

Fear of it all was its own hindrance at the beginning of her recovery. Taking in what felt like a different universe altogether was hard enough. Not being able to see any of her family or friends while she was in so much pain felt impossible to survive. Hearing that the injury to her shoulder came from a gun gave her a whole new twist to the nightmares that awoke her and covered her in sweat each night.

The people caring for her were as gentle and kind as anyone could hope for, but they were not her people. When they spoke to her, there were many words that she did not understand. It took time for her to become comfortable enough even to speak.

It took even more time to open up about her life when she did. More lawmen visited her, introducing them- selves as officers and detectives. They asked too many questions than she had the energy for. They advised her that her family and everyone else who had been on the island were being kept apart and questioned. No one had been mortally injured in the fall of the Good Land, which was a blessing, although Walter was also being treated for the wound to his stomach in the same hospital. Amelia was disappointed when they would not tell her anything about his condition.

The first taste of relief came when she was told that her family had been found unharmed and brought across from the island shortly after she had. When they were finally allowed to see her, they wept tears of relief, grief, and angst all at once. Each visit made Amelia more confident that their lives were not over. It was now simply different. Change was coming in floods that refused to recede.

"Please, Mama?" Sarah begged, sitting on the edge of Amelia's hospital bed, pointing up to the television mounted to the wall with its screen darkened.

"I said no, my little squirrel. No means no," she scolded lightly. "I cannot see why anyone could enjoy all of that noise. They're too strange."

Sarah had taken to television as quickly as a fish to water when the social worker, helping with the newfound mess on the island, switched one on for her. Amelia had asked for it not to be put on again after Sarah had shown her its use on her first visit. She agreed with her mother about its lack of appeal. The stack of books that kept growing on the side table of her room was much more enjoyable. There were more Jane Austen novels than she had ever seen, along with Charlotte Brontë and Louisa May Alcott, whom she had never read nor heard of. Having them freely out in the open and accepted was such a delight. Her mother agreed that there was no issue with her enjoying them now, and they helped soothe her mind while her body healed.

Sarah gave a fleeting pout as she slid from the bed to walk around the room again, inspecting every little detail as if she were exploring a new planet. The shock of it all settled quickly in her curious mind. Amelia was proud of her resilience and made an effort to be just as brave.

"Mary said Walter is allowed to leave tomorrow. He is truly blessed to have not been injured worse," Jane said, changing the subject from the television.

"Are they going back home?" Amelia knew the answer but asked anyway. No one was going home, at least not in the near future. The Shephard had driven the flock from their land when she became lost in her broken mind. Ellen Ward was now a patient of another hospital, one that was better suited to deal with a sickness that had settled into the brain.

"No, Poppet," was all her mother responded.

Her father had once said that you would never see someone's true character more clearly than when they have their back to the wall and your face to theirs. The strain of slowly losing her grasp over her people, knowing they were starting to see her as she truly was, split open a broken piece within Ellen Ward that had been worsening for years.

In the quiet nights of the hospital, when Amelia would allow herself brief moments of reflection, she could see that the Shephard did not want the best for them all – she wanted supreme power. Ultimately, she could not let go of what she never honestly had. Left in the dust was a village that was now home to the mainland's law, who were tearing it apart piece by piece to figure out all of the atrocities that had occurred.

Her parents would not say much about where they were staying other than they were together, with the exception of herself, Walter, and the Shephard, and they were being well cared for. Amelia tried not to think of what would happen to their lives when she was well enough to leave the hospital's care, so she never pushed for more. She could see in her mother's eyes that she was telling the truth; that was all she needed to know. What happened when their new lives began would arrive in due time. For now, she needed to regain her body and spirit. The daily visits from her family helped with that.

"I don't want to go back!" Peter exclaimed, his nose pressed against the window overlooking the town below. Amelia preferred the window covered. There was enough to understand within the room that had become her everything without having to consider what lay outside. "There is so much to see here." He bounded to the bed and jumped up onto the end of the mattress. "Sorry," he murmured when Amelia flinched from the vibrations. "Do they have ice cream here? They brought us ice cream yesterday, and it was the best thing I've ever had!"

"It was so good, Amelia! Mine tasted like strawberries. It was as cold as snow and melted in my mouth," Sarah added.

"And it made you both bounce like crazed rabbits after you had it," their father said, laughing.

Amelia smiled at her siblings, who were licking their lips as if they could still taste the treat. "I haven't had that yet. It sounds like I should."

Sarah opened the door to the restroom opposite the bed and started playing with the sink taps, squealing with delight every time the water appeared. Peter ran in to join the fun, playing with the toilet handle. Amelia could see it from where she lay and was thankful for the bedpan they provided. The roar of water that would wash away their business was off-putting. Thankfully, being indoors, it seemed to smell a lot better than the outhouses she was used to.

"Would you two settle down, please?" their father implored, pulling them from the small room. "I'm going to take them for a bit of a walk to try to settle them down." Gavin took them each by the hand into the hallway. The children's giggles and whoops of excitement faded, and their mother shook her head with a tired smile.

"How have your headaches been?" Amelia asked quietly.

"Actually, I'm surprised that they have not been too harsh lately. With nothing to do all day, the rest must be helping." Jane pulled a chair from against the wall to Amelia's bedside. "How have you been doing? They said you should be able to leave real soon. It will be nice to have us all together again."

"Am I interrupting?" They turned to find Ellie standing at the door.

"Of course not, Elsbeth." Jane stood to welcome her. "You are just the medicine my Poppet needs."

She approached Amelia's side timidly. Her eyes were still puffy even though there was no sign of the tears that had left them in such a sad state. It was the first time they had seen each other since they had left the island.

"I was on a walk while the doctor is with Walter, and I saw your father. He said you were allowed visitors outside of family now," she whispered, looking her over apprehensively. Amelia smiled, looking as well as she could for her worrywart of a friend.

"Such a silly rule. You are family to us," Jane blustered, giving Ellie's back a comforting rub. "You look tired, dear. You should spend some time looking after yourself, not just Walter."

"How is Walter?" Amelia asked when Ellie took her hand. She would never dare to say, but she noticed that she had appeared to have aged ten years in the days since she had seen her.

"He's doing very well now. We are blessed." Ellie pressed a tight smile to her lips. "How about you? I've heard you have been doing your best in here," she looked about the pale pink room, "considering, I suppose."

"I'm healing well. They've been very kind to me," Amelia replied. They stared at each other, both unsure where to start. The days they had been apart felt like years with all that had happened. There was too much to say and too many questions to ask.

"I'm going to let you two have some quiet," Jane said, walking to the door. "I should find your father and see if he's keeping Sarah and Peter in line." She blew a kiss to her daughter and left.

"You haven't braided your hair," Ellie observed, mindlessly smoothing the long blonde plait that ribboned down her back.

Amelia took her loose hair in her hands and twisted it over her shoulder. "No. It's more comfortable like this." Just the thought of pulling it all into the tight style that had been forced on her made her scalp ache more than her knee. She did not think she would ever attempt it again. The thought of cutting it all off like some of the ladies she had seen seemed even better.

"It looks pretty down." She looked to her feet, and then the ceiling, and then back to Amelia.

"Have...," they both started at once and stopped.

"Sorry, go ahead," Ellie said.

"Have you heard much of the Shephard?" Amelia asked, wanting to know and forget the Shephard at the same time.

"No. Only that they say she's very sick." Ellie shrugged one small shoulder. "I'm sure when Walter is on his feet again, he'll find out everything in a day," she chuckled.

"He is good at getting to the meat in the chapter and verse, isn't he?" Amelia agreed. He would know the ins and outs of mainland life in no time. She tried to think of the two of them living life in the world outside of the hospital. Picturing Ellie wearing the trousers some women wore almost made Amelia laugh.

Ellie's eyes landed on the books stacked on the table. "What is all of this?" She walked over and peered at the covers. Her face lit with surprise when she saw what they were. "Are these all from him?"

Amelia looked from the books to her friend, who seemed lighter with whatever thought had just occurred to her. "Him?"

"The boy that came to the village – Cole. Are these all from him?"

Amelia did not know any of them were from Cole. She had not heard word of what had happened to him other than the detectives telling her he was unharmed. "Why would you think these are from him?"

"He has come here every day since we arrived with a stack of books like this." She picked one up and turned the pages, scanning over what she thought to be dangerous contraband. "He said John told him that you love books, so he wanted to make sure you had some." She set the paperback down when she saw the confusion on Amelia's face. "They wouldn't let him see you because he wasn't family. Same with me. That's how I met him." The chair squeaked against the tiled floor when she shifted it to sit. They both grimaced at the ear-piercing noise and then fell into a fit of giggles.

"Why would anyone make a floor that would make that sounds like that?" Amelia asked, playfully covering her ears.

"If I asked all of the questions I have about this place, we would be wrinkled and gray before I finished."

"Isn't that the truth?" Amelia nodded. The laugh they shared felt good. They relaxed into their ways, and Ellie retook her hand, this time more lovingly than concerned. "So, it was Cole that brought those? I thought they were from someone from here." She had always assumed they belonged to the hospital, and they had allowed her to read them to keep her amused.

Ellie leaned into her, mischief dancing on her face. "They are. There's a room I go to when Walter naps or is being tended to. It doesn't have one of those dreadful things, so it's nice and quiet," she added, gesturing to the television. "He was in there reading one of them, and we got to talking. He's very handsome," she covered her blushed face and giggled.

"Ellie! I remind you that you're a married woman now," Amelia teased.

"Oh, stop." Ellie playfully slapped her hand. "He really is very nice. He wanted to see how you were doing, but they wouldn't let him see you. He said he brought a few books every time he came, and they said they would give them to you. Isn't that thoughtful?"

She wondered why he would care so much about a perfect stranger – why she deserved so much care and consideration from him. He was more than thoughtful. "I would have to say yes, he is." She looked at the number of books he had found for her. Finley would have a fit if he saw them all. After all the trouble they had been through, Cole still had it inside to be sweet to her. "Is he okay? Did he get in very much trouble?"

Ellie sat back in the chair, picking at the slippery fabric on the arm. "From what he told me, no. John Clark did not get in as much trouble as you would have thought, either. He has a lot of important friends over here that took care of things." Her parents had not seen or heard from him since *the incident*, as they took to calling it. She was glad to hear he did not fall into hardship because of them. Learning that it had been his land all along made his goodness and humanity even more sure. "I haven't seen him again. I haven't left here, though. I told them I wouldn't leave without Walter."

"Mama said he should get to leave tomorrow."

"That's what they've said. Mary has been here every day to visit. She said they have a room ready for us where they are all staying. It sounds like a comfortable place. Crowded, she said, but comfortable. I guess that's where we'll end up until we know what will happen." Ellie shrugged, the side of her lip tipped into a hooked frown. "I'll still come to see you every day if you'd like. Now that I'm allowed."

"I would like that very much," Amelia asserted. "Hopefully, I won't have to stay much longer. It's so lonely and strange here."

"I'm sure Adam will be here as soon as he hears that more than family are allowed to see you now. I'm sure there are quite a few people who would want to see you." Ellie stood to walk to the window. She looked out the glass at the world below when her eyes twinkled, and a sly grin slid across her face. Turning back to her, she clasped her hands together. "I know there is someone here now who would like to see you very much."

Amelia looked at her questioningly. "Who? Walter? Is he up and around now? I'd love to say hello."

"Well, I'm sure he would, as well," Ellie giggled, looking down from the window and waving her hand quickly. "Cole is here again."

Amelia shuffled to sit up more and combed her fingers through her hair. It seemed inappropriate for him to see her in such a state, lying in bed at that. She pulled the blanket further up her body and untangled her hair more. Ellie squeaked another childlike giggle when she saw her fussing.

"What? They practically have me dressed only in my underthings. It's strange to have visitors when I'm so unsorted," Amelia contended.

"You look fine." Ellie twirled Amelia's hair into one wide curl that rested over her shoulder almost to the bed and smiled.

Amelia frowned. She was not trying to make ado of herself because Cole was coming. The nerves in her stomach flittered, and she felt silly. Maybe she was a little excited to see him. After all they had been through together, they were bound to see each other again. She took the cup from the table that slid across the bed at her lap and sipped the water. It did not taste as fresh as the water she was used to, but it was better than the fizzy drinks and sweet juices they had offered.

"Would it be alright if I left you to visit on your own?" Ellie asked with a pleading look. "I told Walter I would only be gone a short while."

It seemed improper to have him in the room alone with her. She considered that they would hardly be alone with the bustle of people just outside her open door. Her parents would be back soon, and keeping Ellie when Walter needed her would be unkind.

"Of course. Tell Walter I'm glad to hear he's doing well, and I'll see him soon," she told her with a soft grin, hiding the butterflies that had returned to her stomach.

Ellie gave her a kiss on the cheek and a wave as she happily returned to Walter.

Amelia sat quietly, looking over the worn stack of books beside her. It had been so considerate of him to bring her such a wealth of gifts. She wondered how many of them Molly had read. It was kind-hearted of John to have let Cole know how much she loved books, too. So far, everything she had been told of the wretched mainlanders had been proven entirely false.

With everything that had been proven wrong, Amelia now knew that Molly had been right. The settled in her ways woman would not have enjoyed life with so many people and so much noise. Everything moved too quickly. To Amelia, it was both daunting and intriguing.

"Hey," Cole greeted, startling Amelia from her thoughts.

"Hello," she replied, shifting on the bed as best as her bound leg would allow. She was glad to see he did not appear to have any injuries from *the incident*.

"Do you mind if I come in?" he pointed to the chair at her side.

She smiled with a bob of her head. "Thank you for the books. I love them," she said when he was settled in the chair.

"No problem," he replied. "I'm a book lover, too, so I knew you could use a few in here."

"More than a few," she laughed. "That's almost more than Molly had in her whole collection. I've only gotten to a couple of them so far."

"Well, they're yours for whenever you get around to them. John said you liked that sort of genre, and I didn't know anything about them, so my friend Greta helped me find them."

Amelia looked back from the books to Cole, who was having trouble getting comfortable in the chair. "I could not accept such an extravagant gift!" she exclaimed. "There's more than a dozen piled up."

"No, I insist. They're all secondhand, so it didn't cost much," he pushed. "I want you to have them. A start to your own collection."

"Well, thank you," she said quietly. "They mean a lot to me." He gave her a small smile and looked awkwardly around the room, still shifting in his chair. "Did you get in very much trouble?" she asked when he stayed silent.

He gave a hearty chuckle. "My dad took my boat keys away. I don't think I'll be seeing them again anytime soon. Other than that, there's too much going on with everyone else for them to think much of me. Other than the cops. They've had a bunch of questions."

"I'm sorry for all of this. I..."

"Don't apologize, Amelia. None of this is your fault. If anyone should say sorry, it's me. I had no business trespassing over there," he insisted with a frown.

She agreed that it had been unwise of them to have gone to the island but did not blame him for any of the trouble that transpired. "Cole, I don't know what would have happened if you hadn't. If you hadn't told John, things may have been worse." Flashes of her last day on the island pressed their way into her mind. "I don't know what would have happened to Walter if help had not come."

The thought of Ellie being a widow at eighteen years old was too heavy to contemplate. Beyond that, who could say what would have happened if the Shephard had a chance to cross off the last name on her list? Because of Cole, Peter was instead running wild somewhere in the building, smiling from ear to ear.

"I'm sure Walter would have been fine. From what I saw of him, he's a tough son of...," he stopped with a look of embarrassment that Amelia did not understand. "He's a real solid guy."

"He is a good man. I'm glad he is okay," Amelia said, hoping that was what he meant. She was pleased when he nodded. Sometimes, with the way mainlanders spoke, it was as if it were a completely different language.

"I think it's fair to say you're a pretty tough chick your-self," he pointed out, looking at the collection of injuries she had survived.

Amelia laughed at the thought of a tough little baby chick, "I think I'm tougher than that."

Cole forced a laugh to join hers before a clumsy silence fell over them. When Amelia risked a look at him, he was doing the same, and they shared a smile.

"So, do you know what you guys are going to do?" He continued when she looked unsure of the question, "When you're better, and they let you out of here. Are you guys going to go back, or could you stay?"

"I don't know. I don't think it's up to us. After all that has happened, I can't see John welcoming us back," Amelia said regretfully. No one would cast blame on him if he never wanted to see any of them again.

"Old Man Clark doesn't have a mean bone in his body, no matter how anyone jokes about him. He won't turn his back on you," Cole assured. The quiet overtook the room for a bloated minute before he spoke again. "Do you want to go back?"

Amelia did not know how to answer. It changed from breath to breath. There was nothing that seemed to be a clear answer. "I might. I don't know. I guess we'll do whatever my parents decide."

"It's a beautiful island. I could see why you'd want to if it's safer now." He picked up the water jug from the table when Amelia reached for it, and she struggled against the pain in her shoulder. Taking her cup, he filled it and slid it in front of her. "Maybe if it won't get you trouble, I'll save up for my own boat to come visit."

Amelia tried to picture life with mainlanders freely roaming the village and having friendly visits in the cottages. It seemed as bizarre as when she imagined them all living off of the island. "That would be fun, wouldn't it?" She shifted on her pillow, trying to fight off the fatigue that was slipping in.

Cole barked a laugh, rubbing nervously at the scruff of his neck, "Anyways, I should let you get some rest." He rose from the chair and stood at her bedside. "Would you mind if I came another day to visit before you leave?"

She could not fathom why a mainlander whose life must be filled with excitement and packed with days of new things would want to spend any of his time with her. Whatever he saw in her, she hoped he kept seeing it because there was something about him that made her want him to return. "I would like that a lot, Cole." The broad grin on her face betrayed the attempt to sound casual.

"Okay, good. Right, um...I'll see you soon then. Get some rest." He started for the door. "Oh! I almost forgot." He turned back into the room. "I know you like those kind of books, but I wanted to share one of mine with you." He pulled a well-worn novel from the inside of his jacket. "This was my favorite growing up."

She took it from him when he held it out and thanked him. She looked over the colorful cover. There was a drawing of a wooden chest set among dense pine trees. Her breath caught in her throat. Above the chest was a beautiful green hummingbird, its wings frozen in time. The Mystery of Angel Forest's Treasure was written in bold yellow letters above it.

"It's a Choose Your Own Adventure book. They're what got me hooked on reading as a kid."

The book blurred in her eyes as they welled with emotion. "I love it, Cole. Thank you so much for being so kind."

"I hope you like it."

Holding it in her hands, she could feel Molly's spirit looking on, delighted to see what was to come in Amelia's strange new world. Whether the adventures would be in the book she held or the uncertain future that she would soon be swallowed by, she was ready to turn the page. It was time for Amelia's next chapter.

About the Author

Katherine Dempster is a Canadian writer of paranormal and horror thrillers. A lifelong reader and fan of the macabre, she lives in the countryside beside a small lake, pretending every day is Halloween.

You can visit her online at:

Facebook @katherinedempsterauthor

Instagram @katt_dempster

Twitter @para_norma1

Also by Katherine Dempster:

The B.I.T.N. Assignments

-Welcome to Aumbry Valley

-Welcome to Dunhope Manor

Into the Lake

In Sheltered Shadows and Other Short Stories